Mr Kill v

MR KILLJOY

Published worldwide by Apple Loft Press

This edition published in 2025

Copyright © 2025 by S J Richards

S J Richards has asserted his right to be identified as the author of this work in accordance with the Copyright, Design and Patents Act 1988.

All rights reserved. This book or any portion thereof may not be reproduced or used in any manner whatsoever without the express written permission of the author, except for quotes or short extracts for the purpose of reviews.

www.sjrichardsauthor.com

For Jane and Jean

The Luke Sackville Crime Thriller Series

Taken to the Hills
Black Money
Fog of Silence
The Corruption Code
Lethal Odds
Sow the Wind
Beacon of Blight
Tiger Bait
Mr Killjoy
Behind the Ivy

Chapter 1

"I'm concerned about Jack," Stephanie said as she started chopping the last potato. "He's not finishing his meals, and I'm worried that Kelly woman is getting to him."

Larry put his coffee down and sighed.

"You shouldn't worry so much. He'll pull out of it."

"Were you like that when you were his age?"

"No, but I was still at school. This is work, and he's not used to it yet. He's only been at Filchers for three months, and I'm sure his boss isn't as bad as he says she is."

"I don't know. She sounds like a bully to me, and from what he's said, she's taking advantage of him."

Larry shook his head.

"Jack's an office assistant. Photocopying and low-level admin are part of the job, and he needs to recognise that and grow a pair. He's lucky to have anything after giving up on his A-levels the way he did."

Stephanie put her knife down and turned to face her husband.

"It's got worse over the past few days. Don't tell me you haven't noticed."

"He'll get over it."

"Stop saying that."

She heard footsteps and turned around to see Amelia at the bottom of the stairs. Exasperated with her husband's attitude, she decided it was worth seeing if their daughter knew what was up with her brother.

"Does Jack talk to you, Amelia?"

She walked towards her, pursed her lips and shrugged.

"About what?"

"About how he's feeling. How things are at work."

"Not really. Is food ready yet?"

"Amelia, I'm seriously worried."

Stephanie turned back to her husband.

"There's another thing, too. He's spending more and more time in his bedroom."

"He's playing video games, that's all. They all do these days. It'll be 'Call of Duty', shooting up the bad guys." He laughed. "Probably the good guys, too."

Amelia walked over to one of the pans on the stove and peered inside.

"What are we having, Mum?"

"Lamb casserole."

Stephanie added the potatoes and stirred them in.

"It'll be ready in about half an hour."

"Great. I'm starving."

"Amelia, please be serious for a second and stop thinking about your stomach. Do you think your brother's okay?"

"Probably."

Stephanie raised an eyebrow. "Probably?"

Amelia shrugged again.

"If he's got problems with his love life, he's hardly going to confide in his little sister, is he?"

"Love life? What do you mean, love life?"

"I noticed him smiling a few days ago, so I tried to wind him up, asked him if he finally had a girlfriend."

"What did he say?"

"He tapped the side of his nose and said something like. '*Yeah, and she's really into me*'. But then yesterday, when I asked him how they were getting on, he told me to fuck off."

"Amelia!"

"That's what he said. I'm quoting him, that's all. She's obviously dumped him, 'cos now he's full-on back to being a misery-guts."

"That explains why he's not eating," Larry said.

But Stephanie wasn't ready to let go.

"Did he say anything else about her, Amelia? Did he tell you her name?"

Amelia looked from her mother to her father, then back again.

"He was proper showing off, so he couldn't resist telling me something, but he made me promise not to reveal it to anyone else."

"Reveal what?"

"I told you. I promised."

"Amelia!"

"Okay. Don't tell him I said anything, though." She grinned. "She's a lot older than him, that's what he said. Nearly thirty, according to Jack, not that it matters now she's ended it."

Stephanie looked over at her husband and could see by the look on his face that he was thinking the same thing she was.

"What's up?" Amelia asked.

"Nothing, darling. He didn't tell you her name, though?"

"No."

"Look, why don't you go back to your room, and I'll call you when dinner's ready?"

"Okay."

Stephanie waited until she was out of earshot, but kept her voice low.

"Do you remember what Jack said the first week he started at Filchers?"

Larry nodded.

"Only too well. Told us his new boss was 'well fit' if I remember right." He paused. "It can't be Kelly, though, given how he's been complaining about the way she treats him. Unless…"

"What?"

"Well…" He hesitated. "Maybe he likes it, you know, being dominated by an older woman. It's what turns some men on."

"You're talking about our son, Larry. He's only seventeen."

"I'm just saying, that's all. Mind you, from what Amelia said, it sounds like it's ended anyway."

"Yes, but…" She swallowed. "If it *is* her, and they have had some kind of relationship, what happens now? He's still got to go to work and face her every day."

She shook her head in exasperation.

"We've got to talk to him."

"I don't think he'll speak to us."

"Larry, he's suffering. I can see it in his eyes. Go and ask him to come down so that we can have a word."

"I'm not sure that…"

She glared at her husband.

"Larry, please!"

He held his hands up.

"Okay. I'll try."

Chapter 2

Larry knocked on the bedroom door.

There was no answer.

He knocked again, harder this time, and was rewarded with a response, albeit a weak one.

"I'm not hungry."

He bent to the door and raised his voice to be sure he could be heard.

"You've got to eat, Jack."

"Leave it outside."

"It's not ready yet, but your mum and I would like to talk to you."

Larry heard sounds from the bedroom and, a few seconds later, the door was pulled open.

Even though he'd only seen his son that morning, he was shocked by the pallor of his skin, which seemed all the more pale because his eyes were rimmed with red.

He stared into his father's eyes.

"I don't want to talk."

"Whatever's troubling you, we can help. That's what parents are for. You can tell us anything."

Jack shook his head.

"You wouldn't understand."

"Of course we would." Larry tried smiling. "At least give your old mum and dad a chance."

"There's no point."

Jack started to close the door, but his father moved his foot forward to stop him.

"Amelia told us about your girlfriend."

"Fucking snitch!"

"Jack!"

"She promised she wouldn't say anything. What did she

tell you?"

"Only that your girlfriend is older than you, and that she thought you'd been dumped. Is that what's happened? Is that why you're so upset?"

"She doesn't know the half of it."

"Then tell us. There'll be a way through this, Jack. There always is."

"Not through this, there isn't."

"Come on, at least give us a couple of minutes of your time. Talking it through will help, I'm sure it will."

He turned at the sound of footsteps to see Stephanie halfway up the stairs.

"Is he coming down?"

"He doesn't want to."

She reached the door, and Larry made way, hoping that their son would have the decency not to shut it now that he wasn't blocking it with his foot.

The door started to close, but then Jack seemed to have second thoughts and pulled it wide open. He glared at his father, and then at his mother, before spitting his next words out.

"Why can't you leave me alone?"

"Because we're your mum and dad, Jack," Stephanie said.

She wiped away a tear that was creeping towards her left cheek.

"If you're upset, we're upset. Please come down and talk to us."

Jack gave a deep sigh of exasperation before replying.

"We can talk here."

"Whatever's happened, we'll understand." She looked at her husband. "Won't we, Larry?"

"Of course we will."

She turned back to her son.

"Come down to the kitchen and I'll make you a hot chocolate?"

Jack gave a derisory snort.

"A hot chocolate! Like that's going to help."

She waited, sure he was on the verge of confiding in them.

After a few seconds of looking into his mother's eyes, Jack dropped his gaze to the ground and began speaking, his words so quiet that she almost couldn't catch what he was saying.

"I thought she... That..." He sighed again. "I thought she meant everything she said... That it was real..."

He stopped speaking, and she decided to prompt him.

"Real?"

He nodded, his face still bent forward, his eyes still on the carpet.

"Yes. Between us, I mean... And then I... She..."

He hesitated.

It was Larry who prompted him this time.

"What did she do, Jack?"

Jack looked up at this and snorted again.

"*She* didn't do anything. It was me. All me. I thought she was genuine, that she meant every word. That's why... That's why..."

He stuttered to a halt, and it was clear he was struggling to hold himself together.

Again he bent his head forward, his eyes once more fixed on the carpet at their feet.

His parents gave him longer this time, and he started to sniff, close to tears and to breaking point.

Stephanie wanted nothing more than to put her arms around her son, to cradle him and tell him everything was going to be okay.

"Jack?" she said softly.

He sniffed again, but didn't reply.

"Jack," she went on, keeping her voice low, "was it Kelly?"

He looked up at this, his eyes suddenly wide and staring.

"Did Amelia…" He swallowed. "Did Amelia tell you that?"

Stephanie shot a look at her husband before replying.

"She's not worth it. You know that, don't you? I understand that you feel let down, but time is a healer. It'll work out for the best."

"Time is a healer! Is that the best you can do?" He shook his head again. "You're a joke, a fucking joke."

"Jack!" Larry said, "Don't speak to your mother like that!"

This time the door was slammed shut before Larry could react, and they both heard the key turn in the lock.

Stephanie knocked on the door.

"Jack, please."

There was no response.

"Jack!" she repeated.

This was again met with silence.

Larry grabbed his wife's hand and squeezed it.

"I think we should leave him to it for the moment. I'll come back up when the meal's ready and see if I can entice him down."

She shook her hand away and stared at him.

"He's not a pet, Larry! It's not a matter of luring him downstairs with treats."

"I know. I meant…"

She sighed, took a last look at her son's bedroom door, and then turned to lead the way downstairs.

Chapter 3

Stephanie's eyes burned from lack of sleep.

There was one point in the night when she thought she was dropping off, but her husband's regular snoring had soon put paid to that idea.

Larry was still asleep, apparently able to shake off any worries about their son. She wished she had his resilience, but thoughts of the pain Jack was going through were too much for her to bear.

It was a mother's curse, she supposed.

He hadn't come down to eat, despite repeated pleas from both of them through his locked bedroom door. In the end, they'd left his meal on a tray, but when they'd gone to bed it was still there, untouched, the fat starting to congeal. Larry had sealed it and put it in the fridge, trying to assure her that their son would be ravenous at some point in the night and would heat it in the microwave and wolf it down.

She wasn't so sure.

He had looked so desperately unhappy when he'd come to his bedroom door, haunted by demons and utterly distraught. How had that woman got her talons into him like that? He was a decade younger than her, still a teenager, a boy, not a man.

Bitch.

There had to be a way to help him, had to be.

She glanced at the bedside clock and saw it was still only a quarter past five. The alarm was set for 6:30, but it was already growing light outside, and she knew there was no chance of going to sleep.

Clambering out of bed, she tugged her dressing gown tight around her body, suddenly cold and shivery. She didn't bother to creep out of the room. Larry wasn't a light sleeper, and it would take a foghorn to wake him.

She walked along the corridor to Jack's room and put her ear to the door. There wasn't a sound, and she hoped against hope that he had finally succumbed to his tiredness.

The first thing she did when she reached the kitchen was check the fridge. As feared, his meal was still there, and she couldn't see signs of anything else being taken either. There were yoghurts, cheese, cooked sausages, items he would normally snaffle on a midnight hunt for food, but they were all untouched.

She moved to the snacks cupboard, where Jack's favourite Pringles were kept, but the two packets inside remained sealed.

Still, he had to emerge at some point, perhaps refreshed by sleep, realising that not everything had been lost by being shunned by that woman.

She put the kettle on and absent-mindedly dropped a teabag and two sweeteners into a cup, all the time wondering what she could do to help him. Was it worth speaking to someone in Filchers, or would going behind Jack's back be a mistake? It might get him into trouble, making him even more distressed.

The water came to the boil, and she started to pour it into her mug, then jumped in shock when there was a loud thump from above.

From Jack's bedroom.

She looked up instinctively, deciding that he must have needed the loo and stumbled against something in his room in the dark. With any luck, he would have the munchies too, and would appear at the bottom of the stairs at any moment.

But what if he didn't?

Should she take her opportunity now and go up to talk to him? The last thing she wanted was for him to return to the misery of his room and lock himself in.

Before she could decide, there was another thump, even louder this time. A different sound, and coming from the upstairs hall rather than the bedroom.

Then Larry called out at the top of his voice.

"OPEN THE DOOR!"

He sounded panicked.

She thought back to that first thump.

It couldn't be, could it?

With a shaking hand, Stephanie placed the kettle down on the counter and dashed to the stairs.

There was a rattling sound as her husband flicked the handle up and down in an attempt to open the door. Then another two thumps as he banged on the bedroom door with his fist.

"JACK! LET ME IN!"

She took the steps two at a time and shouted up to her husband.

"My God, Larry. What's going on?"

When she reached the top, she saw that he had moved a few feet away.

He turned to look at her for a split second, then twisted and dived shoulder-first into the door.

There was a crack, but it didn't give way.

Undeterred, he stepped back and charged again.

This time, there was a loud snap, and he almost fell through as the door crashed open.

As he stumbled to his feet, Stephanie looked past him to see the limp body of their son, his head bent forward over his chest as he swung slowly from side to side.

She put her hand to her mouth and watched Larry dive towards the coffee table lying on its side a few feet away. He turned it upright, stepped on top and reached up, putting his arms around Jack's buttocks and lifting so that he, and not the rope around their son's neck, was taking the strain.

"Find something to cut him free," he gasped.

Before she could say or do anything, there was a scream

from behind her, followed by a single-word exclamation.

"FUCK!"

Stephanie turned to see her daughter, who had her mouth open and was staring wide-eyed up at her brother.

"Call an ambulance! Now!"

Amelia turned on her heels and headed back to her room.

"The rope's thick," Larry said, still gasping as he held their son up. "Scissors won't do it."

"I'll get a knife."

She raced back to the kitchen, retrieved the paring knife from the block, then returned to the bedroom, pulled out Jack's desk chair so that it was next to Larry, and climbed on top.

Once she was on tiptoe, Stephanie raised her left hand to grip the rope just below the ceiling pendant.

She started sawing, hoping and praying that they weren't too late.

Chapter 4

"Well, Luke?" Edward Filcher asked from his elevated seat at the head of the table. "I say we kick the idea into the long grass. Take it off-piste. Ensure we're on the same page."

The Director of Internal Affairs had reached item five of eleven in the weekly meeting with his subordinates. Numbers one to four hadn't been gripping, but this one took the biscuit.

The last thing Luke wanted was to spend even more time discussing it one-on-one.

"I'm not sure you and I need to talk about this any further, Mr Filcher."

"Mmm. Not so sure." He tapped the side of his more-than-considerable proboscis. "Ethical considerations."

Luke furrowed his brows.

"I don't see how ethics come into it. All they're doing is moving your car parking space."

"Yes, but near the bins! Near the bins! Hah!" He inflated his nostrils, snorted and then shook his head from side to side as if this was the worst calamity to befall mankind. "Thin end of the wedge!"

Luke glanced across at Fred Tanner and saw that he was enjoying the exchange. The Head of Marketing loved to wind their boss up, and couldn't resist throwing in his two penn'orth.

"It wouldn't be cricket, Mr Filcher," he said in his strong Yorkshire accent.

Filcher looked over at him and nodded approvingly.

"Exactly, Fred. Not cricket." He turned back to Luke. "Not cricket," he repeated, still nodding.

"Not if you're using a wedge," Fred went on.

Filcher's head flicked back.

"Eh?"

"It would be golf."

To Luke's surprise, it was the man on his left who spoke next, although, as usual, what Glen Baxter said served more to confuse than to clarify.

"Idiot," the Head of Security said, staring straight at Filcher, a broad, all-teeth-on-show grin spread across his face.

"Me?" Filcher said.

Glen nodded, looked down at his notes, and then back up at his boss.

"Idiot," he repeated, still pleased with himself.

Filcher sucked his jaw in, and Glen's grin disappeared as he reflected on what he had just said.

"Oh! Did I…" He held both hands up. "I didn't mean… Um…" He looked down at his pad again, then back up. "It's 'm' not 't'."

"What in blazes are you talking about?"

Glen paused, put his hand to the top of his head, scratched his buzz cut for a few seconds, then attempted an explanation.

"You're not an idiot."

"That's a relief."

"But you used one of…" He gestured to his writing pad. "…these."

Filcher sighed.

"Explain yourself, man."

"It sounds like 'idiot' but ends in an 'm'."

"Eh?"

"Idiom," Luke suggested.

Filcher still looked confused, but Glen nodded again, and his grin returned.

"The thin end of the wedge, you said. It was an id-i-om." He looked down and slid his finger along as he read from his writing pad. "A group of words established by usage as having a meaning not deducible from those of the individual words."

Filcher shook his head in disbelief.

James McDonald, who headed up Human Resources, hadn't spoken for a while, but decided to intervene in an attempt to move the meeting on.

"I can have a word with Services if you'd like, Mr Filcher? See if they'll reconsider moving your space."

"Mmm. Yes. Excellent." He turned back to Luke. "See, Luke? Teamwork. Cooperation. Vital." He looked across at the newest member of his team. "Don't you agree, ah, Wyn?"

"Oh yes, Mr Filcher," Arwyn Thomas said in his distinctive Welsh valleys accent. "Teamwork makes the dream work."

Luke inwardly cringed at this latest arse-licking comment from the Head of IT, and glanced at Fred, whose widening of the eyes and slight shaking of the head made it clear that he felt much the same way.

James managed to keep his feelings about the matter to himself, in typical diplomatic style, while Glen had become distracted by something caught under the nail of his right index finger.

"Well said," Filcher said, beaming across at the Head of IT. He leaned forward, and for a second it looked as though he was going to pat the man on the head, but he contented himself with a sigh of pleasure.

"Good to have you on board, Wyn."

"Arwyn," Arwyn corrected.

"Yes. Indeed. Excellent decision to transfer you." He tapped the side of his nose. "Took some lobbying, but makes eminent sense. Nonsense having IT in Property Services. Internal Affairs is where you belong. In my fiefdom. My bailiwick."

His chest puffed out as he said this, then he sighed again, a happy man to have increased the size of his empire, and picked up his copy of the agenda.

"Moving on. Ah… Item six. Christmas bonuses."

"But it's only May," Fred said.

Filcher gave him a patronising smile.

"Early planning, Fred. Ensure we hit the back of the net before the goalposts move. Need to keep the ship on the rails."

Fred was about to reply when there was a knock at the door, and Filcher's secretary entered the room without waiting for an answer.

"What's this?" Filcher snapped. "You should know better, Gloria. No interruptions unless it's a matter of life and death."

She ignored him and looked directly at Luke.

"You're needed in reception, Luke."

Filcher's hackles rose.

"A visitor! That hardly constitutes…"

Gloria interrupted before he could finish, her attention still on Luke.

"Leanne says a woman is threatening to murder one of our staff. We thought of calling the police, but since you're here…"

Luke got to his feet and followed her out of the room.

Filcher waved his hand as if urging them on.

"Excellent. Ah…"

The door shut behind Luke and Gloria, and he swallowed, then lowered his voice before finishing the sentence.

"…deal with it, will you, Luke?"

Chapter 5

Luke reached the ground floor to find Leanne perched on the edge of the gold sofa that faced the reception desk, her hands clasped over the hands of the woman beside her, though whether this was to console her or to prevent her from standing up wasn't completely clear.

It was evident that the woman was distressed. She was shaking, and it was clear she'd been crying, but there was more than upset in her face. There was anger there too, deep-seated anger.

Leanne looked up as he approached.

"This is Stephanie," she said, her voice quiet as if speaking louder might reawaken the beast.

As it happened, those three softly spoken words were enough.

Stephanie jerked her hands away and rose to her feet.

"Where is she? Where's that… that… SLUT?"

Luke put his hands on her shoulders.

"Please calm down, Stephanie."

She craned her head back and glared up at him, wriggling her shoulders in an attempt to back away. He held firm and, after a few seconds, she realised that the man towering above her wasn't going to let go.

Her shoulders sagged, and she seemed to visibly deflate.

"The Royal Crescent Room is empty," Leanne said to Luke, still speaking quietly. "Perhaps the two of you could talk in there."

Before he could reply, a man came bursting through the automatic doors and made a beeline for them.

"Stephanie," he gasped. "Thank goodness. I was so worried."

Luke released her from his grip, and the man grabbed one of her hands in his.

She looked up at him, her eyes wide.

"She needs to be dealt with, Larry. For what she's done! Our son…" She swallowed. "He'll never…"

She collapsed into tears and buried her head in the man's shoulder.

A small group of people was watching events unfold, and Luke decided he needed to take the couple where they could talk in private.

"Please, can you come with me?" He indicated the door to the conference room. "We can talk in there, and you can explain what's bothering you."

"What's bothering us!" Stephanie shrieked.

"Shh, Darling. He's only trying to help."

"After you," Luke said, gesturing for them to take the lead.

"Let me know if you need anything," Leanne said as she made her way back to the reception desk.

"Thanks."

He followed Stephanie and Larry into what was the building's largest meeting room. It was impersonal, with seating for sixteen around a rectangular glass-topped table. However, at least it offered some privacy.

Luke pulled out two chairs from the near end and indicated for them to sit down, then pulled a third out for himself.

"My name's Luke," he began, once they were all seated. "I head up one of the departments here."

"Does Kelly work for you?" Stephanie spat. "Is that why that girl fetched you?"

He smiled to try to put her at ease.

"I'm sorry, but I don't even know who you're talking about. I'd like to help if I can, though. Perhaps you could tell me why you're here?"

"Because of that bitch!"

She started to stand, but Larry restrained her.

"Stephanie, this isn't getting us anywhere."

He turned to Luke.

"On Saturday morning, I heard a noise from our son's bedroom. I shouted through to him, but he didn't answer, so I broke the door down." He hesitated before continuing. "Jack had tied a rope around the light fixture and… and…"

He stuttered to a stop, unable to complete the sentence, and then gulped before continuing.

"He works here. Well, worked here. And he'd been in a relationship with his manager. She ended it, and that's why he did it."

"Jack's only seventeen!" Stephanie shrieked. "That woman is nearly thirty."

Luke decided to try to calm her down by concentrating on the bare facts.

"What's your son's full name, Larry?"

"Jack Pickford. He's only been here a few months, working as an office assistant in the Spectra team."

"I see. What's his manager's name?"

"Kelly Gaynes."

"And Jack told you about his relationship with her, did he?"

Larry shook his head.

"No, he told our daughter. She's fifteen and likes to wind him up. Amelia said that he was boasting about it at the beginning of the week and then, on Friday, she teased him about having a relationship with an older woman, and he told her that Kelly had finished with him."

"I see."

Luke paused. The next question was a hard one, but he had to ask it.

"Did you manage to get to Jack in time?"

Larry sighed.

"Possibly. The doctors at the RUH say that he's likely to make a full physical recovery, because he didn't suffer a cardiac arrest. Their concern is that there may be brain damage. Jack's still in a coma, so we won't know if that's the case until he regains consciousness."

"Where is she?" Stephanie said. "I want to know what she has to say for herself."

"I don't think that would be sensible," Luke said. "You need to leave it with me and return to your son." He turned to her husband. "What's your phone number?"

They exchanged contact details.

"I promise you I'll get to the bottom of this. I'll give you a ring as soon as I've spoken to Kelly."

"Thank you, Luke."

He escorted the couple to the exit and watched as they walked to their car. Once he was sure they had left, he returned to reception.

"What was she so upset about?" Leanne asked.

"Their son attempted suicide over the weekend, and they think it was because of something his manager did."

"How awful."

"His name's Jack Pickford, and he's seventeen and works in the Spectra team. I don't suppose you know him, do you?"

Leanne shook her head. "I don't think so."

"What about Kelly Gaynes? He works for her."

She curled her upper lip. "Oh yes, I know Kelly all right. Has she been bullying him? Was that why he did it?"

"Why do you say that?"

"Because it wouldn't surprise me if she had. She's very full of herself, and I've overheard a couple of her staff complaining about the way she treats them."

"Mmm. The Spectra team are on the third floor, aren't they?"

"Yes. At the far end."

"Right. I'll see if she's in and try to get to the bottom of this."

Chapter 6

The Spectra account occupied the end half of the third floor. Most of the forty or so staff had transferred to Filchers when the company had been awarded the contract a couple of years earlier, but this was the first time Luke had had reason to pay the team a visit.

He approached a woman at the first cubicle, and was about to ask where he could find Kelly Gaynes when he heard a voice behind him.

"Sackville. My word, this is a rare visitation."

He turned to see Bernard Fogg, Spectra's client director. They had only met a few times but, on each occasion, he had proved to be overbearing and supercilious.

It also grated that the man insisted on calling him by his surname.

"Hello, Bernard," he said, attempting to smile through gritted teeth.

Bernard snorted. It came from nowhere, but somehow seemed appropriate given his upturned nose and large nostrils gave him an undeniably piggish appearance.

"Not done anything wrong ethically, have we, Sackville?"

He put the emphasis on 'ethically' as if it were a dirty word, and delivered the entire sentence as though he was talking to a three-year-old.

"I don't know yet, Bernard. Possibly."

He let this sink in before continuing.

"I'm looking for Kelly Gaynes. Can you tell me where she sits?"

"Three cubicles along."

"Thank you."

"What's this about?"

Luke ignored him, turned around and began walking towards her desk, only stopping when Bernard spoke again.

"She's not there."

Luke closed his eyes for a second, and sighed before turning back.

"In that case, do you know where she is?"

"You ignored my question, Sackville."

Luke didn't bother responding.

"She reports to me," Bernard went on, and started to advance aggressively.

After a few paces, it dawned on him that Luke had a considerable height advantage, and he stopped in his tracks, before backing away again.

"And?" Luke prompted.

"I am her manager, and I need to know what this is about."

"It's private and confidential. Between her and me. Now, where is she?"

"I'm not sure…"

This time it was Luke who advanced towards the smaller man, only stopping when he was a couple of feet away.

He glared down at him.

"I haven't the time to put up with this, Bernard. Where's Kelly?"

"She'll tell me anyway. And if it's about me, then I ought to be spoken to first."

Luke raised one eyebrow.

"Why would you think it's about you?"

"Oh! I see."

This was an odd response and suggested that he expected any accusations to centre on him. It might simply be the man's belief that he was the centre of the universe, but Luke made a mental note to follow up on it later.

"She's in our meeting room," Bernard continued, pointing to the left-hand door at the end of the floor.

Luke walked to the door, knocked and entered without waiting for an answer.

There were two people inside, seated on either side of a small table. To the left was an attractive, dark-haired woman in her late twenties, while opposite sat a man in thick, black rectangular glasses who looked to be a couple of decades her senior. Although he was older, it was clear from their body language that she was the one dominating the conversation.

She turned and glared at Luke, and he corrected his initial impression. Yes, she was pretty, could even be described as beautiful in the strictly classical sense, but she had a hard edge to her face that made her distinctly unattractive.

"Do you mind?" she snapped.

Luke smiled. "Not at all." He turned to the man. "Would you mind leaving us for a moment? Kelly and I have something important to discuss."

"You can't..." she started to say, but the man had already got to his feet, and Luke held the door open for him before closing it and sitting down.

She sat upright and glared across at him.

"This isn't on. Who are you?"

"I'm Luke Sackville, Head of Ethics. I'm sorry to burst in on you like this, but something has come up that we need to discuss."

"Ethics, did you say?"

"Yes, that's right."

She sighed, and her confrontational attitude dissipated somewhat. "You've found out about our relationship, haven't you?"

He nodded.

"Who told you?"

"His mother."

This seemed to surprise her.

"His mother?"

"She came into the office this morning intent on confronting you."

"But why? Is it the age difference?"

"In part. Ten years is a lot at his age."

"I'm twenty-nine. I'm hardly a child."

"That's the point, isn't it?"

She looked confused by this, and it dawned on Luke that she hadn't heard what Jack Pickford had done.

"I take it you're not aware of his attempted suicide?"

She put her hand to her mouth.

"What? No. When?"

"On Saturday." This seemed to confuse her even more. "His mother told me he did it because you ended the relationship."

She opened her mouth, but no words came out. After a few seconds, she shook her head.

"You've got this all wrong. I didn't end our relationship. As far as I'm concerned, we're still a couple."

"Did you say something that made him think it was over?"

"No." She stood up. "Why don't we get him in here and ask him?"

"We can't. He's still in a coma."

She sucked her chin in and stared at him.

"Was that a joke?"

"I would hardly joke about something like this, Kelly. The doctors say that Jack may have brain damage."

She opened her mouth again, this time for even longer.

"Are you…" She shook her head disbelievingly. "Are you talking about Jack Pickford?"

It was Luke's turn to be confused.

"Who else would I be talking about?"

"Jack and I have never had any kind of relationship. I'm his manager, but that's it. The kid's only seventeen, for heaven's sake."

"But you admitted it. You asked if his mother's concern

was the age difference."

She smiled.

"Yes. That's because Bernard is forty."

*

Luke went straight over to Sam when he returned to the Ethics Room.

She smiled up at him.

"Josh left about thirty minutes ago. He's unbelievably excited about his course." She spotted the grim look on his face. "What's up? Was Filcher's meeting awful?"

"Probably, but I had to leave after half an hour."

"Why? What happened?"

"I don't want to distract Maj and Helen. Let's find somewhere we can talk, and I'll explain. I'd appreciate your thoughts on what to do next."

They found a vacant meeting room, and Luke told her first what Jack Pickford's parents had said, and then about Kelly Gaynes' response when he confronted her.

"And you're convinced she's telling the truth?"

He nodded. "Stephanie and Larry were sure it was her, though." He thought about this for a second. "However, it was their daughter Amelia who told them about the relationship. It could be that she didn't mention a name, and they leapt to a false conclusion. We could do with talking to her, to find out exactly what her brother said."

"Do we need to? It might seem harsh, but if it's not Kelly, then surely it's not our problem."

"It could be another member of the Spectra team." He paused. "Even if it isn't, Jack's a Filchers employee, and his parents are desperate to find out what drove him to suicide. We need to help for their sake."

Sam nodded. "Yes, I guess you're right."

He smiled across at her and put his hand on hers.

"Sam, I don't suppose…"

She smiled back.

"You want me to talk to the daughter?"

"She's only fifteen, and I think it would be less threatening for her."

"Okay. I'm fine with that."

"Thanks."

He gave her Larry Pickford's phone number.

"In the meantime," she said, once she'd entered his details into her contacts, "is there anything else we can do?"

"Not that I can think of. Hopefully, Jack will regain consciousness soon and we'll find the truth out then."

Chapter 7

To say Josh was excited was an understatement.

He was so absorbed in studying the course contents that he only just made it out of the carriage at Bristol Temple Meads before the doors closed.

Criminology and Ethics.

Wowza!

He stood on the platform, the syllabus open at the second page. Boy, did they pack a lot into three days. It started with the factors contributing to criminal behaviour, before looking at the criminal justice system. Only then did it move on to the ethical principles guiding decision-making. And after that…

"Have you still got a girlfriend?"

Josh's brain took a moment to process this interruption, then he looked up and smiled as he realised who had spoken.

"Mandy! Coolio."

He gave her a hug, and then stepped back.

He'd last seen her when the Ethics team helped her mother escape the clutches of a romance scammer, but she looked just as pretty as he remembered, her long brown hair much the same length, her lips full, and her eyes a deep brown.

However, there was something different about her, he was sure of it.

"Well," she said, a twinkle in her eye. "Have you still got a girlfriend?"

She'd floored him with that one the first time they met.

"Uh… No."

"No?"

"Well, yes."

She laughed.

"Make up your mind."

"Leanne and I are still together, but we're engaged."

"Congratulations."

"Thanks. What about you?"

As he said it, he realised what was different about her. It was her tummy. He tilted his head to one side as he studied her midriff.

It was definitely larger.

In fact, she had quite a belly bump.

He looked back up at her, pointed at her stomach and beamed.

"You're pregnant."

She furrowed her brows, looked back at him in horror, and then cast her eyes down to her tummy.

"What? You think I'm expecting?" She swallowed. "I've been eating a lot of chocolate, and I knew I'd been putting on weight, but I didn't realise it was that obvious."

She looked on the verge of tears.

Pissedy-piss-piss.

Open mouth, insert foot.

That was him all over.

"Sorry." He gulped. "Ah…"

Mandy grinned.

"Of course I'm pregnant." She tapped her tummy. "Almost six months."

Josh heaved a sigh of relief.

"You're mean, you know that?"

"And you're as easy to tease as ever." She pointed at the document in his hand. "Are you on the Criminology and Ethics course as well?"

He nodded.

"Uh-huh. I'm still in the Ethics Team at Filchers."

"I'm surprised. Must be pretty boring."

"Oh, I don't know. It certainly keeps us busy."

"What sort of projects do you work on?"

"Quite a wide range. Since I met you we've had to deal with international terrorists, neo-Nazis, police corruption, people trafficking, kidnappings, modern human slavery, organised crime, drug cartels, that kind of thing."

She laughed, assuming he was joking.

"The usual run-of-the-mill corporate nonsense then?"

"Exactly." He paused. "What about you? Are you still with Integrity?"

She nodded. "I'm a fully-fledged investigator now."

"Gucci!"

"Come on. We'd better get going. It starts in forty-five minutes."

*

The course was being held in one of Bristol University's larger lecture theatres. It had twenty rows of banked seating facing a teaching wall, and Josh and Mandy arrived ten minutes before the start and sat themselves on the fifth tier.

The lead presenter was ex-Detective Inspector Philip Angler, now lecturing at the University. His police career had been at Wessex Police, and Josh made a mental note to ask Luke if he knew him.

Angler's delivery was dry, and all he did for the first thirty minutes was tee up the forthcoming sessions. However, he lightened up once he introduced the first topic, 'Understanding Crime', and Josh made copious notes as he ran through the different types of crime and what drove criminal behaviour.

After he'd finished, Josh and Mandy made their way to the building's cafe, and he fetched their drinks while she found a table by the window.

"I see you're being careful with your weight," she said, as he lifted his luxury hot chocolate with cream and extra marshmallows to his mouth.

"Sure am." He grinned and pointed at her tummy. "Unlike you."

"Stop it!"

"You didn't tell me about the father. Are you still an item?"

"Yeah. Leo's great, and we've been living together for nine months now. He has to put up with a lot."

Josh nodded in understanding, thinking about the challenges presented by Leanne for a few days each month.

"With your mood swings?"

She raised one eyebrow.

"No, my working hours."

"Oh. Ah…" He swallowed. "Right."

"They vary from day to day, and sometimes I have to do an all-nighter watching someone's house."

"Is there a lot of variety in what you do?"

"A fair bit of it is personal. You know, people who suspect their other half is having an affair. We do some corporate work too, though. I'm on an unusual case at the moment for Wandsworth Borough Council." She paused. "Quishing."

"Bless you."

"Ha, ha. I take it you haven't heard of quishing?"

Josh shook his head.

"No. What is it?"

"I'm sure you've heard of phishing. You know, where someone gets an email saying they've been left £1 million, and all they have to do is send an admin fee."

"Yes, I've heard of that."

"Well, quishing is similar, only they use QR codes."

"What, people are emailed QR codes?"

"It can be that, but not in Wandsworth's case. For a short period last month they issued a lot more penalty charge notices for their Burr Road car park than is common. They put it down to a random spike, but then they started to receive dozens of emails a day from motorists disputing the fines and saying they'd paid."

"And it's not their systems at fault?"

"No. They thought that was it at first, but when that didn't seem to be the problem, they commissioned Integrity to look into it." She smiled, evidently pleased with herself. "It's my first case as lead investigator, and I managed to find out what was going on pretty quickly."

"Go on."

"I went to the car park, and looked at the machines to see if there were any indications that they'd been tampered with. There weren't, but when I looked at the signs behind the machines, the ones describing the payment options and the parking costs, I spotted residue around the QR code on each one. I had it tested, and it's glue. I'm pretty certain that someone had stuck their own QR codes over the real ones, a QR code that directed the motorist to a false website where they paid for their parking, unwittingly transferring the money into the criminal's bank account."

"What's your next step?"

"Two things. First, I'm going to speak to some of the people who've disputed their penalty charge notices, and see if they can tell me anything useful about the site that the QR code took them to. And second, I've had CCTV installed so that if someone tries it again, we can catch them on film."

"Coolio!"

He paused.

"It'll be interesting to see what our lecturer has to say about quishing, and how common it is. If there's an opportunity, I'll ask him."

*

The day's final session examined the roles of the police, courts, prisons and remand centres. Josh found it interesting, but so far removed from the subject of cybercrime that he felt it best to ask the ex-DI his question when he could get him on his own.

Or perhaps he should leave it altogether.

Mandy sensed his nervousness.

"Come on," she said, as the Q&A session ended and people started to leave. "I'm sure he doesn't bite."

She led the way down to the front of the hall, where Philip Angler was tidying his papers away into a battered brown briefcase. A short, stocky man in his early 50s, he was completely bald with a ruddy face and a sincere, if somewhat intense, manner. The fact that he had transitioned successfully from police officer to lecturer was evidenced by the leather patches on both elbows of his brown tweed jacket.

He fastened the clip on his case and looked up as they approached.

A nervous chuckle emerged unbidden from Josh's mouth, and he looked at Mandy, then back at the lecturer.

"Go on," she said, egging him on. "Ask him."

"Ah… Mr Angler…"

"Yes. Do you have a question?"

"Ah…"

Josh found himself chuckling again, though it was more of a maniacal mini-laugh this time.

"Out with it, lad."

"Ah… What do you know about different types of phishing?"

There.

He'd asked.

He heaved a sigh of relief, and then tried to smile, though it felt very hollow, his cheeks lifting without the lips following.

Angler stared at him for a moment before speaking.

"What are you, boy? Twenty, twenty-one?"

Josh's response came out an octave or two higher than

he meant it to.

"I'm twenty-three."

"Don't you think you're a little old for this level of humour?"

"Eh?"

"Will it make you happy if I answer the question?"

"Ah..." Josh cast another glance in Mandy's direction. "Yes, I guess so."

Angler sighed.

"Fly-fishing, netting and trawling. There. Happy now?"

He picked up his case and started to walk away. As he did so, it suddenly dawned on Josh why the man was annoyed.

"Mr Angler?" he squeaked.

Angler stopped and turned back to face him, a grim expression on his face.

"Yes?"

"It's not because of your name. I mean, I wasn't asking about fishing, I was asking about phishing."

Angler's expression grew even darker, and Mandy decided to come to Josh's rescue.

"Phishing with a P-H," she said. "Quishing and vishing too. We wanted to know how commonplace they are."

"Quishing and vishing. Ah-hah. I see."

He turned back to Josh.

"Did you mean phishing as in fake emails?"

Josh nodded.

"Exactimo."

"May I ask why you're interested?"

Mandy explained about the fake QR codes in Wandsworth car parks.

"My, my," he said when she'd finished. "That's a new one on me. Quishing is generally used to capture people's login details, or to install malware on their devices, but taking money directly is very innovative."

"How would it work?" Josh asked.

"It's simple, really. The person, a motorist in this case, scans the QR code on their phone and is taken to a website that looks like the Council's but puts their money into the criminal's account."

"Wouldn't the website cost a lot to produce?"

"Not necessarily. Thousands of criminals subscribe to services such as FraudGPT on the dark web. For a few hundred pounds a month, they can easily produce malicious code and fraudulent messages." He paused, warming to his subject. "Vishing is on the up too."

"Vishing?" Josh asked.

"It's short for 'voice phishing', where the criminal uses phone calls or voice messages to trick victims into providing sensitive information, like login credentials, credit card numbers or bank details."

Angler smiled, now in his element.

"Cybercrime is a key interest of mine," he went on. "I'll be talking about it in one of tomorrow's sessions, but only briefly. Buy me a coffee, though, and you can pick my brains on it now."

"Gucci!"

"Pardon?"

"He means yes," Mandy said. "I'll treat you to a slice of cake too, if you're interested."

Chapter 8

Josh cut his bacon in two, stuck the end of his fork into the larger piece, dabbed it into the HP sauce on his plate until it had picked up the perfect amount, and then popped it in his mouth.

It was delicious.

"Thanks," he said after he'd swallowed it. "This is terrifico."

Leanne didn't respond, her back to him as she concentrated on the pan of boiling water containing her egg.

She'd insisted on cooking breakfast for both of them, which was good because it meant she'd forgiven him. Okay, she wasn't exactly chatty this morning, had hardly said a word in fact, but he put that down to tiredness.

Her shoulders seemed tense, though, as if she was bottling something up.

Was there a chance she was still annoyed with him for, well, whatever it was she'd been annoyed with him for the previous evening? He'd said something to upset her, that much was clear, but he couldn't for the life of him work out what it was.

He cut himself a piece of sausage, dipped it in the sauce, and tried to recall exactly what had happened.

She'd been keen to hear about the first day of the course, so he'd run through the contents of the afternoon sessions, told her how impressive DI Angler was, and, of course, he'd mentioned running into Mandy.

That was when her frown had appeared.

The frown.

The one accompanied by teapot arms and the single word reply of '*Really?*' to everything.

As far as he remembered, all he'd done was say that Mandy was looking good.

Hadn't he?

Now that he came to think about it, he might not have used exactly those words, but it was close. He'd been careful to avoid saying she was 'pretty' or 'attractive', that was for certain.

He wasn't stupid.

The cooker alarm pinged, and Leanne lifted her egg onto her plate, turned around and dropped into the seat opposite.

He looked across at his fiancée as she started buttering her toast, and reflected on how lucky he was. Even when angry, she was beautiful, gorgeous in every way imaginable, great to chat to, pretty as hell. She had the perfect figure too, with curves in all the right places, and…

"SHITTEDY-SHIT-SHIT!"

There was a loud clatter as Leanne's knife slipped from her hand.

"What is it, Joshy? Is your sausage undercooked?"

"No, it's fine." He hesitated. "Curves in all the right places. That was what I said, wasn't it?"

She furrowed her brows.

"Yes."

"When I was telling you about Mandy?"

"Yes."

"And that's what upset you?"

"Yes."

The frown from the evening before was back in full force now, the only difference being that its accompaniment was 'yes' rather than 'really'.

"But, I didn't mean her, ah…" He gestured vaguely towards Leanne's breasts.

"Oh. And that's supposed to make me feel better, is it? I'm supposed to be pleased that you only fancy her curvaceous arse?"

"I didn't. I don't. She doesn't... Well, she might have..."

"Joshy!"

He swallowed.

"I meant her tummy. She's got a curvaceous tummy."

"And that's what you fancy about her?"

"Yes... I mean, no. Of course not."

"Then..."

"She's pregnant."

She raised both eyebrows and sucked her jaw in.

"Pregnant?"

Josh nodded.

"Why didn't you say so?"

"Because you want children, and, well, *you're* not pregnant."

She shook her head and smiled for the first time that morning.

"What are you like? Yes, I want children, but not now. I want them once we're married, and when we're both ready." She reached for his hand. "I want it to be just you and me for a while."

"You're not broody?"

"No, I'm not broody." She squeezed his hand and looked into his eyes. "Do you want to have children? And if so, when?"

Josh smiled.

"I think four would be good."

"Four years?"

He shook his head.

"Four children."

"Wowza!"

"Hey! That's my word."

"Four children?" she repeated.

He nodded. "Not all at once, though."

"Well, that's a relief. Have you thought when you'd like us to start trying?"

"Not until we're married, but perhaps, what do you think?" His voice rose an octave. "Perhaps quite soon after?"

She smiled.

"Is it you that's the broody one, Joshy?"

"Yes, I guess." He held his index finger and thumb out, leaving a tiny gap between them. "Maybe a teensy bit."

Chapter 9

Luke waited until Sam had fastened her seat belt and then set off for the twenty-minute drive from the farmhouse to Filchers' head office on the Lower Bristol Road in Bath.

"Well," she said, after they'd been driving for a few minutes and were approaching the village of Hinton Charterhouse, "what do you think of the VW so far?"

He considered this for a few seconds.

"The lack of engine noise is disconcerting, but I'm getting used to it. It's certainly comfy, and feels a lot more spacious than the Beemer. What about you?"

"It definitely makes things easier with Wilkins." She laughed. "Or at least, it will do once the dog guard arrives."

It was less than a week since Luke's company car had been exchanged for a silver Volkswagen ID7 Tourer, an all-electric hatchback. They'd taken Wilkins out in it for the first time over the weekend, and it had taken the cocker spaniel less than thirty seconds to discover that he could fit through the gap between the back seat and the roof. Before they knew it, he was sitting between them at the front of the vehicle.

Luke had ordered the dog guard as soon as they'd returned to Norton St Philip.

The phone started ringing.

"It's Josh," Luke said, as he tapped on the screen to answer the call.

"Hi, Josh. How was the course yesterday?"

"Brillianto. And Mandy's on it. You remember Mandy?"

"Mandy Jones? Yes, of course I remember her. How is she?"

"Still at Integrity and seems to be doing well. She's pregnant, too." He paused. "Our main instructor is Philip

Angler. He was a DI with Wessex Police, and I wondered if you knew him."

Luke smiled. "I remember Fishy. I worked with him on a couple of cases. He was a boon wherever technology was concerned."

"He's an expert on the ishings."

Luke and Sam exchanged a look.

"The ishings?" Sam asked.

"Oh. Hi, Sam. Yes. Phishing, quishing, vishing. He knows loads about all of them. AI too. Plus, the deep web and the dark web. Chatbots, deepfake, malware, you name it, he knows it."

"It sounds like you're impressed," Luke said. "Although I have to admit I didn't understand anything you just said."

"It's coolio."

"I'll take your word for that. But why are you ringing, Josh, or is it just to bamboozle me with high tech?"

"Ah, no. It was for advice, actually." He hesitated. "It can wait."

"Don't mind me," Sam said.

Josh remained silent.

"Is it something to do with work, Josh?" Luke asked.

"Not exactly."

"Not exactly?"

"Well, not at all. It's personal. I, ah…" His next words came out in a rush. "Have you ever been broody?"

"I can be gloomy sometimes, I guess."

"No, not that. I mean, if you think back, guv, way back, decades back, back when you were my age…"

"I get the picture, Josh."

"Back before Chloe and Ben were born, did you want children, or was it just Jess?"

"It was both of us."

"And were you broody, wanting children so much that it was almost a physical pain?"

Luke didn't have to think about his answer.

"No."

"Ah… Gotcha."

"What you need to do," Luke went on, as he recognised that Josh wanted more than a simple 'no', "is tell Leanne how you feel. Then you can agree on when to start a family. That's what Jess and I did."

"Thanks, guv. I'll do that." He paused. "I'll have to go, my train's pulling in."

"Okay. Bye, Josh."

"Bye, guv. Bye, Sam."

The line went dead.

"Where's Josh's real dad?" Sam asked after a few seconds.

Luke thought about this before answering.

"I don't know, to be honest. He's not on the scene, and Josh has never mentioned him."

He was about to say more when he replayed Sam's words in his brain and shot her a look.

"What do you mean, his *real* dad?"

She was smiling, almost laughing.

"Haven't you noticed?"

"Noticed what?"

"It's you he comes to whenever he needs advice, and it's not just work. He asked you how to propose, didn't he? And now he's asking your advice on when he and Leanne should have children. Next thing, he'll be asking you to walk him up the aisle."

He returned her smile.

The phone rang again, and he accepted the call.

"Hello. Luke Sackville."

"Luke, this is Ambrose. Are you in the office?"

"Not yet. I should be there in the next fifteen minutes."

"Good. Would you mind coming straight up to see me? I'll explain why when you get here." He paused. "Please can you pick Edward up on the way? This is something he ought to be in on."

"Okay, Ambrose. I'll do that."

He hung up.

"I wonder what that's all about," he mused.

"It's intriguing," Sam said. "Although that's not a word you should be using."

He glanced across and saw that she was smiling again.

"Go on. Why not?"

"Because the correct expression in your extended family is 'mucho intrigo'."

"Ha, ha."

Chapter 10

When Luke reached the corridor leading to the executive offices, he spotted his boss standing behind Gloria, his eyes focused on her monitor as she typed rapidly on the keyboard.

"Every Thursday," he said. He bent forward and jabbed his finger at the screen. "No meetings after two. Must be on the tee by...."

He spotted Luke in his peripheral vision and stopped mid-sentence, but didn't move a muscle.

"Ah..." he went on, without looking up. "Yes..." He jabbed at the screen again. "More tea. For meetings after 2 pm. More tea."

She furrowed her brows and turned to look up at him.

"I don't understand. Weren't we talking about meeting your caddy?"

"No, Gloria," he snapped, shaking his head as if she were being stupid. "We were talking about tea. To go with coffee. Tea!" He harrumphed. "For meetings. Ah... In a tea caddy. Keeps it fresh."

He waved his hands dismissively and looked up as if he'd noticed Luke for the first time.

"Ah! Good morning, Luke. Gloria and I were, ah..." He paused for a second. "We were discussing refreshments."

"So I heard."

"How can I help? Need a rundown of yesterday's meeting? Want to catch up on the six items you missed?"

That was the last thing Luke wanted.

"No," he said. "I need to take you to see Ambrose."

Filcher's eyes widened in horror. For him, being taken to see the chief executive was akin to being taken to the

Headmaster's study for being a very naughty boy.

"Oh! Because of the, ah…?"

He swallowed and pointed at Gloria's monitor.

"It's nothing to do with what you were discussing with Gloria, Mr Filcher," Luke said. "He rang me on my way in and said he needed to see both of us."

"I see. Excellent." He breathed a sigh of relief and turned his attention back to his secretary. "We'll talk later, Gloria. About the, ah…"

He pointed at the screen again.

"The refreshments?" she suggested, a barely concealed smile on her face.

"Indeed. Hah!"

He turned back to Luke.

"Right. Mustn't keep our CEO waiting. Wait here, Luke."

"But he wants to see both of us."

"Yes, but you report to me. I report to him. Line of control. Line of management. Important to respect the hierarchy. He will tell me what's needed. I will relay the information to you. Then, if appropriate…"

He was interrupted by a shout from the end of the corridor.

"Edward! Get a move on!"

Filcher froze mid-sentence and turned slowly around.

"Of course, Uncle."

"Be quick, will you?" Ambrose went on. "You're both keeping my guests waiting."

"Both?"

"Yes, both of you. I want both of you to join us."

"Naturally. As I thought. Excellent."

Luke glanced at Gloria, who had her hand to her mouth to prevent a snort of laughter from escaping, and then followed Filcher down the corridor.

Ellie, Ambrose's personal assistant, looked up as they approached her desk.

Mr Killjoy

"I'm about to phone for some drinks," she said. "Strong black coffee for you, Luke?"

"Yes, please."

"And for you, Mr Filcher?"

"Tea, please." He hesitated for a second, and flicked his eyes towards Luke, before adding, "Bring it in a caddy. A tea caddy, not a golf caddy."

"In a tea caddy?"

"Yes. It keeps it fresh."

"Edward! Move yourself!"

"Sorry, Uncle."

He pushed past Luke and rushed through the door into Ambrose's office.

Luke gestured for Ambrose to go first, and then followed him in.

A man and a woman stood up from either end of one of the two William Morris-covered linen sofas that made the room so relaxed and welcoming, and so very different from Filcher's stuffy, mahogany-filled office.

He didn't recognise either of them.

The woman was fifty or so, slim and around five feet five. Her blonde hair was cut in a short bob, and she wore a plain white shirt, black jacket and matching slacks. She was elegant, and could have easily passed for one of Filchers' board directors. However, there was something about her bearing that told Luke instantly that she was a police officer.

Her colleague was in his early forties, and harder to assess. He had short brown hair, his main distinguishing feature being a neat handlebar moustache, one end of which he was twirling with his right hand. His clothes were more formal, a grey suit, pale blue shirt and navy blue paisley tie.

Filcher marched past the woman, eyes fixed on the other guest, his chauvinistic antennae leading him to the automatic conclusion that the man had to be the senior of the two.

"I'm a director," he said pompously, and held his hand out. "Edward Filcher."

The visitor shook Filcher's hand briefly, and then looked across at Ambrose.

"Please sit down, Edward," Ambrose said.

"Of course," Filcher said. He snapped his hand back to his side, executed a military about-turn and marched to the second sofa, where he turned around again and dropped down vertically onto the edge.

"In fact, why don't you all sit down, and I'll make introductions."

They did so, and Ambrose pulled over a visitor's chair for himself before continuing.

"As Edward has mentioned, he is one of our directors."

"Internal Affairs," Filcher said. "Very important…"

Ambrose glared at him, and he stuttered to a stop.

"However, it's Luke that I felt it most important you meet since you'll be working closely together." He gestured to the woman. "Luke, Edward, this is Jean Scarrott. She's an assistant chief constable with Avon and Somerset Police."

"Pleased to meet you," Jean said, and Luke thought he detected an East Midlands accent. "I've heard a lot about you from the chief."

Filcher puffed his chest out like a hawk.

"I'm sure you have," he said.

"I'm sorry, Edward. I wasn't referring to you."

The air went out of him like a softly punctured balloon. She smiled across at Luke.

"Sara has told me what excellent support you and your team have been providing."

"That's very good of her, Ma'am."

Ambrose gestured to the man beside her.

"And this is Dominic Watts."

"Hello," Dominic said.

"Dominic is with…" Ambrose paused. "Before we

start, I need to emphasise the importance of keeping everything we say a secret."

"A secret," Filcher repeated, nodding sagely.

"What we are about to discuss must remain between us and us alone."

"Us alone."

Ambrose closed his eyes for a second before continuing.

"If it were to get out, it could have serious implications."

"Serious…"

"Enough!"

"I was just…"

"Well, don't." He paused. "As I was saying, if news of this escapes, it could not only impact the investigation, but also do irreparable damage to our company. Indeed, I thought twice before asking you both to join us."

"I'm sure Luke can be trusted," Filcher said.

Ambrose fixed his eyes on his nephew.

"So am I. And you, Edward? Do I have your word that nothing will escape your lips once you're sitting in Boodle's with your cronies after a couple of brandies?"

"Of course, Uncle." He tapped the side of his nose. "Of course."

Chapter 11

There was a knock at the door.

"Come in," Ambrose called.

Ellie entered with a tray. She placed it on the coffee table between the sofas, and Luke was amused to see that she had brought a silver storage jar with 'English Breakfast Tea' embossed in black on the side.

They helped themselves to drinks, Filcher making a great display of closing the storage jar quickly after removing a teabag.

"Keeps the tea fresh," he assured everyone, before removing the bag quickly from his cup to ensure his drink remained as weakly flavoured as possible.

"Jean," Ambrose said. "Perhaps you could outline why you're here?"

"Of course, Ambrose."

She paused to gather her thoughts.

"I'll begin with some background. I joined Avon and Somerset from Nottinghamshire Police a month ago and, because of my experience there, the chief constable asked me to take on cybercrime as part of my portfolio. My main focus is cyber-dependent crime, and by that I mean crime that can only be committed through the use of technology. A good example is hacking to steal customer data."

Jean took a sip of her coffee before continuing.

"Keeping one step ahead of criminals is always difficult. However, when it comes to computers and networks, it's particularly hard. They're able to expand their activities across country borders with minimal effort, and increases in processing power and the advent of artificial intelligence have made their lives easier all round."

She paused again.

"The only element in our favour has been the fact that the general criminal community lacks the IT skills needed to fully exploit the latest developments. However, that's all changing with the advent of cybercrime enablers who offer criminals an all-in-one solution."

She held her hands up.

"I hope I'm not losing you with all this."

"Not at all, dear lady," Filcher said in his most condescending tone.

He nodded knowingly.

"All-in-one solutions," he went on. "Oh yes. I fully understand."

"You do?"

"Yes. I have one myself."

She raised one eyebrow at this.

"You have one yourself?"

He nodded.

"It's made by Hewlett-Packard and it can print, scan, copy and fax. Wonderful machine. But did you know that faxing is out of fashion? Can't understand why. So convenient."

She stared at him for a moment or two before turning to the man seated at her side.

"Dominic, perhaps you can pick it up from here."

"Happy to, Ma'am."

He called her Ma'am, and yet Luke had been sure he wasn't a police officer. Was he losing his touch after a year off the force?

"I work for the National Crime Agency," Dominic said, which Luke knew made him a civil servant but also 'triple-warranted', with the powers of police, customs and immigration officers.

That explained his mistake.

"More specifically," he went on, "I'm a senior investigator for the NCCU, the National Cyber Crime Unit, which is a command within the NCA. Perhaps I should start by explaining what we mean by an all-in-one solution."

"Didn't I just do that?" Filcher asked.

"Edward?" Ambrose said.

"Yes, Uncle."

"Be quiet."

"Yes, Uncle."

"Please carry on, Dominic."

"As the ACC was saying, most criminals lack deep technology skills. This has been seen as an opportunity by unscrupulous, IT-literate individuals to create and offer services that make cybercrime in its many forms easy to implement. Such all-in-one services are usually bought on subscription, and almost exclusively via the dark web."

"Not printers, then?" Filcher asked.

Dominic managed to keep a straight face as he replied.

"No. Not printers."

He returned his attention to Luke.

"One example is, or should I say was, LabHost, which sold technology for scammers. It enabled them to send their victims messages to trick them into making payments online."

"You used the past tense?" Luke asked.

Dominic gave a grim smile.

"Closing the service down is one of our few successes. After a two-year operation, working with the Met and overseas law enforcement bodies, we made 37 arrests. The person behind it, who I'm pleased to say is now serving time at his majesty's pleasure, made over £1 million from the venture before we caught him."

"I take it you've now uncovered another similar service?"

"Yes. It's called ByteIt, but its abilities make LabHost pale by comparison. ByteIt is a more wide-ranging and advanced offering, and takes full advantage of artificial intelligence. It's also being continually updated to keep pace with the latest developments."

Mr Killjoy

"I'm with you so far," Luke said, "but what I don't understand is your presence here." He smiled. "I know we've helped with investigations in the past, but only on the periphery, and none of my staff could be described as tech gurus."

"Midge," Filcher said.

Luke turned to look at him.

"Midge?"

"Yes. He's good with IT. Tall man. Very, ah…"

He pointed at the sleeve of his suit jacket.

"Black?" Luke suggested.

"Indeed."

"Do you mean Maj?"

Filcher nodded.

"Maj. That's the fellow. He's from Africa, but despite that…"

"Enough," Ambrose said. "You were saying, Luke?"

Luke returned his attention to the NCCU investigator.

"To put it simply, Dominic. Why are you here?"

"Because the man behind this latest criminal service is operating, at least in part, from this building." He paused and smiled wryly. "He doesn't make many mistakes, but we intercepted an email that he sent without using a VPN."

"VPN?"

"Virtual private network. They're used to disguise the originating computer's location."

"I see. You seem certain it's a man behind this?"

"Ah. You're right to pick me up on that. It could be a woman, but it's easy to fall into that trap because of what he, sorry, he or she, calls themselves."

"Which is?"

"Mr Killjoy."

Chapter 12

It was another half an hour before the meeting finished, and Luke immediately returned to the Ethics Room and called the team together.

"We're going to be working on a new project," he began, once they were all seated around the meeting table. "It's a meaty one too, but before I tell you more, please can I have an update on where you've got to with your current investigations? Sam, perhaps you could begin."

"Sure. I'm working on two cases, although the harassment turned out to be a false alarm. I met with Cynthia Fowlds this morning, and she's retracted the accusation against her colleague."

She turned to Helen and Maj to explain the background.

"Cynthia and the other woman both work in Marketing. They argued after work, and Cynthia contacted me last week, saying her colleague had pushed her over and she'd needed stitches for a head wound. However, she was quick to go back on her word when I explained how severe her accusation was and what the potential consequences might be."

"Did she lie about the injury, then?" Maj asked.

Sam laughed.

"She wasn't lying about her head wound, but it was nothing to do with her workmate. Cynthia told me it happened in the bedroom, but that was all I could get out of her."

"How have you left it?" Luke asked.

"I spoke to Fred Tanner, who told me the two women have never got on. He's agreed to monitor the situation and separate them into different teams if necessary."

"Good," Luke said. "What about the other case, the Pickfords?"

"Is that the attempted suicide?" Helen asked.

Sam nodded.

"Yes. It's still possible that the reason Jack did it was because Kelly Gaynes dumped him. I'm hoping to find out more when I speak to Amelia, his younger sister. She told her parents that he'd confided in her about his relationship with Kelly."

"Any progress on setting that up?" Luke asked.

"I finally managed to get hold of Larry Pickford just before you got back, and I've arranged to see him, his wife and their daughter at the hospital this lunchtime."

"Has their son regained consciousness?" Luke asked.

"Unfortunately not. There's been no change by all accounts, and he's still in the ICU."

"Okay."

He turned to Helen.

"Helen, are you any further on with that invoicing problem?"

"What's the issue there?" Maj asked.

She turned to face him.

"About a month ago, Finance received an invoice from Acedesk for call centre equipment. It wasn't a large amount, just under £400. One of the team, Harry Mullins, checked that the goods had been received and then transferred the funds. However, last week Acedesk sent an email saying payment was overdue."

Maj looked confused.

"I don't understand. It sounds like an administrative error with Mullins paying the wrong supplier. What's it got to do with ethics?"

Helen smiled.

"Because this is the fifth time it's happened. Different suppliers each time, but it was Harry Mullins who made all five payments, and it appears that they all went to the same bank account. It was his manager who rang and asked if we could look into it."

"Do the destination accounts belong to Mullins?" Sam asked.

"That's the thing. According to his manager, all five payments were paid into the same account, although it's impossible to tell whose it is. It's in Switzerland, but that's all I can tell from the bank codes."

Helen turned to Luke.

"I'm seeing him tomorrow afternoon at two. Is there any chance you could join me?"

"Yes, that's fine." He paused. "Maj, I saw your email saying there was nothing further to do regarding the Hardy case. What's the situation with the other one? Gus Walker, wasn't it?"

"That's the one, and we can close that one too. I've passed the files to HR to deal with. Walker was definitely making fraudulent expense claims, and it's now down to them to decide how to deal with him."

"Which means you're free, which is good because Mr Killjoy needs your help."

Maj's eyebrows shot up.

"Mr who?"

Luke smiled.

"Ambrose called me upstairs to meet ACC Jean Scarrott from Avon and Somerset Police, and Dominic Watts, who's an investigator in the National Cyber Crime Unit. They're pursuing a criminal calling himself Mr Killjoy, who they believe to be a Filchers employee."

"What makes them think that?" Helen asked.

"They intercepted an email from him, and apparently he forgot to use a virtual private network which gave his location away."

He looked over at Maj.

"Does that make sense to you?"

Maj nodded.

"If he forgot to use a VPN, then the lack of a proxy means they can find his location using crawling, traceroutes, and geofeeds. What's more, Filchers uses static IP addresses, which makes the process a whole lot easier than if they were dynamic."

"That's what I thought," Helen said, but was unable to keep a straight face.

"What you've just said, Maj," Luke said, "might be complete gobbledygook to the three of us, but is the very reason I want you to work full-time on Project…"

He drew to a halt.

"We need a project name."

"It's a shame your son's not here," Sam said.

"Why would we need Ben?" Helen asked, then saw the look on Luke's face and grinned. "You meant our wee Josh, didn't you, Sam? He certainly looks up to you, Luke and, now I come to think of it, I guess it is much like a father-son relationship."

"Don't you start."

"Static," Maj said. "We could call it Project Static, because of the static IP address." He smiled. "I'm conjuring my inner Josh."

"Gucci!" Helen said.

"Incredibilo!" Sam added.

Luke held both hands up to stop them, but he was also smiling.

"Okay, Project Static it is. Helen, please can you wheel the whiteboard out so that we can capture what we know so far."

"Wowza," Maj said. "A crazy wall."

Chapter 13

"Helen," Luke said, "can you summarise where we've got to."

"Aye, nae problem. It's not as if there's much."

She pointed to the board.

Project Static

ByteIT toolkit

Multiple products including FishIt

Accessible at byteit.onion

Mr Killjoy

"ByteIt is a set of offerings on the dark web," she went on, "which can't be reached using Google. Is that right, Maj?"

"Yes. Anyone wanting to access the dark web needs to use a browser such as Tor. There are others, but that's the main one. Unlike Google, it allows users to access the Internet anonymously. Website locations are also hidden, using a technique called onion routing, and that's why, as it says there…" He gestured to the fourth line on the board. "…sites on the dark web have '.onion' as their suffix rather than '.com' or '.co.uk'."

Helen tapped the last entry.

"And we know that someone calling themselves Mr Killjoy is behind ByteIt, because that was the name on the email intercepted by Dominic Watts at the National Cyber Crime Unit."

"Can I have another look at that email, Luke?" Maj asked.

Luke clicked a couple of times on his phone and then passed it over.

Maj read the contents, rubbing his chin as he did so.

To: *[hidden]*
From: *[hidden]*
Subject: *Welcome to ByteIt*

Hello potential client,

Thank you for expressing an interest in ByteIt, a comprehensive set of tools designed to simplify the use of technology. You are one step away from leveraging products such as FishIt, our first and most successful offering.

"The product changed everything for me. It was easy to use and I tripled my earnings within weeks."
FishIt customer

For a low monthly subscription fee, you will be able to harness world-leading software. What's more, as an incentive to join, I can offer you a 20% discount for the first three months if you sign up in the next week. All you have to do is enter the promotion code ALLIWANTIS20 before you complete your payment details.

Best wishes
Mr Killjoy

"If I didn't know better," he said, as he passed the phone on to Sam, "I'd think this was an above-board offering."

"Spooky, isn't it?" she said, after reading the email. She turned to Luke. "You didn't say how they managed to intercept it."

"Dominic wouldn't tell me the details, but he did say

that GCHQ in Cheltenham had helped, and that it was something to do with searching for tagwords. Maj, do you know what he would have meant by that?"

"I imagine they used their processing power to trawl through servers looking for emails containing the word 'ByteIt'." He paused. "Has Dominic tried signing up himself?"

"Yes, countless times, but he hasn't been able to get past the welcome page."

"Mmm. I suspect they've implemented something to detect intruders or bots, probably like 'captcha' but more sophisticated."

"What put them onto ByteIt in the first place?" Helen asked.

Luke gave a wry smile.

"A disgruntled and, from what I heard, somewhat stupid customer. He'd been using FishIt to send emails asking for charity donations, but used his personal bank account. When he was caught, he blamed ByteIt for what had happened and was only too happy to tell the police everything he knew."

"But he didn't know what the other products in the suite were?"

"Unfortunately not."

"Okay," Maj said. "What happens next? You said I need to devote all my time to this."

"Yes. Dominic plans to come back in later in the week so that you can meet him. In the meantime, there are a couple of tasks he wants you to make a start on. Give him a ring and he'll run you through them."

"Will do."

Chapter 14

It was a monster, that was the problem. Big, much too big.

Having an electric car was good for the planet, Sam knew that, but did the VW have to be so enormous? The boot could swallow ten of Wilkins and still have room for a suitcase or two.

The lack of an engine was unnerving too, and she worried that pedestrians wouldn't hear her coming, and might step suddenly into the road.

It was for that reason that she was determined to drive slowly, even though she'd already had to give a middle finger to one irate motorist who'd mouthed obscenities at her as he accelerated past.

She turned right by the now-closed Weston pub and headed up towards Combe Park. As she did so, her thoughts turned to the Pickfords.

When Kelly Gaynes had spoken to Luke, she'd categorically denied having anything other than a platonic relationship with Jack. And yet Amelia had told her parents he'd been showing off about it, proud of the fact that he was dating an older woman.

Had the seventeen-year-old made the whole thing up? Was he inventing a relationship purely to impress his younger sister? If that was the case, it had to be something else that had driven him to try to kill himself. The way he had been found, and the fact that he was still in a coma, made it clear he had been genuinely distressed. This was no cry for help, it was an attempt to end his life.

After parking, she walked towards the RUH's main entrance and texted Larry Pickford to say that she'd arrived. He replied immediately.

I need to see you alone. Meet me in the Atrium cafe.

The coffee shop was directly in front of the main doors, and there were several groups dotted at tables, and a small queue at the serving counter. As she cast her eyes around, a man appeared through the double doors at the end of a corridor to the right. He was in his early forties, so the right age, but it was the haggard, haunted look on his face that told her this had to be Jack's father.

He saw her looking in his direction and speedwalked over.

"Sam?"

"That's me."

She smiled and offered her hand.

"Pleased to meet you, Larry. I only wish it were in better circumstances."

"Me too," he said.

He shook her hand briefly and then looked around at the seated patients and relatives.

"We can't talk here."

He headed towards the exit, and she followed a couple of steps behind. Once outside, he turned right and continued for twenty paces or so before stopping and turning back to face her.

There had clearly been a development, something bad, and Sam decided the best thing was to come straight out and ask him.

"Has Jack's condition deteriorated?"

He put the base of his palm to his forehead, closed his eyes for a split-second, and then let out a deep sigh.

"No. He's much the same, still in a coma. It's my wife. It's Stephanie." He hesitated. "She's…" He breathed deeply, in an attempt to pull himself together. "This whole business has messed with her mind, and she seems to be having a mental health crisis."

He sighed again.

"I'm at my wits' end. As if Jack wasn't enough to deal with, but now…"

"Where is your wife?"

He nodded his head towards the building.

"She's in there, by his bedside. I told Amelia to stay with her, whatever happens, even if she says she's popping to the loo. I'm worried she'll try to track that Kelly woman down again and, if she does, I don't know what she might do."

"Luke talked to Kelly, and she says that there was never anything between her and your son."

"She's lying. He told Amelia all about it."

"That could well be the case, but I need to talk to your daughter to find out exactly what was said."

"Are you saying you don't believe me?"

This was proving difficult, and no wonder. The man was under immense stress.

"Of course, I believe you," Sam said, keeping her voice slow and unemotional in an attempt to calm him, "but if Kelly *was* the cause of what happened, it's vital I find out exactly what Jack said."

He thought about this for a few seconds before replying.

"I'll go back to the ICU and ask Amelia to come and speak to you."

He started to walk away, but Sam put her hand on his arm to stop him.

"Have you spoken to anyone about your wife, Larry? About her emotions, her struggle to cope?"

He turned back.

"I haven't had a chance."

"I think you should make it a priority." She gestured to the building they were standing beside. "It's not as if there's a shortage of health professionals in there. Why don't you speak to one of the doctors treating Jack? I'm sure they'll be understanding. It sounds to me as though Stephanie needs to be on anti-anxiety tablets, or at the very least something to help her sleep."

He looked at her for a second before speaking.

"I guess you're right."

This was what she wanted to hear, but it was said with a heavy heart, and Larry's shoulders slumped even further.

She watched as he returned to the entrance doors, a broken man, then picked up her phone and called Luke.

"Have you seen Amelia yet?"

"No. Larry's gone to fetch her, but I'm worried about his wife. And him, for that matter."

She told him what Larry had said, and what she'd suggested.

"It's an awful situation," Luke said when she'd finished. "Keep me posted, won't you?"

"Will do. Love you, Luke."

"Love you."

She hung up, returned to the cafe and sat at one of the vacant tables, all the while keeping her eyes on the doors that Larry had used. Sure enough, a couple of minutes later, a teenage girl appeared. She looked tired, but not as heavily burdened with worry as her father had been.

Sam stood up and walked over to her.

"Amelia?"

"Hi. Sam, is it?"

"That's right. Can I get you a drink?"

"A Diet Coke, please."

"Have a seat and I'll fetch it."

She bought their drinks and, on impulse, a slice of coffee and walnut cake.

"I thought you might like this," she said, sliding the plate over to Amelia.

"Thanks."

The young girl picked up the fork, broke off a generous piece, and slid it into her mouth.

Sam waited until she'd finished before speaking.

"It must be awful, seeing your brother in that state."

Amelia opened her can of Coke and tipped it into her glass.

"Yeah. He's my brother, and he can't half be a pain, but... Yeah, it's awful."

She took a sip of her drink.

"Amelia, I'd appreciate it if you could talk me through exactly what Jack said to you."

"About his girlfriend?"

Sam nodded and reached into her bag for her writing pad and pen.

"Do you mind if I take notes?"

Amelia shrugged.

"Whatever." She picked up her glass again. "There's not much to tell you, though."

Sam sensed that the girl was worried sick about Jack, but trying to act cool. As much as anything, she was probably being brave for her parents' sake.

"When did your brother first mention that he was seeing someone?"

"Dunno. Last week sometime."

"Amelia, this is important. Please try to remember exactly when it was."

"Why does it matter?"

Sam smiled.

"Because we need to establish who this woman is, and if I have dates it might help."

"You don't need dates for that. It's Kelly Gaynes, his manager."

"Did Jack tell you it was her?"

She shrugged again.

"Kind of."

"Did he tell you it was her, or not?"

"Can't remember."

Sam could see that being sympathetic and gentle wasn't getting her anywhere and decided on a different approach.

"Amelia," she said, her voice harsher than it had been, "you're starting to piss me off."

"You can't talk to me like that."

"Your brother has tried to take his own life. Don't you think you owe it to him to help? You need to tell me exactly what he said."

Amelia glared at her for a moment, then her bottom lip started to wobble, and Sam leaned over and grasped her hand.

"I know this is hard for you, incredibly hard."

The young girl drew her hand away from under Sam's, took a deep breath and began speaking.

"It was last Monday after school. Mum and Dad were still at work. I went up to my room, and Jack was coming out of the shower with a towel around him. I asked him if he was getting himself cleaned up 'cos he finally had a girlfriend."

"Hasn't he had one before?"

"Yeah. He went out with Nancy Cleverley for a bit, but that finished months ago. I said it to wind him up, that was all."

"And you succeeded?"

She nodded.

"He said something like, *'Yeah, I've got a girlfriend. A proper one. And she's really into me.'*"

"Could he have been inventing it?"

She thought about this for a second.

"He could have been, I suppose, but I don't think so. He seemed proper pleased with himself."

"What did you say next?"

Her cheeks reddened, but she didn't say anything.

"Amelia?"

"I asked him if they'd done it."

"And?"

"He grinned and said, *'What do you think?'*, and I said, *'You want to be careful you're not caught. I bet she's not even sixteen.'*

That was when he said it."

"Said what?"

"That she was older."

"What exactly did he say?"

"He said, '*She's twenty-seven, so there*', then blew a raspberry at me and went into his bedroom."

"And that was it. That was all he said?"

"Yeah. Until after school on Wednesday. I asked him if they'd done it again, and he told me to fuck off."

"That was it? He didn't say she'd finished with him?"

"No. All I got were those two words, then he went into his room and locked the door."

"And you didn't speak to him again after that?"

"No."

"He didn't actually tell you his girlfriend's name?"

"No, but Mum and Dad are convinced it's his boss."

"Thanks, Amelia." Sam closed her pad. "That was very useful."

Amelia shrugged again.

"I dunno. Not as if it's going to make him better, is it?"

She stood up.

"If that's all, I'll get back."

"I hope he wakes up soon."

"Yeah." She picked up her glass and drained the last of the Coke. "Thanks for the drink and the cake."

"No problem."

Sam watched as the girl stood up and headed back towards the ICU, then finished her own drink and started the walk back to the car.

She rang Luke on the way.

"I've just finished talking to Amelia."

"And?"

"She's convinced Jack was telling the truth about having an older girlfriend, but he didn't actually tell her her name."

"That's interesting. What did he say?"

"Only that she was twenty-seven. Oh, and he didn't say

that he'd been dumped, either. He was upset and told his sister to, and I quote, fuck off, and she assumed that was why, but he didn't say it in so many words."

"It… Hang on, did you say twenty-seven?"

"Yes."

"Kelly Gaynes is twenty-nine."

"Is she?" She considered this for a moment. "Perhaps she lied because she didn't want Jack to think she was too old for him."

"It's possible, but if so, why not say she was in her early twenties? There's not a lot of difference between being ten or twelve years older."

"That's true. What does it mean, Luke?"

"It probably rules out Kelly being involved. I believed her when she poo-pooed the idea of being in a relationship with Jack, and what Amelia said about his girlfriend being twenty-seven seems to confirm it. However, finding out who this twenty-seven-year-old is isn't going to be easy."

Chapter 15

Mr Killjoy tapped impatiently on the desk, irritated that the others were yet to join the meeting.

Punctuality was important. Vital even. Being late showed a lack of effective time management, and such a failure often flowed into other areas. The three members of his team needed to be precise in everything they did, be it updating and testing code, amending the website or keeping account of income and outgoings.

An avatar appeared on his central monitor, but this was a much more complex and detailed representation of a person than might be used in a video game. It was a photo-realistic image of the younger Malfoy from the Harry Potter films, with the dining hall of Hogwarts School used as the background.

"Sorry I'm late," the avatar said, the lips almost perfectly synced to the words.

"It's not good enough, Draco," Mr Killjoy typed in. "You were supposed to join two minutes ago."

He hit return, and the image of Voldemort in the bottom right-hand corner of the screen spoke the words.

He nodded in satisfaction. It was only the second time they had used this new approach, rather than the previous text-based system that had used Telegram, and it seemed to be working well.

There was a pause while the accountant typed his response, and then his avatar spoke again.

"It looks like I've beaten the other two."

Draco's face was expressionless, but Mr Killjoy suspected this wasn't echoing what was on the accountant's face. He would be smiling, pleased with himself for being the first of the three to join.

"Stay connected while we wait for the others."

He sat forward in his chair and rapped his fingers on the surface again, impatient to get on.

Where were they?

There were two monitors on either side of the one showing a now motionless Draco. Both were blank, save for a message in green on a black background reading, 'Awaiting Connection'.

He glanced up at the six screens above the three meeting monitors. They told him all he needed to know about his operation, displaying everything from website interactions to bank balances. At this very moment, two people had items in their baskets. He watched as the screen refreshed to show a purchase had been made, and was pleased to see it was for PhishIt, which would net him £400 a month.

It was amazing to think he could control a global organisation from this hidden room in his house. But on the other hand, why should he be surprised? As with everything he did, the space had been planned to the last detail.

The left-hand screen flickered into life, displaying an image of Gilderoy Lockhart. The one on the right followed seconds later, this one showing Bellatrix Lestrange.

Gilderoy started to speak, and Mr Killjoy held his hand up to stop him, forgetting for an instant that they could not see the real him, only the image of the Dark Lord, whose hands were not in shot.

"It's been a good day," Gilderoy said.

Mr Killjoy typed and sent his response.

"Until now. You're late, both of you."

Voldemort spoke his reply and, a split-second later, Bellatrix started speaking.

"I'm not late, am I? I was stuck in traffic on the way home."

He sighed. The delay caused by the need to type made

free-flowing discussion difficult. He decided to deal with it head-on.

"Gilderoy, have you made further progress with auto-interpretation from speech to avatar?"

He waited impatiently for the response, which took even longer than usual. The reason became clear when the avatar spoke for almost half a minute.

"I'm still working on it. It's a challenge because of the inherent built-in latency, coupled with the need to use strong encryption and firewalls to prevent interception. My algorithms take account of this, but still have to be fine-tuned. More testing is needed before I'll be confident enough to implement an improved version."

Mr Killjoy knew all this, but his team had to be ultra-efficient if ByteIt was to continue to make stellar progress, and that went for their internal solutions as much as for customer-facing products.

"That's all very well, but the current system is unsatisfactory. You need to sort it out as a matter of urgency."

"I'll have it done in the next couple of days."

"Be sure you do."

He waited for Voldemort to speak his words before typing again.

"I want to keep this brief, and only have two items to cover: sales and R&D. Let's start with sales. Bellatrix, how were our e-commerce numbers last week?"

"Up on the week before. New subscriptions for our three legacy products are down, but we had no cancellations."

"Can you be more specific?"

"We had five new subscriptions for RansomIt, four for SexIt, but none for PayIt."

"And what about our new products?"

"FishIt has seen only a slight increase, but ChatIt is beginning to take off. Twenty-two new subscribers last week."

"Excellent. Draco, what does this mean for revenue?"

He continued to ask questions for several minutes.

"Okay," he typed, once he was sure he had the complete picture, "Has anyone got any ideas on how to revitalise PayIt?"

It was Bellatrix who got in her reply first.

"I could highlight it on the welcome screen, and add some invented reviews from happy customers."

Draco spoke next.

"What about a discount for new subscribers?"

Mr Killjoy considered these ideas for a few seconds.

"Let's do both of those. Bellatrix, ensure you amend the website today, and include the offer of a 20% discount for new subscribers."

He waited to ensure this was taken on board before continuing.

"Okay. Now to research and development. Draco, Bellatrix, I don't need you for this, and you've got a lot to do, so you can both sign off."

"Goodbye," both avatars said almost simultaneously before their screens went blank, leaving only Gilderoy on the central monitor.

"Have you completed testing of FakeIt?" Mr Killjoy asked.

"Yes. It's ready to go. There were a few challenges with one of the characters, but I've fine-tuned the natural language nodes. The artificial neural networks have multiple layers now too, and that's resulted in a higher level of machine learning."

"Good. Send me the scripts to check. Once I've okayed them, we'll go for it. For this first experiment, I want you to manage the interactions, but link me in so that I can follow everything."

"Will do."

The screen went blank, and Mr Killjoy rocked back in

Mr Killjoy

his chair and reflected that the members of his team were performing well in their respective roles.

Draco was a numbers man at heart, an old-fashioned bean-counter, but he was also a man who understood what drove the business forward. His modelling had enabled them to quickly identify the winners and losers in their products, enabling investment to go where it was most likely to reap rewards.

That was where Gilderoy came in. Mr Killjoy was no novice when it came to technology, but Gilderoy was a true genius, and almost geek-like in his urge to keep abreast of the latest developments in artificial intelligence. This latest idea, the one they had provisionally called FakeIt, had only been in development for a few weeks but had the potential to be a big earner.

Bellatrix, meanwhile, understood the ins and outs of website design and e-commerce. She also handled any customer queries or problems. In effect, she was the administrator for the operation.

Pseudonyms had been a good idea. He knew their real identities, of course he did, but keeping them from knowing who the others were, and indeed who he was, helped to minimise risk.

Chapter 16

Richard Harding pushed his glasses up onto the bridge of his nose, dunked his first soldier, and was gratified at the amount of yolk coating the bread when he lifted it to his mouth. These were large eggs, which needed to be boiled for precisely 4 minutes and 45 seconds. Any more and they ceased to be sufficiently runny, any less and the white would be watery and viscous.

Not that he was a pedant, but it was important to get things right. Later, he'd be buying lunch from the staff canteen, where the standard of cooking could best be described as woefully inadequate. Even their sandwiches were poorly put together, and as for their omelettes…

He shook his head as he remembered the cardboard-like mass of yellow and brown they had served him two days earlier.

His wife saw the concern on his face.

"Sorry, Darling. Have I overcooked them? I used Alexa to set a timer, so they should be okay."

"No, Emma. The eggs are perfect, thank you. I was thinking about something else."

"You're not fretting about promotion again, are you?"

He hadn't been, but now she'd mentioned it, he knew he wouldn't be able to shift it from his mind.

"You'll get it in good time," she went on, as he dunked his second soldier. "I'm sure Graham will move on before long."

"I'm not so sure." He swallowed his toast and reached for another piece. "I've been his deputy for three years, and he feels like a permanent fixture."

"You could always look for a job as Chief Accountant somewhere else. It's not as if you owe Filchers anything."

Mr Killjoy

"I could, but…"

His phone pinged and he retrieved it from his pocket, read the text that had come through and involuntarily sat up ramrod straight in his chair.

"What is it, Richard?"

He reread the message and looked across at his wife.

"It's from Gillian Ley. It's not like her to contact me directly."

"She's Filchers' Finance Director, isn't she?"

He nodded. "My boss's boss. She wants me on a Zoom call." He looked at his watch. "In five minutes."

"Does she say what about?"

"Only that it's confidential."

He passed the phone over, and she read what was on the screen.

Good morning, Richard. You are required to join a sensitive and confidential Zoom call with the Filchers Executive Team at 8 am today. Details to follow. Gillian

There was another ping, and Emma passed it back.

Richard clicked to read the new message.

"It's the site address and password."

He stood up and retrieved his briefcase.

"I'll use the study."

"What about your eggs?"

He dunked one more soldier, put it in his mouth and shrugged.

"Sorry, no time."

"Good luck."

He raced upstairs, removed his laptop and cable, plugged it in and pressed the on button.

As he settled into the desk chair, and waited for his computer to power up, he wondered why he had been invited to an Executive meeting alongside, or possibly instead of, the company's Chief Accountant. It wasn't as if

Graham was on holiday.

Most likely, the meeting was a last-minute thing, and they hadn't been able to get hold of his boss. Yes, that was probably it. Regardless, it was a chance to impress, and he found himself slightly nervous as he keyed in the website details and then the password.

Two windows opened on each side of the screen, Gillian on the left with him on the right. He minimised the view of himself.

"Good morning, Gillian."

She smiled stiffly.

"The others will be with us in a moment, Richard."

"Who else is…"

She interrupted him before he could finish.

"Ah, here they are now."

The window showing Gillian shrunk to take up the bottom left quarter of the display, and two new windows opened at the top. He immediately recognised Filchers' silver-haired CEO on the left.

"Oh. Hello, Ambrose."

Again, there was a slight pause before he replied, presumably due to a poor connection.

"Good morning, Richard." He smiled before continuing. "Thank you for joining. And I see Cora's with us. Good morning, Cora."

Cora Evans, recently promoted to head up the Technology and Communications sector, echoed his smile.

"Hi, Ambrose."

"Is Graham joining us?" Richard asked.

Both Gillian and Ambrose seemed hesitant about replying, but it was the CEO who eventually answered.

"Unfortunately not, Richard. For reasons I would rather not divulge on the call, he will soon be leaving our employ. Please come to my office later this morning, and I'll explain everything."

Richard's heart gave a little leap. This was his chance.

"Of course, Ambrose."

"However," Ambrose went on, "the reason for this meeting has nothing to do with Graham. We are on the verge of an acquisition which we have had under wraps for some time. Cora, could you explain, please?"

This time, there was no pause as Cora began.

"Filchers will be buying InfoLaunch, a privately owned company that specialises in customer relationship management software. Have you heard of InfoLaunch, Richard?"

"No. I must admit I haven't."

She smiled again.

"I'm not surprised. They have been very much under the radar, but their founder, Martin Fuller, has put together a ground-breaking product. They pitched it to us, but Ambrose, Gillian and I saw the potential, and Filchers intends to purchase the company outright."

"The reason for this call," Gillian said, "is that we are at a very sensitive stage of the negotiation. Martin Fuller has accepted our offer of £20 million in principle, but contracts are still to be finalised. However, we are aware that Bannermans has also been sniffing around."

"To that end," Ambrose cut in seamlessly, "we have agreed to transfer £200,000 to Mr Fuller as a gesture of goodwill. In return, he has guaranteed not to talk to other potential purchasers." He paused. "Richard, I am right, aren't I, that you are able to access our bank accounts from home?"

"Yes, Ambrose."

"Excellent. Please transfer the funds as soon as we've finished this call."

Richard hesitated for a second before replying.

"Ah... Strictly speaking, I ought to have written authority."

Ambrose raised one eyebrow.

"This is urgent as well as confidential, Richard. Is my

word not good enough?"

Richard swallowed.

"Of course it is, Ambrose."

He looked at the bottom left display to see that Gillian was tapping on her phone.

She looked back up.

"I've sent you the bank details."

A split-second later, his phone pinged and he looked down to check it contained what he needed.

"Have you got it?" she went on.

He nodded.

"Yes. It's everything I need."

"Good. Message me back as soon as the transfer has been completed."

"I will do, Gillian."

"And thank you for this," Ambrose said. "I appreciate your help."

"It's no problem. I'll see you later."

He ended the call, and smiled to himself as he logged into Filchers' bank account. This had to be his moment, his time.

After years of waiting, he was going to be Chief Accountant. It was long overdue, but nonetheless exciting. The extra money would come in handy too.

But first, he had to transfer the funds, not that he was expecting any problems. The Faster Payments System had an upper limit of £1 million for business transfers, and he had the necessary security accreditation.

He hesitated before entering the one-time password sent to his phone, but only momentarily. A stickler for due process, he would normally have insisted on something in writing. However, he understood the need for speed, and besides, he could take a form for Ambrose to sign when he saw him later in the morning. That way, he could cover all eventualities.

A few seconds later, he received confirmation that the

money had been transferred successfully. He texted Gillian and received an immediate, if typically curt, response.

Good.

Smiling to himself, he returned his computer to his briefcase and returned downstairs, pleased to be able to share the good news with Emma.

Chapter 17

It was Luke's turn to get the drinks in, and he was on his way to the canteen when his phone rang. He pulled it out of his pocket and saw that it was his son.

"Hi, Ben. It's not like you to ring at this time of day."

"Hi, Dad."

This was said in a flat monotone, immediately telling him something was wrong.

"What's up?"

There was a pause before an answer came.

"It's over between us, between me and Pippa." He hesitated again, and Luke could tell that he was finding it a struggle to hold himself together. "We had an almighty row, and she told me we were finished and that she never wanted to see me again. Then she threw her engagement ring at me and stormed out."

Luke's heart sank.

"When was this?"

"Yesterday evening. I've tried ringing, but she's not answering. And, you know, I can't even remember what kicked it off." He laughed, but there was no humour in it. "We were planning what to do over the summer, and the next thing I knew she was shouting at me."

"Won't you see her at lectures?"

"There aren't any today." He swallowed. "I love her, Dad. I don't want it to end."

"Why don't you go round to her hall of residence?"

"That's where I am now. I spoke to one of the girls on her floor, and she was surprised to see me. She told me that Pippa wasn't there last night, and she'd assumed she was at mine."

"She probably stayed with a friend."

"Maybe."
"What do you mean?"
"It's nothing."
"Out with it."

Ben hesitated for a second before replying.

"There's this guy on our course, Ryan. He's okay, except he flirts with Pippa, and she seems to like it. I wonder if that's why she's ended it between us. If the row was a pretence, a way of dumping me so they can be together."

"Pippa wouldn't do that."

Another pause.

"No. You're right, Dad."

The phone went silent for a few seconds. His son sounded defeated, but Luke knew he'd regret it if he didn't try his damnedest to get her back.

"You need to track her down and apologise, Ben. There'll be two sides to what happened. Something you said has upset her, but I'm sure your relationship is strong enough to survive it. Think of who she might be staying with. Who are her best Uni friends?"

"Tilly and Charlotte, I guess."

"Do you have their numbers?"

"No, but I know where Tilly lives, and if she hasn't seen Pippa, she can tell me where to find Charlotte. I'll walk to Tilly's now, it's only fifteen minutes."

He sounded more positive, which was at least something.

"Let me know how you get on, won't you?"

"I will, Dad."

Luke hung up, hoping that what he had said was true, that Ben and Pippa's relationship was strong enough to survive what must have been an almighty bust-up.

He made his way to the canteen, where a few people were waiting in line, and joined the back of the queue.

A few seconds later he felt a tap on his shoulder.

"Good morning, Luke."

He turned to see a grinning Glen Baxter holding an oversized mug in one of his oversized paws.

"They mix this for me every morning," he went on, lifting the mug to reveal that it was full to the brim. The contents were purple and looked to have the texture of wallpaper paste. "It's good for my constipation."

"I think you mean your constitution."

"Yes, that's it."

He nodded his head towards his right bicep.

"Helps my guns. Protein's important, but they need carbs as well."

"So it's got both protein and carbohydrates in it?"

"Uh-huh. Oats, Greek yoghurt, blackberries and chicken breast. All blended together."

"Isn't that a bit of an odd mixture?"

"Yes, but you have to expectorate to accumulate."

"Speculate."

Glen shook his head.

"Not at all. My vision's perfect."

Luke was now at the head of the queue. He ordered, paid, and waited for the drinks to be poured, hoping Glen had said his piece and would now clam up.

He didn't.

"I'm responsible for martial war."

Luke sighed, closed his eyes for a second, and then turned back around.

"You're responsible for martial war?"

"Yes… No… Hang on. Ah… It's not martial war, but almost."

"Martial arts?"

"No. Ah… Martial fire! That's it. I'm a responsible marshall… for fire."

"You mean you're a fire marshall?"

Glen's grin widened.

"Not just *a* fire marshall. *The* fire marshall. For the entire precipice. The whole building."

Mr Killjoy

"Congratulations."

"Thanks."

Luke took the cardboard coffee tray from the woman at the counter and turned to leave, hearing Glen's words as he did so.

"Morning, Miriam. I'm a smoothie."

His phone rang again before she responded, and he quickly walked to a table and put the drinks down, hoping it was Ben with good news.

It wasn't.

It was Ambrose.

"Luke, you need to come up to my office. Please bring Maj as well if he's free. Dominic Watts is here, and he's made a breakthrough."

Chapter 18

Luke and Maj arrived at Ambrose's office clutching their still-hot coffees.

"You can go straight in," Ellie said.

They went inside to find Ambrose and Dominic seated on the sofas.

"Ah, Luke, Maj," Ambrose said, as he and the investigator got to their feet. "Thanks for coming up. Dominic, I don't think you've met Maj, have you?"

"No, but we spoke several times on the phone yesterday. Good to meet you, Maj."

They shook hands, then everyone sat down, Maj beside Dominic, while Luke joined Ambrose on the sofa opposite.

"As I said on the phone," Ambrose said, "Dominic has some good news to share. And before you ask, Luke, he has requested that we keep the number of people who know this information to the absolute minimum, which is why Edward isn't here."

"I think we may be on the verge of catching our man," Dominic began. "We've had two breakthroughs. First off, we now know the names of two more of the offerings within ByteIt. You'll remember, I'm sure, that FishIt is the system they sell to generate phishing emails."

They all confirmed that they did.

"Well, we now know that there are two other subscription services called PayIt and SexIt."

"That's excellent," Luke said. "How much do you know about them?"

Dominic gave a dry smile.

"Very little as yet and, if I look a little tired, it's because getting this far kept me up until four o'clock this morning. After many attempts, I finally managed to access the homepages for both PayIt and SexIt, although neither page would let me go further. When I clicked on 'More Details', a message came up saying there would be a 24-hour delay while my credentials were checked."

He pressed a few keys on his phone, then passed it to Maj.

"That's PayIt. Swipe right to see the homepage for SexIt."

Maj looked at the two screenshots, then passed the phone to Luke, who held the phone so that both he and Ambrose could view the screen as he flicked between the images.

PayIt's homepage had the word 'PayIt' at the top, a button at the bottom saying 'More Details', and in the background a photo of an invoice for electrical work.

SexIt's homepage was laid out in the same way, but the photo was of an attractive twenty-something brunette who was smiling at the camera.

Luke passed the phone back.

"And you've no idea what PayIt and SexIt actually do?"

"I can't be certain, but my guess based on what you've just seen…" He tapped the screen of his phone. "…is that PayIt enables criminals to send out fake invoices, while SexIt gives them the ability to blackmail people."

"Through sextortion?" Luke suggested.

"Quite possibly."

"I've heard the term," Ambrose said, "but what is sextortion exactly?"

"Most often," Dominic said, "it's when criminals threaten to share sexual images of the victim unless they are paid. SexIt may well give them the ability to target people through dating apps, social media, webcams, or pornography sites, using a fake identity to befriend the target. Once they've done that, they ask for intimate photos or videos."

"You said you'd had two breakthroughs?" Luke

prompted.

"That's right, and the second one is in large part down to Maj."

"Me?" Maj said, surprised.

"You remember we discussed Filchers' use of static IP addresses?"

"Yes."

"Well, I took your advice and used a ping-based IP geolocation method instead of relying on the ISP's self-reported location information."

"Which means?" Luke asked.

Dominic smiled.

"I now know exactly where the person behind that email, the person calling themselves Mr Killjoy, sent it from. Or at least, I do within a few square feet."

"Have you got the GPS coordinates?" Maj asked.

"Sure."

"I've got an app with a plan of this building," Maj said as he transcribed the coordinates from Dominic's phone onto his own. "Everyone in Security was given it, and I didn't see the point of deleting it when I joined the Ethics Team."

He hit the return key and smiled.

"That makes sense." He looked up. "It looks like Mr Killjoy is in our IT department."

"On the first floor?" Ambrose asked.

"Yes. More precisely, he or she is in one of six cubicles at the far end of the office."

Ambrose stood up, opened the door and called out to his PA.

"Ellie, please can you find the names of the people occupying the last six cubicles in IT, the ones at the end of the first floor?"

"Will do, Ambrose. By the way, Richard Harding was here a few minutes ago. Are you free to see him? There's nothing in your diary, but he said it was vital he see you this morning."

"I could see him now while you're obtaining those names for me. Ask him to come up, will you?"

He returned to his office.

"I'm sorry, but would the three of you mind stepping outside for a few minutes. Our deputy chief accountant needs to speak to me urgently."

They left the room.

"Can you tell me where the gents is?" Dominic asked.

Luke pointed down the corridor.

"It's the first door on the right after the lift."

"Thanks."

He headed for the loo and, a minute or so later, Richard Harding walked down the corridor, seeming not to even notice Luke and Maj, so focused was he on seeing the CEO.

"Can I see him?" he said, his eyes fixed on Ellie and his voice breathless.

"Yes, go straight in," she said and smiled, but it wasn't returned.

Richard turned away and walked into Ambrose's office, closing the door firmly afterwards.

"He seemed on edge," Luke said.

Ellie nodded. "Yes. I wonder what's happened."

Chapter 19

Luke and Maj had only been waiting for a couple of minutes when the door to the CEO's office opened and Ambrose stepped out.

"Luke, would you mind joining us?" He noticed that Dominic wasn't there. "Ellie, please give my apologies to Dominic and tell him that something urgent has come up. Sorry, Maj. I'll be as quick as I can, but this may take some time."

Luke followed Ambrose back in to find Richard Harding bent forward on the front edge of one of the sofas, his head in his hands.

He looked up at Ambrose when he heard them approach.

"What about Cora?" he asked, his eyes staring and his voice shaky. "Or Gillian? They can back me up."

Ambrose walked over and put his hand on the younger man's shoulder.

"Richard, I fear you are having a breakdown of some kind."

"No. It's not that. I know what I heard, and they were there when you said it."

Ambrose turned to Luke.

"Would you mind staying with him while I ask Ellie to fetch a doctor?"

"I don't need a doctor! I'm not hallucinating. Ambrose, please."

"Tell me what happened," Luke said.

"I can't." His eyes flicked back to the Chief Executive. "You told me yourself that it's highly confidential. Just after you told me that Graham was leaving the company."

"What's confidential?" Ambrose asked.

"The purchase of..." He hesitated. "...the software company."

"Believe me, I didn't say anything about purchasing a software company. Why would we do any such thing? Filchers' business is outsourcing, not software."

"But you did. It was..." He hesitated, still unhappy to reveal what he had been told in confidence.

"Out with it, Richard. Whatever it is, you can say it in front of Luke."

Richard swallowed.

"InfoLaunch. The CRM company. You're buying it for £20 million. That was what the £200,000 to Martin Fuller was for."

"I assure you..." It was Ambrose's turn to hesitate as he took in what the other man had said. "What £200,000? And who's Martin Fuller?"

Luke was now totally confused, both by what the two other men were talking about, and also by Richard's fervent belief that he had been in a meeting which Ambrose had no recollection of.

Was Richard imagining the whole thing, or could it be Ambrose who was mistaken?

"I came in halfway through this," he said. "Richard, please can you run me through exactly what happened?"

He sat down in the hope it might calm the other man down.

"Please start from the beginning."

"Okay." He took a deep breath. "I was having breakfast with my wife when I received Gillian's text. This was just before eight this morning."

"Can you show me?"

"Sure."

He clicked on his phone a couple of times and then passed it over.

Good morning, Richard. You are required to join a sensitive and confidential Zoom call with the Filchers Executive Team at 8 am today. Details to follow. Gillian

Luke pointed to the number displayed above the message.

"Ambrose, is this Gillian's number?"

Ambrose pulled out his phone, called up her contact details and compared it to the number on the screen.

"No."

"It has to be," Richard said, desperation in his voice. "Who else would send it? Or could it be Mollie, her PA? Yes, that must be it."

He seemed to be clutching at straws, and Luke was more confused than ever. Was it possible that Richard's hallucination had stretched to sending himself a text message? Surely not.

Then was it Ambrose who was lying? He found that even harder to believe.

"What happened next, Richard?"

"I went straight up to the study and dialled in. Gillian was already on the call, and Ambrose and Cora joined shortly after I did."

"Was I wearing this?" Ambrose asked, gesturing to his white shirt, pale blue tie and grey waistcoat.

"No. You had a white shirt, but your tie was green, and you didn't have a waistcoat."

"And where was I?"

"I'm not sure. At home, I assume. You were seated in front of a bookcase."

"I assure you that I was here well before eight this morning."

Luke had been listening closely to this exchange and was beginning to understand what might have happened.

"Richard, did any of the others on the Zoom call strike you as odd in any way?"

"There was a lot of hesitation, but I guess that's down to the novelty of it."

"Anything else?"

He thought about this for a second.

"Cora's earrings were certainly odd. They were pretty, don't get me wrong, but to have Christmas trees dangling from her ears in May struck me as a touch eccentric."

"Christmas trees?"

"Yes. They were about this big…" He held up his thumb and forefinger with an inch gap between them. "…and white."

"With tiny red and green jewels dotted around to simulate baubles?"

"Yes. How did you know?"

"She wore them at a party back in early December for Filchers' senior staff."

Luke remembered them well because he and Cora had been dating at the time, and he'd bought them for her as part of her birthday present.

He turned to Ambrose.

"If you remember, you hosted a mini-awards ceremony, and Cora gave a short speech of thanks on behalf of her team."

Ambrose nodded.

"Yes, I remember."

"And I wouldn't mind betting you wore a green tie that evening." He turned his attention back to Richard. "You mentioned £200,000 being paid to someone called Martin Fuller?"

"Yes. I transferred the funds straight after the call as instructed."

"What's going on, Luke?" Ambrose asked.

"I am fairly confident a crime has taken place."

"I assure you…" Richard began.

Luke held his hand up.

"Not by you, Richard. My prime suspect would be Mr Killjoy."

Richard looked at him as if he were crazy.

"Mr who?"

"Ambrose, do you mind if I ask Dominic to join us? He knows much more about deepfake than I do, and I suspect that's what's been used here. Someone set up this Zoom call and used artificial intelligence to produce simulations of you, Gillian and Cora with the sole purpose of stealing £200,000. And from what Richard has said, it seems that he was successful."

"I see. Yes, Luke. Please ask Dominic to come in."

Chapter 20

Luke left the room to find Ellie and Maj deep in conversation.

"Have either of you seen Dominic?"

They looked up and shook their heads.

"He hasn't returned from the loo," Maj said.

"I hope he's okay. He was looking very pale, but I put it down to his late night. Perhaps I ought to check…"

He stopped mid-sentence as a high-pitched ringing sounded from speakers embedded in the ceiling.

A split-second later, Glen Baxter appeared at the top of the stairs twenty yards away. As he turned towards them, Luke saw that his face was serious, the trademark grin absent from his face.

He ran towards them, his bulk making it more of a cumbersome waddle than a graceful gallop.

"FIRE!" he shouted. "Everyone needs to leave the building."

Ambrose emerged from his office, Richard following slightly after.

"Is this a drill, Glen?" Ambrose asked, his voice raised but still barely audible above the incessant screeching of the alarm.

Glen shook his head. "No. You need to get out."

Gillian Ley, her secretary, and others from the executive team, appeared from further down the corridor.

"What's happened?" Gillian asked.

"Fire on the floor below. The sprinklers are on, but you need to leave the building as quickly and calmly as possible. Don't use the lifts."

This was a side of Glen that Luke hadn't seen before. He was being supremely efficient and, for once, not muddling his words.

"Fire wardens," Glen went on, "will guide you to the trembly points."

As people started walking towards the stairs, Luke called across to Glen.

"Our visitor's in the gents. I'll check on him first."

"Okay, but be quick."

Glen headed further along the corridor, opening office doors as he went to check that no one was inside.

Luke ran to the gents, pushed the door open, shouted "DOMINIC!" at the top of his voice, then pushed each of the stall doors open to ensure he wasn't there.

All four cubicles were empty.

This left him in a quandary. He couldn't imagine that Dominic would simply wander off, unless the gents had been closed when he tried to access it. Maybe that was it. Perhaps it was being cleaned, and he'd gone to another floor.

In all probability, he was one of the many people now heading out to the car park. But what if he had been more than simply tired? What if he'd been ill and had collapsed and was now unconscious?

Luke decided to check the loo on the next floor down.

He joined the mass of bodies on the stairs, then left the group at the bottom of the first flight, and pushed through the double doors to the corridor beyond. He immediately smelt smoke and, despite the blaring alarm, could hear the hissing of water escaping from the sprinklers to his right. Beyond them, he caught a faint orange glow.

The gents was a few yards to the left, and he dashed in, checking each of the four cubicles.

Again, there was no sign of Dominic.

He ran out to find that another sprinkler had come on. The air temperature was increasing, a sure sign that the fire was advancing.

It was clear that continuing to look for the NCCU

investigator would be foolhardy. He needed to join everyone outside, and hope that he'd find him at one of the assembly points.

He was about to pull open one of the doors to the stairs when Glen came barging through.

"Luke! Why aren't you outside?"

"I was looking for my visitor."

"You need to go. Now!"

There was a loud bang, and both men turned toward the source of the noise to see a fluorescent light had escaped its mount and clattered to the corridor floor. It was evident the fire was moving towards them, the orange glow now brighter and interspersed with flickering flames. Water was cascading from regular points along the ceiling, but didn't seem to be having much impact.

Glen started to move towards the inferno, and Luke immediately grabbed him by the arm.

"We need to get out."

Glen shook his arm away.

"Can't. Randy."

The combination of sprinklers, crackling flames and screeching alarm was making it impossible to make out what Glen had said. It sounded like 'Randy', but surely…

Then he cottoned on.

He hadn't said 'Randy' at all. He was referring to his deputy, Andy Collins.

He put his mouth to Glen's ear.

"Did you say Andy?"

Glen nodded, pulled his phone out and held it up for Luke to read.

In the Abbey Room. Door won't open.

He put the phone back in his pocket, turned and headed down the corridor towards, rather than away from, the conflagration.

"I'm coming with you," Luke shouted, but Glen showed no sign of having heard him.

The Abbey Room wasn't far. It was on the right-hand side, no more than fifty paces down the corridor. Less than a twenty-second walk in normal circumstances.

But these were far from normal circumstances. Fifty paces could well take them into the centre of the fire.

Glen was right, though. They had to try. Andy, and whoever he was meeting, were trapped, and they had to do their damnedest to free them.

After ten or so steps, they reached the first of the activated sprinklers. Within seconds, both men were drenched to the skin. Despite this, Luke could sense that the air temperature had risen even further, and was able to taste smoke in the back of his throat.

There was a loud bang, and both men stopped dead in their tracks as part of the ceiling crashed to the ground twenty yards ahead of them.

This side of the Abbey Room.

Glen sped up rather than slowed down, his hand now over his mouth to keep the fumes at bay.

Luke followed suit.

There were almost continuous cracks and crackles above them now, as small pieces of the ceiling fell, accompanied occasionally by larger chunks, but they continued on. After a few more steps, they were forced to squeeze through the gap between the collapsed ceiling and the wall, no mean feat given Luke was a sturdy 6ft 6 and Glen had the build of an overnourished rhino.

The heat was almost unbearable, and Luke could feel sweat forming on his brow. The smoke was also thickening with every step. Despite this, there was enough visibility for Luke to see that they had almost reached the meeting room.

Two more paces and they were there.

It was immediately obvious why Andy was stuck inside. A heavy rectangular ceiling tile had fallen against the door, the top of it preventing the handle from moving.

Glen and Luke grabbed one side each and heaved it away. Glen immediately reached for the handle, but Luke grabbed his arm and mouthed 'hot'.

Glen nodded, pulled the bottom of his shirt out, wrapped it around his hand, grabbed the handle, pressed it down and pushed the door open.

Andy, and a young woman Luke didn't recognise, rose to their feet. They had been crouched on the floor in the far corner of the small windowless office, the only position where the water sprinkler in the centre of the ceiling couldn't reach them.

It was slightly cooler inside, but the fire was advancing rapidly, and Luke knew that the room wouldn't survive for much longer.

"Thanks," Andy said breathlessly as Glen ushered them both outside.

"Glen!" Luke shouted. "You go first. I'll take the rear."

Glen nodded and headed outside, only pausing to ensure the others were behind him.

He led the way back down the corridor, his hand again over his mouth.

Another tile dropped, almost catching the side of Glen's head as he swung to the left to avoid it. He stumbled but managed to stay upright, only for there to be a massive crash as several tiles dropped at once, a few paces in front of them.

They stopped moving as more chunks descended, then took two steps back as a large portion of the ceiling ahead collapsed.

Their escape route was blocked.

Chapter 21

Luke turned and was shocked to see how close the flames were, their spitting tongues of orange now no more than fifteen paces away.

It was as if the fire sensed victory and was surging forwards, intent on destroying everything in its path.

Everything and everyone.

The loudest noise yet was accompanied by another section of the ceiling crashing to the ground, and Luke watched in horror as a portion of the floor collapsed under it. This threw small particles into the air that were greedily swallowed up by the advancing inferno.

A split-second later, the walls on either side started to cave in.

He turned back again.

Was there time to clear the rubble in front of them?

Did they have any choice?

Glen moved as if reading his mind, grabbing large slabs of ceiling tile and heaving them to one side. Andy joined in, but Luke could see it was hopeless. The fire was almost on them and, even if all four worked at it, there was no chance of moving the mountain of rubble in time.

He looked around.

There had to be another way.

The Abbey Room was only five yards behind them, but what was the point in returning to it? It was windowless, and would be…

That was it.

A window.

They needed a window.

Luke tried to remember the layout of the floor. Each was different, but wasn't there another office, a larger one, an office with a window facing out onto the rear of the building?

He grabbed Glen's shoulder and put his mouth to his ear.

"Jane Austen."

Glen looked at him as if he was mad.

"Isn't she dead?"

Luke shook his head and gestured to a door that was only faintly visible. It was on the other side of the corridor, almost opposite the Abbey Room and close to being engulfed by the blaze.

"Over there. The Jane Austen Room."

This time he didn't wait for a reply.

Covering his mouth, he staggered across to the door, pulled his shirt out of his trousers and used it to protect his hand from being burned as he grasped the handle.

He pressed down.

Nothing happened.

The fire was roaring now, moving ever closer.

He was about to push on the handle again when there was another crash behind him, followed immediately by a woman's scream.

Turning, he saw that Andy was lying on his side, blood oozing from a cut on his temple. The woman was bent over him, Glen still heaving up massive slabs of ceiling in a vain attempt to clear a path.

Luke leaned down on the handle and barged his shoulder into the door.

It gave way, and he stumbled inside to find a space mercifully free of smoke. To his relief, there was indeed a window. It was closed, and he knew it would have a restrictor to stop it from opening more than a few inches.

Not that that was going to stand in his way.

He dashed back to Glen's side, and again put his mouth to his ear.

"There's a window."

Glen immediately understood, left what he was doing and lifted Andy onto his shoulder as if he were no heavier than a rag doll. Luke ushered the woman into the room, waited until Glen had entered and then closed the door.

The room had filled with smoke in the few seconds this took, but they had a route out now.

If they were quick.

Luke lifted one of the chairs positioned around the meeting table, swung it back over his head and crashed it into the windowpane.

It bounced off.

He swung again, putting every ounce of power into the action. Seventeen stone was too much this time, and the pane shattered, glass raining down onto the ground outside.

There was no time to waste. He rushed to the window, looked down and saw, to the right, two firemen, each holding hoses and directing pressurised water at the flames.

He cupped his hands around his mouth and shouted down.

"UP HERE!"

A third fireman heard this, looked up, and gestured to a fourth to climb into the caged platform on the back of one of three parked fire engines. He then ran around to the cab and manoeuvred the vehicle closer to the building.

A few seconds later, the hydraulics cut in and the platform rose, then inched its way towards their window.

Luke held the woman's arm as she stepped up onto the chair. She stepped up and over the windowsill, and the fireman helped her down beside him.

Next, Luke and Glen passed the unconscious Andy through and onto the fireman's shoulder.

Glen stepped onto the chair and was about to follow, when the fireman saw his size and held his hand up.

"Wait there. Back in a second."

The platform pulled away and down to the ground, and Luke watched as the woman was helped off. Andy followed, two paramedics lifting him onto a stretcher before wheeling it away to a waiting ambulance.

There was an explosion behind them as the door to the meeting room fell inwards. This was accompanied by a surge of heat alongside a stream of tumbling smoke.

Sweat was dripping from both men's chins, and Glen started coughing as the smoke began to hit the back of his throat.

Luke was relieved when he heard the hydraulics operating again, bringing the platform back to the window.

Seconds later, the fireman held his hand out. Glen grasped it and heaved his way over and into the metal cage.

Luke followed, flames at his rear as he stepped across to safety.

*

Sam ran into his arms as Luke stepped off the platform.

"God, I was so worried."

She stepped back and nodded her head in the direction of the window he had escaped from. It was now engulfed in flames.

"When I saw you up there…"

He smiled and stroked her cheek.

"I'm okay, and relieved we were able to get to Andy in time. Do you know how he is?"

"They took him straight to hospital to check him over, but he came to as they were putting him into the back of the ambulance. I guess we'll know soon if he's badly hurt."

"Do you know if anyone else was caught in it?"

"No, but the fire took hold very quickly, and look at the state of it now."

Most of the left-hand wing of Filchers head office was no more than a pile of masonry, but the fire crew seemed to be having some success in stopping any further spread.

Glen walked towards them, his face and the top of his head covered in flecks of grey and white, and his expression deadly serious.

"I'm going to the front to check the rooster."

Luke raised one eyebrow. This was a new one.

"The rooster?"

Glen nodded.

"The fire wardens will have pulled together a list of everyone outside. I need to check it against the visitors' book."

"Ah. You mean the roster?"

"That's what I said."

"Please can you check my guest is safe? The man I was looking for on the first floor. His name's Dominic Watts."

"Will do."

Glen marched off, and Luke turned to Sam.

"He was amazing in there. It was a side to Glen I've never seen before."

She punched him on the upper arm and smiled.

"You weren't so bad yourself."

He sighed. "I hope no one else was hurt. Have you heard anyone say how it started?"

She shook her head.

"No, but I heard someone suggest it was in the server room on the first floor."

"Mmm. I wonder if one of the computers overheated."

Chapter 22

Mr Killjoy rocked back and smiled as he scanned the monitors positioned on and above his desk.

There were six fire engines in attendance, with their crews stationed on either side of the burning wing of Filchers' head office. Several firemen were using high-pressure hoses to fire jets of water into the roof and walls of the building, while two were talking to a woman rescued from a first-floor window. Three others were in discussion with fire wardens, doubtless checking whether anyone was missing and unaccounted for.

They'd soon find out the truth.

It was a shame innocent people were likely to be caught in the inferno, but collateral damage was unavoidable. A fire like that would spread like…

His smile broadened.

…like wildfire.

All in all, he was pleased with what he had achieved.

Doubly so.

He had killed two birds with one stone, literally with respect to the first, and figuratively when it came to the second. That was two problems eliminated, freeing him to concentrate on acquiring new customers and growing the business and the brand.

And making money.

The NCCU investigator had been getting too close, but Mr Killjoy knew he had only himself to blame. It was a rare mistake, emailing from Filchers without using a VPN, and could have given the game away. Fortunately, he'd had the presence of mind to react quickly.

He was sure he'd eliminated him in time.

And, by starting the fire in the server room, he'd

destroyed the database containing the original email, all trace of it vanished in…

He was almost laughing now as he completed the thought.

…a puff of smoke.

Oh, the irony!

An added bonus was the sense of control and power that creating this mayhem gave him, making nonsense of his father's continual accusations when he was young that he would never amount to anything.

Well, he amounted to something now.

Stick that up your jacksie, Daddy dearest.

His phone pinged, and he saw that it was the message he'd been expecting.

He'd known she'd panic and be in touch with him at the first opportunity, ignorant of the fact that he not only knew what had happened, but had been the instigator.

She had no inkling of his real identity.

Mr Killjoy had deliberately led her to assume that the man who recruited her into the ByteIt team was based somewhere in the north of England. Little did she realise that they not only shared an employer, but also worked in the same department.

He also had information he could use against her if he needed to.

Yes, he controlled her completely. She was nothing but a marionette, and he was the puppeteer, directing her every move.

Sure enough, the message demonstrated her growing anxiety.

There's been a fire where I work. I had to leave my laptop behind. Can we talk?

He'd known she'd contact him about the fire, but what she said about her laptop was concerning. He replied with a 'yes', and seconds later she kicked off a Zoom call.

The facial features of the avatar remained calm and controlled as Bellatrix Lestrange delivered what the web developer typed. However, the words themselves demonstrated how agitated she was.

"My hard drive has all my code. What if someone gets hold of it?"

"Was it encrypted?"

He waited while Lord Voldemort delivered this, and it only took a couple of seconds for Bellatrix to voice her reply.

"Yes."

"Then what is the problem?"

"The database is protected, but I had a file open containing the draft of a new home screen for one of our services."

"You mean you were working on it while you were in the office?"

"Yes, but where I sit, I have my back to the wall. No one can see my screen."

He knew exactly where her cubicle was, and hence that she was telling the truth, but to be working on it so brazenly, with others nearby, was foolish to say the least.

"I expect better of you."

"I know. I'm sorry, but what should I do?"

"It's simple. You find where your laptop is, and you reclaim it before some prying busybody sticks their nose where they shouldn't."

"But I don't know what they've done with it."

"Then find out, and do it now."

"Okay."

"Get back in touch when you've resolved the issue and not before."

He ended the call before the Dark Lord had finished speaking, keen to ensure that it was he who had the last word.

Chapter 23

Luke and Sam walked around to the front of the building to find people were beginning to disperse, either to their cars or to catch a bus.

Glen was standing in front of the entrance doors, leafing through sheets of paper on a clipboard and shaking his head.

"Are people missing?" Luke asked.

He looked up, his face and hair still covered in specks of plaster dust, and sighed.

"Yes, I'm afraid so. There are four unaccounted for." He looked down at his clipboard. "Marcia Brown from HR, Jane…"

He stopped speaking when he realised that a woman was walking briskly towards them, waving her arm to gain his attention.

"What is it, Clarissa?"

"We've located one of them," she said. "Jane Briers."

"Thank goodness. Any of the others with her?"

"No. She left on her own before the wardens took a roll call. The stupid woman decided to use the opportunity to do some shopping."

"Well, at least that's one we know is okay."

She left them, and Glen put a line through one of the names on the top sheet.

"Are there now three people unaccounted for, then?" Luke prompted.

Glen nodded. "Yes. Marcia Brown, who I mentioned, Peter McIntyre, from one of the government sector teams, and your visitor, Dominic Watts. There's a chance they dodged the roll call as Jane Briers did, so they might yet be fine."

Mr Killjoy

He cast his eyes at the smouldering wreckage that was once the west wing of a four-storey office building.

"My worry is that one or more of them was caught in there, and if that's the case…"

He didn't have to finish the sentence for his meaning to be clear.

"Helen and Maj are over there," Sam said, pointing to a bench on the far side of the car park. "Let's go and check they're okay."

They hadn't moved more than five yards when Luke's phone rang. It was Josh, but on looking at his screen, he saw that he'd missed a call from Ben.

He turned to Sam.

"Ben's tried to ring, but this is Josh. He must have heard about the fire. I'll speak to him, ring Ben back and then come and join the three of you."

She headed off towards the others, and he accepted the call.

"Hi, Josh."

"Hi. I heard all about it."

"I'm not surprised. Did you see it on your news app?"

Josh laughed.

"Very funny, guv."

Luke was shocked by this response.

"Did I hear you right? Did you say that you think this is funny?"

"Only that you should think it would be on the news." He chuckled again. "I mean, it's a big event for you personally, guv, but it's hardly the sort of thing they'd talk about on the BBC."

This struck Luke as wildly inappropriate, and he wasn't prepared to let the younger man get away with it.

"You're being incredibly insensitive, Josh. We're talking about people who are missing."

"Yes, but she's back now, isn't she?"

"One of them's back, but there are three who might

still be under the wreckage."

Josh paused before letting a single, short word escape his lips.

"Eh?"

"There are three missing who might be under the wreckage. And if they are, I don't give them much chance of surviving. There's nothing 'funny' about it."

There was silence at the other end.

"Well? What do you have to say?"

Josh's voice went up an octave.

"Wreckage?"

"Yes. The entire west end of the building has been burned to the ground. Christ, I was lucky to get out myself."

"I, ah…"

"You're sorry?"

"Yes… No… I mean…"

"Out with it."

"Are you saying there's been a fire at Filchers?"

It was Luke's turn to hesitate.

"You didn't know?"

"No." The panic was evident in his next words. "Do you know if Leanne is okay?"

"She's fine. I saw her a minute ago with Carys."

"Thank goodness. What about Sam, Helen and Maj?"

"They're safe too." He paused. "If you weren't talking about the fire, Josh, what were you talking about?"

"Ben and Pippa. He managed to track her down. Oh, Leanne's ringing. Speak to you later, guv."

The line went dead, and Luke immediately clicked on Ben's number to ring him back. He answered straight away.

"Dad, are you okay? The fire's all over the news."

Luke almost smiled at the irony of this.

"I'm fine, and so's Sam. I've just spoken to Josh, and he said you found Pippa."

"Yes, I couldn't get hold of you, so I gave him a call."

"And?"

"I think we're going to be okay. I apologised, like you suggested, and then so did she."

"Where was she?"

"At Charlotte's."

"Do you know what upset her?"

"It was me saying how lovely Somerset was, and how great it would be if we could stay at the farmhouse over the summer. Apparently, I was over the top about it, and she thought I was having a dig at Manchester."

"I hope you said sorry."

"I did, yes."

"Good. I'd best go, Ben. I'll give you a ring this evening."

"Bye, Dad."

Chapter 24

Luke was listening to 'A Devil's Share', the fictional DCI Bone's eighth outing, and enjoying every minute.

The book was gritty in places but, in the latest chapter, Mullens had taken his dad and his dad's friend from their care home to a pub with hilarious results, and Luke found himself laughing out loud, despite the events of the previous twenty-four hours.

TG Reid was a skilled writer, and an audiobook was a great way to wind down.

He turned the audiobook off as he approached the Good Bear Cafe, parked, and walked inside, immediately spotting his friend and ex-colleague, Detective Inspector Pete Gilmore, at their usual table in the far corner.

Pete waved him over.

"I've ordered coffees and our usual breakfasts."

"Cheers, Pete." Luke dropped into the chair opposite. "Thanks for saying you'd meet up this morning."

"No problem. What's happening about somewhere to base yourself?"

"Ambrose, our Chief Executive, is on the case. He sent an email to staff yesterday evening asking everyone to work from home while he finds temporary office premises."

Pete lowered his voice.

"Between you and me, there's a possibility the fire was started deliberately."

"Really?"

Pete nodded.

"The Chief Fire Officer told me that there are two things pointing to that being the case. First, they believe the fire started in the server room, which doesn't make sense because there are no heat sources and the electrical infrastructure is sealed off. Second, and more crucially, they found several small piles of white residue around the server room floor. They've sent samples off for testing, but they believe they're the remains of an accelerant used to initiate the fire and help it get hold quickly."

"What about the three people who are missing? Have you heard whether they've been found?"

"Did you know any of them?"

"Only the man, and I don't know him well."

Luke decided not to say any more about Dominic, who had specifically asked that his involvement with Filchers be kept secret.

Pete sighed.

"I'm sorry to say they found two bodies about an hour ago, though 'bodies' is overstating it by all accounts." He gave a grim smile. "By all accounts, they were charred to a crisp."

"Do they know who they are?"

"Not yet. Sally's performing the post-mortems this afternoon."

Luke was pleased she was conducting them. While more than a touch eccentric, Sally Croft was an excellent pathologist.

"Any chance I could attend?"

"As a consultant to Avon and Somerset Police, I don't see why not. In any case, I thought you'd ask, which is why I've already warned her that we'd both like to be in attendance."

"Both of us?"

"The chief rang me this morning and asked me to be SIO. If this was arson, then we're looking at involuntary manslaughter at the very least."

A waiter appeared with their coffees, and Pete took a sip of his coffee before continuing.

"Can you think of any reason why someone would deliberately start a fire at Filchers' head office? Could it be a disgruntled employee? Perhaps someone who's been passed over for promotion, or been dismissed?"

Luke forced himself to shake his head, but his brain was working overtime as he began to connect the dots.

Dominic Watts had been close to catching the so-called Mr Killjoy, and now he was missing, feared dead, after the fire. It also seemed likely that it had been started deliberately.

Was it possible that the investigation and his disappearance were connected, that the fire was started to mask the murder of the NCCU investigator?

He didn't believe in coincidences, never had. However, the link was a weak one, and he decided not to share his thoughts with Pete until he had more to go on.

Another thought occurred to him.

Pete had also suggested that the arsonist might be someone who had been passed over for promotion. This brought to mind Richard Harding, the Deputy Chief Accountant, but he appeared, on the surface at least, to be the victim of a scam rather than a criminal.

A scam using deepfake technology, which must have been carried out by someone with advanced IT skills.

The kind of person who might create a suite of systems for criminals with limited computer knowledge.

The kind of person who bigged himself up by using the name Mr Killjoy.

"Penny for them."

Luke smiled.

"Sorry, Pete. I was miles away. Ah, here's our breakfast."

Chapter 25

Victoria Park would not have been Luke's first choice for a meeting to discuss a highly sensitive and confidential investigation. However, needs must and, with Filchers' head office out of action, it would have to do, at least for today.

Fortunately, the weather was being kind. The sky was cloudless, and the temperature was already touching on 18 degrees, and looked set to hit 20 by lunchtime.

Sam was waiting on the bench when he arrived.

He kissed her on the cheek and then dropped down beside her.

"You said we ought to meet, but that was it," she said. "What's this all about?"

He smiled.

"Some ideas I've had, that's all. I'll explain when the others get here."

"You won't have to wait long." She nodded her head, and he turned to see Maj and Helen walking towards them.

"What's that?" he asked, pointing at the rectangular cardboard box that Helen was carrying. It was about 2 feet by 3 feet, but only a few inches deep.

Helen grinned.

"It's a wee substitute for the whiteboard."

He was about to respond when he heard a familiar voice.

"Crazy wall!"

They all turned to see Josh jogging towards them.

"It's not a whiteboard, it's a crazy wall." He turned to Luke. "I got the message, guv. What's this all about?"

"Project Static."

"Eh?"

"Bear with us, and all will become clear."

Helen opened the box, pulled out a corkboard and a packet of coloured pushpins, and placed the board face up on the bench with the pins beside it.

"We also got these," Maj said, producing Post-its and pens from his pocket and adding them to the mix.

"Great," Luke said.

"Not sure how much privacy we've got though," Sam said.

"Ach, we'll be fine," Helen said. "There'll nae be many who are interested in our ramblings."

"I'm interested," Josh said. "Project Static, did you say, guv? Is it to do with electricity? Lack of movement?"

"Be patient," Luke said, "and I'll explain everything."

"I took a photo of the whiteboard before we left yesterday," Helen said. She clicked on her phone a couple of times and held it up so that everyone could see the image.

Project Static

ByteIT toolkit

Multiple products including FishIt

Accessible at byteit.onion

Mr Killjoy

Josh's eyebrows furrowed as he scanned the photo.

"Fish and Onions? Is the project something to do with food shopping?" He paused. "And who's Mr Killjoy? Is it Mr Filcher? Because he's not exactly a bundle of laughs, so it would make sense if it was him."

"No, it's not Edward Filcher," Luke said. "Someone calling themselves Mr Killjoy has created a package of tools to simplify cybercrime. The suite is called ByteIt, and different elements, including that one..." He pointed to where it said 'FishIt' on the whiteboard image. "...are bought by monthly subscription on the dark web, where websites use the suffix .onion rather than .co.uk or .com."

"Wowza! Why are we involved?"

"A National Crime Agency investigator, Dominic Watts, intercepted an email from Mr Killjoy that was sent from our head office."

"What does that mean we're looking at? Fraud? Theft?"

"Both of those." He paused. "And potentially murder."

"Murder!" Sam exclaimed. "What on earth are you talking about?"

"Dominic is now missing, and it seems likely that he died in the fire yesterday. If that's the case, I don't think it was through bad luck. It's a coincidence too far, and I have a hunch it was Mr Killjoy's doing."

"Couldn't Dominic have just been in the wrong place at the wrong time?" Maj asked.

Luke shook his head.

"I don't think so. He said he was going to the gents on the second floor. What reason could there be for him to go to the floor below, unless he was encouraged or forced to do so?"

"Is that all we know?" Josh asked, pointing to the photo of the whiteboard.

"No, we now know quite a bit more. In addition to FishIt, there are two other subscription services within ByteIt called PayIt and SexIt."

Helen wrote the three onto Post-its and pinned them to the corkboard.

Josh pointed at them.

"Do we know how they're used?"

"Not in detail, but FishIt suggests something to do with sending emails that appear to come from legitimate companies. Dominic suggested PayIt might enable the sending of fake invoices, while SexIt may give criminals the ability to blackmail people through sextortion."

Helen added a few words to the Post-its.

"In addition," Luke went on, "in the last couple of days, Dominic, with Maj's help, found out which part of the building Mr Killjoy is based in."

"How did he do that?" Josh asked.

Luke turned to Maj.

"Something to do with pinging or ponging, wasn't it?"

Maj smiled.

"Dominic used a ping-based IP geolocation method, which revealed that the email he intercepted was sent from one of six cubicles used by the IT department."

"What's more," Luke said, "Ellie, Ambrose's PA, emailed me this morning with the names and contact details for the people who sit in those cubicles."

He opened the email and transcribed five names from his phone to Post-its, and then pinned them to the board.

"Why five and not six?" Sam asked.

"The sixth, Evelyn Brindberg, has been on maternity leave for several months, so we can rule her out." Luke hesitated. "Oh, I nearly forgot. There may be a fourth element of ByteIt."

He wrote 'FakeIt' on a fourth Post-It, pinned it to the board and added the words 'deepfake'.

They all spent a few seconds studying what was now on the corkboard.

PROJECT STATIC

ByteIt Components

FishIt (fake emails)

PayIt (fake invoices)

SexIt (sextortion)

FakeIt (deepfake)

Mr Killjoy Suspects

Zara Opray (web developer)

Naomi Simmons (systems analyst)

Miles Barrington (software engineer)

Jordan Fellowes (software developer)

Charlie Wallace (database engineer)

"To be honest," Luke said, "FakeIt is not necessarily a product, but what I *am* certain of is that deepfake was used to con Filchers out of £200,000."

He explained about the AI-driven Zoom call used to con the deputy chief accountant, Richard Harding, into transferring £200,000 from a Filchers account to a Martin Fuller.

"Could Richard be lying?" Helen asked when he'd finished.

"The idea occurred to me, but I'm inclined to think not. The story's too far-fetched to be an invention, and his body language suggested to me that he was telling the truth."

He pointed to the list of potential suspects.

"Do you know any of these five?"

They all shook their heads except for Sam, whose cheeks started to redden.

"Sam?" he prompted.

She pointed to the last name but one.

"I know Jordan."

"You do? How?"

"I… I went out with him a couple of times."

"Was this in the last few weeks?" Helen asked, a twinkle

in her eyes.

"No, it was not!"

Sam glanced across at Luke and saw a glimmer of a smile on his face.

"It was nearly two years ago. Jordan asked me out, just for a few drinks, then we went out again, but I could see it wasn't going to go anywhere, so I ended it."

"Could he be Mr Killjoy?" Luke asked.

"He could be. I mean, I hardly know him, but he's certainly arrogant enough."

"Arrogant?"

"Yes, he's very full of himself. That's why I didn't want to see him again. He kept talking about what a wonderful software developer he is, how lucky Filchers is to have him in the IT department, how he'd thought about setting up his own business." She paused as she remembered their two nights out. "God, he's boring. Talks about himself non-stop."

"Perhaps he *has* set up his own business," Maj said.

"Aye," Helen said, "and called it ByteIt."

She hesitated for a second, then her eyes widened, and she pointed at the Post-it with PayIt written on it.

"Harry Mullins."

Luke smiled. "I was thinking the same thing."

"Who's Harry Mullins?" Josh asked.

It was Helen who answered.

"He's in Finance. Luke and I are seeing him this afternoon because, on five occasions, he's made payments to the wrong bank account."

"Sorry, Helen," Luke said. "I'm going to have to bow out of that meeting."

"Nae problem."

"Sam, perhaps you can talk to the two female suspects." He smiled. "Probably best you stay away from Jordan Fellowes."

"Ha, ha."

"Maj, you tackle the three men. I suggest the two of you work up an excuse so that none of them suspect what we're really up to."

They agreed that they would.

"What about me, guv?" Josh asked, a pleading note in his voice.

"Rather than throw you in at the deep end on Project Static, we've got another case you can pick up."

"What's the project name?"

"It hasn't got one. Sam, please can you run through where we've got to with the Pickfords?"

"Move," Josh said, then saw Luke's eyebrows go up, and added swiftly, "I didn't mean you should get out of the way, guv. That should be the project name. Project Move." He grinned. "You know, because Pickfords, well, they move people, don't they? From one house to another house. They're a removals…"

Luke raised one hand.

"I get the picture."

He looked at his watch.

"I need to leave if I'm going to make it to Flax Bourton in time for the post-mortems. Sam, I'll leave you to bring Josh up to speed…" He hesitated, then, much to Josh's delight, concluded with, "…on Project Move."

Chapter 26

After Luke had left, Helen returned the corkboard to its box, and she and Maj headed off.

Sam was about to speak when she saw that Josh was still smiling, pleased that he had named another investigation.

"Sit down and wipe that off your face," she said, gesturing to his grin, "and I'll update you on where we got to with the Pickfords."

"Gotcha."

He mimed zipping his mouth closed, then sat down on the bench beside her, pulled out his notepad and opened it to a blank page. Slowly and carefully, he wrote 'PROJECT MOVE' in capital letters at the top, then underlined the words, nodded to himself approvingly, and looked across at her, his pen poised to take notes.

"Go for it."

She hesitated for a second while she pulled her thoughts together.

"The case centres on Jack Pickford, a Filchers employee. He's seventeen and works on the Spectra account. Last Friday, he attempted to hang himself in his bedroom, and his parents believe it was because of his manager, more specifically because they'd been in a sexual relationship and she'd dumped him. However, it appears they're wrong."

"Has Jack told you that?"

"No. He's still in a coma, but Luke spoke to his manager, Kelly Gaynes, and I spoke to his younger sister, Amelia, and we're convinced it's a misunderstanding. It does appear that he was in a relationship with a woman in her late twenties, and that she ended it, but the person in question is not Kelly."

"What do you suggest I do next?"

"You need to speak to his parents, explain why we're confident it's not his manager, and ask them who else they think it might be. At the moment, his father's distraught, and his mother's in an even worse state and seems to be on the verge of a mental breakdown. It's important that we find out who this woman is as soon as possible."

"Got it. What are his mum's and dad's names?"

"Larry and Stephanie. Their son's still in intensive care, so they'll most likely be at the RUH. I'll text you Larry's phone number."

*

Josh waited until Sam had left before calling Larry Pickford, who picked up after five rings and immediately let out a very audible yawn.

"Excuse me." He swallowed before continuing. "This is Larry."

"Larry, my name's Josh. I work with Luke and Sam."

"Oh. Hi, Josh. Sorry about the yawn. I was trying to catch up on some sleep."

"I understand. Any improvement in Jack's condition?"

"No change, I'm afraid. How can I help?"

"I was wondering if I could come to the RUH and talk to you."

This provoked an immediate response, and from the tone of it, Josh could see that Sam had been right. Larry Pickford was wound up tighter than a 10-day clock.

"Have you confronted that woman? She needs to be dealt with? It's awful what she did. He's only seventeen. Has she admitted it?"

"We've talked to her, but I'd prefer to go through what she said face to face, if that's okay?"

"Not at the RUH, not with my wife there. Could you come here, to our house? We live on Park Lane. Number 42."

That was a bonus. Josh could see Park Lane from where he was sitting.

"Yes, I can do that."

Five minutes later, he rang the doorbell of a semi-detached house that had to be worth well over a million pounds. It was Georgian, he thought, whatever that meant. Or perhaps Victorian. It was old, anyway, and grand, set over four storeys, with the front door on the first floor and approached over a stone walkway.

He rang the bell, which gave a resounding 'boing-boing' that made him confident it would have been heard inside.

Not to mention halfway down the street.

Larry opened the door a couple of seconds later.

Josh knew, from what Sam had told him, that Jack Pickford's father was no older than Luke, but it was hard to believe. It was partly his grey hair, but also the bags under his eyes. He had a haunted look, and no wonder, given what he'd been through over the preceding week.

"Hi, Larry."

"What did she say?"

"May I come in?"

"Sorry. Yes. How rude of me. Sorry."

He opened the door, and Josh walked into a large hallway with several doors leading off.

"We'll go in there," Larry said, gesturing to an open doorway on the right.

Josh entered what he assumed was the lounge, although rather than facing a television, the two pale green sofas were at right angles to each other and facing a grand piano, which was very much the focus of the room.

"Please," Larry said, indicating the furthest settee.

Josh sat down, and Larry perched on the front edge of the other sofa.

Josh smiled.

"We spoke to..."

He stopped mid-sentence.

Launching into Kelly Gaynes' innocence wasn't the way Luke would approach a situation like this. He'd spend a few minutes talking about subjects unrelated to the investigation. Josh had seen him do that to put the interviewee at their ease. As a consequence, they more readily opened up when it came to the conversation proper.

That was what Josh should do.

All he needed to do was find something unrelated to the suicide attempt and talk about that.

And above all, remain calm and in control.

That was essential.

Calm and in control.

Josh was staring into space as he considered his options, and Larry raised one eyebrow.

"Are you okay?"

"Ah... Sorry. I was, ah..."

He looked around for inspiration and found himself gesturing to the Steinway.

"Are you a pianist, Larry?"

"No, that's my wife."

Josh stared at the piano.

"That's your wife?"

As soon as he said it, he realised what the other man meant and a snort of laughter escaped his lips.

"Sorry... You mean she.... I mean, she's not the piano.... Obviously..." He swallowed. "Is your wife a professional musician?"

Larry was about to reply when Josh screamed.

"AAAGH!"

He wagged a shaking finger at the piano's keyboard.

"There's a... LOOK!... It's moving!... There!... That green thing!"

He shrank back into the sofa while at the same time

wagging his finger again, even more violently this time.

There was a half-smile on Larry's face as he replied. "That's Matilda."

"Matilda! What do you mean, Matilda?"

He glanced at the other man as if he had completely lost his mind, then returned his attention to the monstrosity perched on the black and white keys. As he watched, it started rubbing a pair of skinny green forelegs together, its beady eyes seeming to focus on Josh as if intent on making him its next victim.

It walked slowly along the keys.

"Christ, it's moving. The thing's moving."

"Matilda is my daughter's pet. She's a praying mantis. Do you want me to put her away?"

"Definito. It's mahoosive. AAAGH! Look! It's coming nearer!"

A horrible thought occurred to him.

"Can it…" He swallowed. "Can it fly?"

It shot at him like a stone from a catapult before Larry had the chance to reply. Josh ducked, and it flew over his head, then around the room before returning to the piano.

Larry laughed, rose to his feet, calmly walked to the Steinway and cupped his hands around the insect.

"I'll put her back in her cage."

"Please. And lock it. Make sure it's locked."

*

Josh took a sip of his tea, which was going some way to making him feel better after his ordeal.

He attempted a smile.

"Sorry about that, Larry." He lifted his cup. "Thanks for the tea."

"No problem. You were saying that you spoke to Jack's manager?"

"Yes."

Josh put his cup down and held his hand out flat to check it was steady before continuing.

"Based on what she said, and what your daughter told us, we're convinced that there hasn't been any kind of relationship between her and your son."

"But Amelia said he'd been in a relationship with an older woman?"

"Yes, but not Kelly Gaynes."

Josh gave this a moment or two to sink in.

"Larry, can you think of anyone else it could be? Amelia told us the woman in question is twenty-seven. Has he mentioned anyone else he works with, or do any of his friends perhaps have older sisters?"

"There's no one I can think of."

"Have you thought of searching his room to see if there are any clues to the woman's identity?"

"I've already done it, and there's nothing."

"Did you notice anything odd about his behaviour? For example, was he out more often than usual in the run-up to what happened last week?"

"The opposite, really. He's been spending more and more time in his room, and I did wonder if this was purely an online relationship, you know, someone he met on an app like Tinder." Larry paused. "There is one thing that's got me baffled. I checked his bank account, and there's a debit of £500 which has taken the balance down to single figures."

"When was this?"

"Last Wednesday."

"Would that be before he told Amelia the relationship was over?"

"Yes. The day before. I wondered if perhaps he'd bought this woman a gift." He hesitated. "It even occurred to me that she might be a prostitute, although if she was, why would she finish with him?"

"Was the money paid to a company or an individual?"

"There wasn't a name, just a reference. It said 'KW-13', that's K, W, then a dash, then 1 and 3 as digits."

Josh made a note of this.

"And you don't know anyone with the initials KW?"

"No."

"Perhaps you could explain the circumstances to the bank and see if they can tell you who the recipient was?"

"I'll try."

"Would you mind giving me the names and numbers of Jack's closest friends? I'd like to have a word with them and see if they know anything."

"Of course. There are three he's close to, Euan Broscombe, Isaac Staples and Matthew Rogerson, but I haven't got their phone numbers. I know where Isaac lives, though, so perhaps you could start with him. His address is 23 Lynfield Park. That's in Upper Weston."

"Thanks, Larry. I'll do that. And if you get anywhere with the bank, please let me know."

Chapter 27

Luke had just pulled into a parking space outside Flax Bourton mortuary when his phone pinged, and he looked down to see it was an email from Ambrose.

To: All Filchers Employees
From: Ambrose Filcher, CEO
Subject: Fire at Head Office

Dear Colleague,

It is with immense sadness that I write to inform you that three people died in yesterday's fire. My thoughts are with their family and friends at this sad time. I will send a further email when the police permit me to reveal their names.

Thank you for your forbearance while we deal with the aftermath of this tragedy. Fire officers are looking into possible causes, and I ask you please not to speculate, and not to participate in the various conspiracy theories being touted on social media.

Meanwhile, hard as it is, we must carry on with business. The senior team has managed to obtain temporary premises, and our Director of Internal Affairs will email you shortly to provide details.

Best wishes
Ambrose

He had only just finished reading it when a second email arrived, an email in which every word was imbued with Edward Filcher's pomposity and tactlessness. It was evident that Gloria had not been given the chance to edit it before he'd hit the send button.

To: Filchers Staff
From: Director of Internal Affairs MA (Oxon)
Subject: Fire at Head Office

Dear Subordinate,

You will have heard from our CEO that three people burned to death in yesterday's fire.

This was unfortunate.

I remind you that the event has not created the opportunity for a holiday, nor to slack. You are required to continue working. We cannot monitor your activities, but your manager will expect you to fulfil your duties as you would normally.

I have obtained temporary office accommodation for our most important employees at numbers 23 to 27, Gay Street, and at the Bath Travelodge. If you are one of these, the attachment will tell you where you are based.

If you are not one of our most important employees, you must continue to work your normal office hours from home or other suitable locations. No claims for expenses will be accepted.

Yours sincerely and fraternally
E Filcher

Luke was about to click on the attachment when the email vanished, and the message 'email recalled' appeared at the top of his inbox.

"Thank goodness for Gloria" was his immediate thought, accompanied by the hope that it had been recalled before

too many recipients had had the chance to read it.

Luke was about to knock on the pathologist's door when another ping heralded a second, much-improved email which had Gloria's hand all over it.

To: *Filchers Staff*
From: *Edward Filcher*
Subject: *Fire at Head Office*

Dear Colleague,

Further to Ambrose's email, I confirm that the Executive Team has obtained temporary office accommodation at numbers 23 to 27, Gay Street, and at the Bath Travelodge. This will be available for use from next Monday.

Unfortunately, there is insufficient space to house everyone, and I apologise if you are not listed in the attachment. Please rest assured that we are doing everything we can to find additional premises to tide us over until we can return to our head office.

Thank you for bearing with us at this difficult time.

Regards
Edward Filcher

Luke turned at the sound of footsteps to see that Pete had arrived.

"Hi, Pete." He nodded to his phone. "Ambrose has emailed saying that three people died in the fire. I thought they'd only found two bodies?"

"It's three as of an hour ago, and an ambulance is on its way here with the third body now."

"Do you know why it took so long?"

"It was in a part of the building that had only partially collapsed, and they had to reinforce the structure before they could properly search."

The door behind them opened, and Luke turned to see Sally Croft beaming across at them. As usual, her clothes and hair reflected her extroverted nature, on this occasion an orange rinse complementing her choice of lilac slacks and blouse.

"Good afternoon, boys, and welcome to the madhouse. You're just in time for my first onslaught into these poor people's bodies." She lifted up her phone. "And I've just heard a third one is on the way, so it's going to be a busy afternoon. You know where the PPE is. Let's get going."

Two minutes later, Luke and Pete followed her into the examination room, where blanket-covered bodies lay on the first two of three metal tables. Nina, Sally's assistant, was standing by the first table, a notepad in her hand, while beside her stood a metal table covered with an array of scalpels, knives and saws.

Sally nodded to Nina, who pulled back the blanket to reveal the severely burned body of a woman. Her sex was apparent by the shape of her body, but her face was so badly charred and covered in blisters that Luke would not have been able to recognise her had she been his best friend.

"What are you looking for?" Luke asked.

"As in any post-mortem, my main aim is to identify how this poor woman died. In this case, I need to differentiate between injuries sustained before the fire and those caused by the fire itself."

She began her visual inspection, bending forward to study the woman's face before moving on to her arms, legs and then torso.

"Scalpel, please," she said when she'd finished.

Nina passed her the instrument, and she bent forward to the woman's chest.

Chapter 28

"It's vital," Sam said, "that if we're right, and Mr Killjoy is one of these five people, we don't give him or her any reason to suspect what we're up to. Mr Killjoy is clearly very smart, and potentially dangerous too."

Maj considered this for a few seconds.

"You're right. We have to find a reason why we, members of the Ethics Team, need to speak to them. What's more, it has to be a topic that Mr Killjoy might be uncomfortable talking about. We can't expect him or her to slip up, but their body language may give us a clue as to whether they're concealing something."

"The fire's the obvious subject, given we think Mr Killjoy may have had a hand in it." She flicked her fingers, then smiled. "Got it! Let's say there's concern that the fire took hold so quickly, and we're checking whether there were any flammable materials around."

They spent a few minutes working this idea up.

"I suggest you go first," Maj said, once they were happy enough to proceed, "and talk to the two female suspects."

"Good idea. Mr Killjoy is most likely a man, so it would be best to try out our approach on the women first."

"I agree, but we can't be certain that's the case, so tread carefully, won't you?"

"Don't worry. I will."

*

Ellie had provided phone numbers and, once Maj had left, Sam took a deep breath before ringing Zara Opray.

"Zara."

"Hi, Zara. I'm Sam Chambers from the Ethics Team."
"Oh. Ah… Hi."
"I was wondering if I could have a word with you."
There was a momentary hesitation.
"Sure. What about? I haven't done anything wrong, have I?"
Zara spoke softly, and Helen thought she detected a touch of Geordie in her accent.

She decided to try to set the woman's mind at ease. The last thing she wanted was for her to refuse to meet up.

"No, not at all, Zara, and don't worry, this has nothing to do with ethics. The Chief Fire Officer has asked Ambrose Filcher if it's possible that items were hanging around which helped the fire get hold so quickly, and he's pulled together a small team to make enquiries."

"What kind of items?"
"It could be as simple as paper, but more likely something flammable such as sun cream."
"I didn't have any sun cream."
"I'm sure you didn't, but it's possible the cleaners left cleaning fluids behind. If they were alcohol-based, that could have helped to fuel the fire."
"I don't remember seeing anything like that."
"Do you think we could meet face to face? If we talk things through, it might spark a memory."

There was another pause before she replied.
"I suppose so."

She spoke again, but more quietly, and Sam realised she was talking to someone else.

"Zara, is Naomi Simmons with you?"
"Yes. Why?"
"We're speaking to everyone based on the first floor and, if you're together, it would make sense to talk to both of you at once."

"Okay. Just a second." The phone went quiet for a few seconds, then she came back on the line. "Naomi's fine

Mr Killjoy

with that."

"Great. Where are you?"

"We're at Naomi's house. It's in Walcot."

Sam heard the other woman hiss something, but couldn't make out the words, then Zara spoke again.

"Can we meet at Walcot House? It's a cafe near here."

"Sure."

*

Thirty minutes later, Sam walked through the doors of the cafe to find an elegantly furnished room that looked more suited to cocktails and dining than to coffee and cake. There was a well-stocked bar to the left, and several rectangular tables down the middle, all of which were set with cutlery and napkins for either two or four people.

To her right lay a series of alcoves with comfortable-looking, semi-circular, tan leather seating set behind marble-topped circular tables. It was at the second of these that she spotted two women deep in conversation who had to be Zara Opray and Naomi Simmons.

It was Naomi, the younger of the two women, who spotted Sam first, and indicated as much to her colleague who turned and smiled nervously.

Zara wasn't as Sam had expected from their phone conversation. They'd only talked briefly, but her withdrawn and reticent manner had led Sam to assume she would be unmemorable and fade into the background. In reality, she was anything but, her stand-out feature being short hair that was dyed a not-so-subtle shade of iridescent pink.

However, she spoke softly, as she had on the phone, and it was clear that her personality did not match her appearance.

"Hi, Sam. I, ah…" She swallowed and gestured to the other woman. "This is Naomi."

Naomi smiled, exhibiting a set of sparkling white teeth that would have given Glen Baxter a run for his money. She had big blue eyes, a petite button nose and thick brown hair that fell in curls over her shoulders. Sam knew men whose eyes would be out on stalks, but there was something about her smile that seemed false, almost as if she was trying too hard.

Or concealing something.

However, Sam had already made one false assumption, and was determined to give the woman the benefit of the doubt.

She smiled back.

"Hi, Naomi. Mind if I squeeze in?"

Naomi shuffled along to the centre, and Sam slid in beside her, then signalled to a waiter who came over and took their orders.

"Thanks for seeing me, both of you," she said, once he had left.

"No problem," Zara said.

Naomi didn't say anything, her focus now on the immaculately lacquered nails of her left hand, which she was inspecting one by one.

"As I said to Zara on the phone, I'm trying to discover whether there was anything left lying around on the first floor that might have helped the fire."

"Paper," Naomi said without looking up, and Sam thought she detected a Liverpool accent, though it was only slight.

"Paper?"

"There's always paper." She held her index fingernail up to look at it more closely as she added, "For the printer."

"How much?"

"Three or four boxes."

"That would have caught fire, there's no doubt about that, but it wouldn't act as an accelerant. Did either of you see anything that might have helped to promote the fire?"

"Like foam?" Zara suggested.

"Yes, or it could be an ignitable liquid. Something like turps or motor oil."

"I left my nail varnish behind," Naomi said.

She lifted her head to look at Sam and held her middle finger up. She was staring at the end of it, and it could have been an innocent gesture, but Sam had a suspicion that the insult was intended.

"Hermes Rose Porcelaine," she went on, her finger still extended. "Cost me £50, it did."

"It would have to be something considerably bigger, perhaps a cleaning spray or a solvent-based detergent of some kind."

"Wouldn't it be more sensible to ask the cleaners?"

Sam chose to ignore the sarcasm that was oozing from the woman as she said this.

"Good idea. I will."

Naomi stared at her for a second or two longer, then lowered her hand and started to inspect her ring finger.

Their drinks arrived. Sam lifted her cappuccino to her lips and decided to change tack.

"You were both lucky not to get caught up in the fire, given that the fire brigade believes it started very near you. I take it you're both full-time, so you were there when the alarms went off?"

"Of course we're full-time," Zara snapped.

"I was on the third floor," Naomi said, again without looking up.

"The third floor?"

"Yes. When the alarm went off, I was with one of the managers on the Spectra account, running through system changes we're making."

"That was lucky."

"Yes." She sighed, took one last look at her nails and then added, in an exasperated tone, "If that's all, do you mind if I leave?"

"What about your coffee?" Zara asked.

"I'm not thirsty." She turned back to Sam, and nodded her head to indicate that she needed to move. "Do you mind?"

Sam slid out, and Naomi squeezed past, then headed towards the exit without another word.

"She can be like that," Zara said, as Sam returned to her seat, then lowered her voice to a conspiratorial whisper. "That wasn't true what she said about running through changes."

"What do you mean?"

"She was up there chatting to her friend. She's always doing it."

"Her friend?"

"Yes. They're like peas in a pod, Naomi and Kelly. Like peas in a pod. They were at school together, and have been friends ever since, even though there are two years between them."

"Is Naomi the younger of the two?"

"Yes. She's only twenty-seven and Kelly's nearly thirty."

Chapter 29

The Edwardian terraced house didn't look large enough to accommodate six apartments, but that was how many buttons there were on the buzzer next to the front door.

The fourth from the top read 'Mullins', and Helen pressed it. There was no satisfying buzz, but a voice spoke a few seconds later.

"Alright?"

"Hi, it's Helen."

"Sound. Nice one."

These words were enough to tell her that the occupant was an out-and-out Scouser, but there was no click to unlock the door. She was about to press the button again when she heard footsteps on the stairs and, a few seconds later, Harry Mullins pulled open the door.

He was in his early sixties, no taller than Helen, and thin as a rake. He stared at her through thick-rimmed glasses as if she had landed from outer space. After a few seconds, the stare transitioned into a series of rapid blinks.

"Harry?"

After a few seconds, he stopped blinking and grinned.

"This about the dodgy invoices, like?"

"Yes. Is there a cafe we can go to so that you can explain what happened?"

"No."

"No?"

He pointed down at his bare feet.

"No trabs."

"Shoes?"

He nodded, blinked a few more times, then said, "I'll fetch 'em," and closed the door again.

A few minutes later he reappeared, now wearing a pair

of blue trainers that matched the colour of his 'Queen' t-shirt and baggy denims.

"There's a cafe at the Tesco," he said, pointing to the supermarket at the end of the road.

"Aye. That'll do."

They headed off, and Helen sensed he was desperate to ask something. Was he on edge? His manner was certainly unusual. Perhaps he was concerned because he was up to no good and had been rumbled.

But what he said next wasn't what she had expected at all.

"Strong accent."

He must have seen that she was struggling to understand him, and she was about to speak some words of reassurance when he spoke again.

"Is it because you're Scottish?"

She smiled to herself.

"Yes, from Edinburgh."

"Nice one. I'm from Everton, like. Always followed the toffees, I have. Always."

*

Tesco's cafe was mercifully quiet, and Harry was staring out of the window when she returned with their drinks.

"Ta," he said as she passed him his glass.

He gestured around at the empty tables.

"Good time to come. Gets chocka in here, like. Came with our kid on Saturday, took ages to get served. I was proper gutted."

"Perhaps we can talk about those invoices?"

"Can do, but all I did was pay 'em. Did all the checks, then paid 'em."

"I'm sure, but didn't you notice they were all to the same account?"

Mr Killjoy

He shook his head.

"I do a lorra payments. A lorra lorra payments. No way can I remember all the numbers."

"Okay. I understand that, but it seems a wee bit odd that you were the person to handle all five invoices. There are other payments clerks, aren't there?"

"Aye. Three."

"Then why you? How are invoices allocated?"

"It's a cap."

Helen was confused. Was this a Scouse expression that had passed her by?

"A cap?"

He shook his head.

"Norra cap. It's a cap. A system, like. An IT system."

"An IT system?"

"You gorrit. Itsacap. I-T-S-A-C-A-P. Stands for IT System to Allocate, Check and Pay."

"Ah. I see. The system chooses who the payments go to."

Harry nodded, took a glug of his lemonade and held the glass up.

"That's boss, that. Ta."

"Nae problem. Harry, do you know who configures the system?"

"One of them IT thingios. Analyst or programmer."

"Do you know which one?"

"What it is is one of them on the first floor. Always the same one. An IT kidda. The wool."

"The wool?"

"Aye."

He knocked back the rest of his drink, put his hand over his mouth in a failed attempt to disguise a very audible burp, then rose to his feet.

"Gorra go." His grin returned. "Payments don't pay theirselves. Ta fer the drink."

She watched him leave and thought through everything

he'd said.

There was certainly no indication of guilt, and she was inclined to believe Harry when he said that all he did was process the invoices passed to him by the IT system.

But that still left the question as to why all five had been assigned to him.

She decided her best bet was to ring his manager and see if she might know why.

"Hello, Kylie Dobson."

"Hi, Kylie. It's Helen. I've been following up on those invoices."

"Oh, thanks. Are you getting anywhere?"

"I'm not sure. I've just met Harry, and I think he's an innocent in all this. All he says he did was process the invoices sent to him by ITSACAP. Does that make sense?"

"Yes. ITSACAP makes the allocations."

"What I'm wondering is why he was sent all of the fraudulent invoices, rather than them being split across the four payments clerks."

There was silence at the other end.

"Kylie?"

"To be honest, I don't know why, but, well…" She hesitated. "The truth is that Harry's not the brightest. Of all my team, he's the least likely to spot something odd going on."

"Are you suggesting they could have been sent to him because he was the most likely to approve them for payment?"

"Exactly."

Chapter 30

Maj bought himself a flat white and took it to a table in the centre of the Costa Coffee.

He'd chosen the branch nearest to Filchers' head office, or what was left of the head office, and glanced around, pleased with his decision. It was open plan, about half-full, and far from the kind of place you might conduct a probing interview. That made it ideal. It was important that the meeting was non-confrontational. The three suspects had to believe that all he was doing was asking questions, to ensure that Filchers hadn't been at fault by inadvertently helping the fire to get hold.

Whichever of them was Mr Killjoy, and he was 99% sure it had to be a man rather than a woman, and therefore almost certainly one of the three, they would be on edge. The last thing he wanted was to give them reason to suspect he was onto them.

He had arrived early and, after checking no one was watching, pulled out a sheet of paper from his pocket to remind himself of what he knew about the three men. Unfortunately, it was very little, because all he'd been able to do was access their HR records, and even that had required calling in a favour.

Miles Barrington was 35 years old and a senior software engineer. He'd been with Filchers for just over a year, having previously worked for a software company. According to his CV, he'd obtained a double-first in Mathematics at Oxford University, so he was clearly bright.

Jordan Fellowes was 33, and the man Sam had briefly dated and had described as arrogant. He was a software developer who, in the two years he had been with Filchers, had asked for promotion on four separate occasions. His request had been declined each time, most recently by Miles, who was his current manager.

Charlie Wallace, 41, was a database engineer. He also reported to Miles, and was the longest-serving of the three, having joined as a graduate trainee nearly two decades earlier.

Maj returned the sheet to his pocket, checked his watch, and took a sip of his drink, which was still hot, almost scaldingly so.

He looked over at the counter and saw that there were two men in the queue. They were talking to each other, and about the right age, and he was about to stand up and walk over when there was a tap on his shoulder.

"Maj, fancy seeing you here."

"Oh. Hi, Glen."

Glen Baxter was all smiles.

Well, not quite.

If truth were told, he was all pumped-up, steroid-fuelled muscle coupled with a bristly, greying number one haircut.

The grin was there, though.

As was a plate of hard-boiled eggs.

Eight hard-boiled eggs.

Glen saw where he was looking and nodded to them.

"Eggs are a complete protein. Good for muscle building and very nutrinious."

"Nutrinious?"

He nodded.

"Uh-huh. They contain enema acids too."

"Do you mean amino acids?"

"Exactly. Mind if I join you?"

"Ah…"

Glen sat down opposite before Maj could say more, grinned across at him and pushed first one egg and then a second into his mouth.

A few seconds later, the two men from the counter

walked over.

"Maj?" the taller man asked.

"That's me."

"I'm Miles, and this is Charlie."

Charlie raised one hand.

"Hi."

Glen looked up at the two men, his cheeks now distended by the eggs so that he looked like nothing less than a hamster preparing for winter.

"Eegh, ugh, eegh," was all he managed to say.

"This is Glen," Maj said. "Thanks for coming, guys."

"No problem," Miles said. "Ah, here's Jordan."

Maj turned to see a man approaching who was clearly, like Glen, a bodybuilder. Unlike Glen, however, he had a full head of brown hair, and a mouth that was not stretched to breaking point by two boiled eggs.

"What's this all about?" he said. "I haven't got all day."

"Come off it, Jordan," Miles said. "It's not as if you're busy."

"Do you want to grab a drink?" Maj asked.

Jordan shook his head.

"Nah. Let's get this over with. You wanted to know if we'd seen flammable stuff before the fire. Is that right?"

"Marshal."

This was from Glen, who had managed to swallow both eggs and was grinning as he jabbed his right thumb into his chest several times.

"Marshal," he repeated. "Me."

"Glen is the fire marshal for Filchers," Maj explained.

"Is that why he's here?" Miles asked.

Glen shook his head. "Here for the nutriniousness and the enema…" He coughed as a piece of egg repeated on him. "…not enema, the, ah…" He tapped the side of his temple a couple of times, as if trying to force the correct word out, all the while beaming like the proverbial Cheshire Cat. "…the amino acids."

"All I wanted to check on," Maj began, choosing to ignore the Head of Security, "is whether any of you saw materials lying around that might have helped the fire to get such a strong hold."

"Accelerants, you mean?" Charlie asked.

"Yes, anything solvent-based. Perhaps a spray can left behind by one of the cleaners."

"It'd take more than a pint of detergent to get a fire going," Miles said. "What do the fire brigade think started it?"

"I'm not sure they know yet."

"There was a lot of paper," Jordan said. "Would that have done it?"

"Don't be an idiot," Miles said. "Paper might burn, but it's not an accelerant. An accelerant is something that has a high burn temperature and a high heat release rate. A road flare, for example."

"There's no need to patronise me."

But this was like water off a duck's back. Miles was in his stride, enjoying showing off his knowledge about everything and anything.

"Turpentine would be a good option," he went on. "A petroleum distillate would be effective, too. Kerosene, for example, or motor oil."

"Did any of you see anything like that?" Maj asked.

"Yeah," Jordan said, sarcasm oozing out of him. "There are always jerrycans of petrol lying around in the IT department."

"No need to act like a tosser," Miles said. "He's only asking."

"You're the tosser. Always showing off about your extensive fucking knowledge."

"I take it," Maj began, keen to break things up before a fight started, "that none of you saw anything."

"Not a thing," Miles said.

"Me neither," Jordan chipped in.

Mr Killjoy

Maj turned to the third man.

"Charlie?"

"No. Nothing."

"Okay. Well, thanks for your time, guys."

"Fucking waste of it, if you ask me," Jordan mumbled under his breath, before turning and heading for the exit.

"Egg, anyone?" Glen said, holding out his plate, his grin turned up to eleven. "I can't manage the last one."

Chapter 31

Luke felt shattered, and yet all he'd done was watch and listen. How Sally could do the job every working day of her life was beyond him.

He rapped the fingers of both hands on the top of the steering wheel, a hundred thoughts going through his mind, almost forgetting that Pete was in the VW's passenger seat.

"He was murdered, then?" Pete said quietly.

Luke sighed.

"It looks like it."

He paused, then turned to look at his friend.

"Pete, would you mind going to your car while I make a phone call?"

Pete furrowed his brows.

"What do you mean? We were both there, so if you're telling Ambrose, you hardly need to keep it from me."

"Please, Pete. It's not Ambrose."

"You can't…"

Luke held his hand up.

"I'll explain everything, but first, I need to make a call. Trust me on this."

Pete sighed, looked at Luke for a second or two, and then opened the door and climbed out.

Luke waited until the Detective Inspector was almost at his car before making the call.

It was answered immediately.

"ACC Scarrott's office."

"Hi, this is Luke Sackville. Is the ACC there?"

"She's with the Chief at the moment. Can I…"

Luke interrupted before she could finish.

"I need to speak to her urgently, in fact it would be good to speak to both of them. They'll want to hear this.

Can you patch me through, please?"

There was a click, a few seconds of silence, then another click, and the Chief Constable came on the line.

"Luke, this is Sara."

"Good afternoon, Ma'am. I gather ACC Scarrott is with you?"

"She is, yes. Give me a moment." There was a pause. 'You're on speaker."

"Hi, Luke," Jean said.

"Hi, Ma'am. I'm in my car in the mortuary car park. DI Gilmore and I have just sat in on all three post-mortems."

He swallowed, aware that he was about to impart devastating news.

"I'm sorry to say that Dominic Watts had a fractured skull, and Sally believes the injury was inflicted before the fire."

He heard one of the women at the other end gasp, and there was a pause before Jean spoke.

"What makes her think that?"

"The nature of the wound. He'd been hit with considerable force, more than she would expect if the injury was caused by falling masonry. Sally thinks the weapon used might have been a hammer."

"Was he dead before the fire got to him?" Sara asked.

"Sally doesn't think so. He had particles in his respiratory tract, and over 50% carboxyhaemoglobin in his blood."

"Does that mean that he was knocked out, and left somewhere in the belief that the evidence would be destroyed?" Jean suggested.

"It looks like it. He was found in the server room, which was at the centre of the fire. I suspect that whoever knocked him out put him in there, then locked the door before setting light to the building."

"Jean told me there was accelerant found," Sara said. "God. How awful."

"Ma'am, how do you want to proceed from here?"

"What have you told DI Gilmore?" Jean asked.

"Nothing as yet."

"I think you should tell him everything. In fact…" She paused. "Luke, can I put you on silent for a moment while I speak to the Chief?"

"Of course."

There was a click, and he waited, wondering what it was that she needed to speak to Chief Constable Gough about.

A couple of minutes passed, then the ACC came back on the line.

"This is unorthodox, but the Chief has agreed that you should be the senior investigating officer for this investigation. Are you okay with that, Luke?"

"Yes, Ma'am."

"Good. We need to move quickly to stop this so-called Mr Killjoy before he or she kills again. Tell Pete everything and continue using your team, but make sure they tread carefully."

"I will, Ma'am. Are you okay if we continue referring to the investigation as Project Static? It's a name one of my team came up with."

"Yes, that's fine. Oh, and bring Ambrose up to speed, please, but don't involve that idiot he brought along to our first meeting."

"You mean my boss?"

"He's your boss, is he? I don't envy you there." She paused. "Keep me up to date. I'll ring the NCCU now and speak to Dominic's manager."

∗

Luke opened the passenger door of Pete's Renault, climbed in and summarised his conversation with the chief and the ACC.

"So, you're going to be SIO," Pete said when he'd finished. "An ex-officer as senior investigating officer. That's a first."

"You're sure you don't mind my taking over?"

"Of course not, and it's not as if I'm off the case. Besides, it'll be good to be working together again."

"We're close to catching him, Pete, I can sense it, but if Mr Killjoy gets any inkling that we are getting close, heaven knows the lengths he or she might go to to protect themselves."

"You're right. The bastard set off a fire that killed not just the target but two other innocent people as well."

Luke paused to pull together his thoughts.

"We're going to need an incident room. I don't want to use Avon and Somerset Premises, and I'm not sure the places Filcher has secured will work. I'll have a word with Ambrose and see if he has any ideas."

"What do you want me to do, guv?"

"Don't you start. I get enough of that from Josh. Stick with calling me Luke."

"Will do."

"Can you run checks on our five suspects, see if that turns anything up?"

"No problem."

"Thanks."

Luke returned to his car, and spent a few minutes making a mental list of what to do next.

He needed to ring Ambrose first, after which he needed to ask the ACC for approval to bring two subject matter experts into the team.

Once they were on board, he'd call a team meeting so that everyone was up to speed, him included. Having spent all afternoon in the mortuary, he hadn't had the chance to catch up with Sam, who had been talking to the two female suspects, nor Maj, who was interviewing the three men. Plus, he wanted to hear how Helen had got on with Harry

Mullins. He was convinced there was a link between those fraudulent invoices and one of the ByteIt services, but whether that would help them pinpoint Mr Killjoy was another thing.

It was going to be all hands on deck, which meant pulling Josh off the Pickfords investigation, or Project Move as he had christened it. It was a shame, but catching Mr Killjoy was a priority, and he couldn't afford for a valuable member of his team to be off pursuing an unrelated case.

He hesitated as two thoughts occurred to him.

First, did he really consider Josh to be a valuable member of the Ethics Team?

This made him ponder. The lad could be immature some, no, correct that, most of the time, but he had drive and initiative, and he was smart too.

Yes, on reflection he was most definitely an important member of the Ethics Team.

Second, and more importantly, was there a chance that Jack Pickford's attempted suicide was related in some way, that he had tried to kill himself because of something Mr Killjoy had done?

But if so, what possible connection was there?

Chapter 32

Luke was about to call Ambrose when Sam rang.

"Hi, Sam."

"Hi. What was the outcome of the post-mortems?"

"Sally's certain that Marcia Brown and Peter McIntyre died in the fire. It seems that they were plain unlucky to be in the wrong place at the wrong time."

"And Dominic Watts?"

"That's a different story. He suffered a fractured skull, which Sally believes happened *before* the fire started. It's likely that he was knocked out with a hammer, or something similar, and then locked in the server room."

"By Mr Killjoy?"

"Has to be. He must have spotted that Dominic was homing in and decided to take drastic action."

"How dreadful."

"How did you get on with Naomi Simmons and Zara Opray?"

"That's why I'm ringing. Naomi Simmons is a friend of Kelly Gaynes, Jack Pickford's manager and, get this, she's twenty-seven."

"The age Jack's sister said his girlfriend is."

"Exactly. And, according to Zara, Naomi is forever popping up to the Spectra account."

"Mmm. She could well be the person Jack was in a relationship with." He paused. "Could she be Mr Killjoy?"

"I don't think so. I can't say I liked her, in fact I found her obnoxious, but I don't see her as a murderer."

"What about Zara?"

"Even less likely. She's very timid, almost withdrawn."

"Okay, that's good to know."

"What happens next, Luke?"

"There's a lot to tell you, but it'll have to wait for now. I've got a few phone calls to make, then I'll head home. Aside from everything else, I need to arrange a venue for the extended team to meet."

"The extended team?"

"Yes. I'll explain later. Love you, Sam."

"Love you more."

He hung up, took a deep breath and then rang Ambrose, knowing that the CEO would be devastated to hear that the fire had been started deliberately. He thought of Filchers' employees as family and went out of his way to meet each and every one of them. He would be appalled to learn that their deaths had not been accidental.

"Those poor people," Ambrose said, once Luke had updated him. "I'd only met Marcia once, but I knew Peter well. And as for what you said about Dominic, well, it beggars belief."

"I have a favour to ask."

"Ask away."

"ACC Scarrott has asked me to be SIO, and I need somewhere for the team to meet."

"Could you use one of the meeting rooms in Gay Street, or a conference room at the Travelodge?"

"I don't think that would work. DI Gilmore will be with us, plus there are a couple of others I'm hoping will join the team. We'll need to keep out of sight of other Filchers staff."

Ambrose thought about this for a second.

"What about here?"

"Here?"

"Yes. At my house. I'm lucky enough to have a cinema room in the basement, and I'm sure that would work with some shuffling around of chairs."

"That would be great. Where do you live?"

"The Circus in the centre of Bath. Number 7."

"Can I arrange for us to get together tomorrow?"

"Of course."

Luke ended the call and rang Josh who answered straight away.

"Hi, guv."

"Hi. How did..."

Josh interrupted before he could finish, almost spitting his next words out.

"I was attacked, guv."

Luke was horrified.

"Attacked?"

"She dive-bombed me, but I managed to duck out of the way."

"She? I thought you were seeing Larry Pickford."

"I was. It was Matilda who attacked me. She's green."

"She's green?"

"Uh-huh. With big beady eyes. She can fly too. And get this, I googled them and, after they mate, they bite the male's head off. That could have been me."

He hesitated for a second before continuing.

"Not that we mated, guv. I mean, a praying mantis is an insect, but still." He swallowed at the memory. "It was terrifying."

Luke was smiling as he replied.

"I'm sure it was. How did it go with Larry Pickford?"

"He gave me the names of three of Jack's friends. I'm on the way to see one of them now."

"Can you ask if Jack's ever mentioned Naomi Simmons? Not only is she twenty-seven, she's also a friend of Kelly Gaynes, and a frequent visitor to the Spectra account."

"Will do, guv."

"Also, I need someone's contact details."

He explained why and then added the person to his contacts.

Next, he rang the assistant chief constable.

"Hi, Luke."

"Ma'am, I want to add two people to the team for Project Static, and neither are serving police officers, so I thought I ought to run them by you."

"Fire away."

He explained who the two were, and why they were needed.

"That's fine with me."

"Thank you, Ma'am. I'm going to get everyone together tomorrow morning. Is there any chance you could come along to say a few words?"

"I'll be happy to."

"We're using a room at Ambrose's house. It's number 7, The Circus. Could you be there for 10 am?"

"Yes. I'll see you then."

He hung up and retrieved the number he'd obtained from Josh, mentally crossing his fingers that the person on the other end of the phone would say yes to joining the team.

Chapter 33

Luke was pleased when he got through first time.

"Philip Angler."

"Hi, Philip. This is Luke Sackville. I don't suppose you remember me?"

"Sackville, did you say. Give me a moment."

Luke could almost hear the cogs turning.

"Ah! I remember now. Operation Turncoat, wasn't it?"

"Well remembered."

"My, my, that is a blast from the past. Must have been six or seven years ago. Wasn't Applejack the SIO?"

"He was indeed. And yet we still managed to bring the gang to justice."

Philip laughed.

"Yes, he was a bit of a useless article. Still is, I dare say. Anyway, how can I help? Didn't I hear that you made DCI?"

"I did, but I left the police last year and now work for a private company. One of my staff was on the course you ran this week. Josh Ogden."

"Josh works for you? Smart lad. His girlfriend's very bright too."

"You met her?"

"Yes. Mandy's a lovely girl. Baby on the way, and I'm so pleased for them both. Anyway, how can I help?"

Luke decided that correcting him about Mandy could wait for a later date. He was keen to get to the point.

"I gather from Josh that you're keeping pace with developments in cybercrime."

"I certainly try to. I should warn you, though, that I don't take assignments for private companies. I do the odd bit of consultancy for Wessex Police, but lecturing takes up most of my time. Has something happened at your company?"

"Yes, but… It's not…" He hesitated. "Philip, what I'm about to tell you is highly confidential. Do I have your word that you won't tell a soul?"

Philip chuckled. "Now you've got me interested. Don't worry, I can keep a secret."

Luke ran through everything that had happened, from his first meeting with ACC Scarrott and Dominic Watts, through to being asked to be SIO on Project Static.

"As you'll gather," he concluded, "Mr Killjoy is technology-savvy."

"Very much so, from what you said. His development of ByteIt is interesting, with parallels to FraudGPT, which incorporated WormGPT, although he seems to have taken it a stage further. The use of deepfake is also fascinating. There was a similar incident in Hong Kong last year, but this one sounds more sophisticated." He paused. "This Mr Killjoy is one smart cookie. I take it you want me to join the team."

"Please."

"I'd be happy to."

Luke gave him the details for the next day's meeting and then retrieved the number of the second person on his list.

He hesitated before phoning.

This call would be different, very different.

Philip Angler became excited when talking about his sphere of expertise, but he was still restrained, intense almost.

The next person on his list was anything but restrained, a larger-than-life character who not everyone liked, but who Luke would trust with his life.

He was disappointed when the call went straight to voicemail, and left a message hoping it would be picked up without too much delay.

"Hi, it's Luke. Can you give me a call as soon as

possible? I need your help."

He hung up, took the handbrake off, and headed home.

*

Luke had only been driving for five minutes when his phone started ringing.

He took a deep breath and then accepted the call, prepared for an onslaught on his ears.

"Hi, Misty. Thanks for ringing back."

"No fucking problem!"

This was almost shouted, but that was par for the course for Misty Mitchell, Private Investigator, a woman whose build was almost on a par with Glen Baxter's, but who had a much wider vocabulary, albeit a vocabulary that incorporated more than its fair share of choice Anglo-Saxon expletives.

"Is this a social call," she went on, "or are you after something? If you're asking after my welfare, I'm as dandy as Korky the cat, but if you're seeking my assistance, there's no chance."

"I take it you've got lots of work on."

"Abso-fucking-lutely. I'm busy as a vampire at a blood bank. Scrotes and weasels don't catch themselves, and believe me there are loads of them out there, most of them shagging my clients' partners."

"It's largely infidelity you're dealing with, then?"

"Yeah. The odd stalking, but mainly couples playing hide the sausage."

"Must be boring, doing the same thing day in, day out."

"Stop circling round the fucking wagon, Luke. If you're trying to tempt me, get on with it."

"I'm hunting a cyber criminal."

"I take it you don't mean he's a fucking robot, you mean he's using technology to steal money."

"Not directly. He provides computer services to other criminals by subscription, and I know you've got your tendrils into no end of low-level villains."

"I'm well connected, yeah, but the numpties I deal with haven't got the brains of a beheaded chicken between them. Computers aren't their thing."

"But that's the point. He makes it easy for criminals with no IT knowledge to send phishing emails, fake invoices, the works."

He explained the way ByteIt worked, and the services within it.

"Well, screw me until my lady garden glows!" she exclaimed when he'd finished. "He's cornered the market there, hasn't he? I can think of no end of losers and wasters who'd sacrifice their dear old granny for products like those."

"And that's why I'm ringing."

"You want me to put feelers out? See if anyone's subscribed?"

"Exactly."

"How come you're doing this, Luke? You're not back in the police, are you?"

"Almost."

He explained about being SIO under the sponsorship of an assistant chief constable.

"Well, that sets my tits-a-tingling," she said when he'd finished. "Haven't you gone up in the world? And that's saying something given you're already taller than a giraffe on fucking tippy-toes."

"I'm getting the team together tomorrow morning so that everyone's up to speed. Are you okay to come along?"

"I'll be there. Oh, and Luke."

"What?"

"Give my best to Sam."

"Will do."

Chapter 34

Josh descended from the bus, studied the map on his phone for a second, then headed up Trafalgar Road, turning right at the top onto Lynfield Park.

Number 23 was at the top of the road on the left, a thirties, semi-detached house with an integral garage. It was set behind a waist-height stone wall and boasted a bow window and a neat, well-tended garden.

He pushed open one of the double gates, and had walked a couple of yards up the drive when he heard a voice immediately behind him.

"Hello."

He swung around, trying to locate the person who'd spoken, then looked down to find a woman in dungarees staring up at him through thick glasses. She had been hidden by the wall and was on her knees, a trowel in one hand and a plant in the other.

"Can I help?" she asked.

"Hi. I'm Josh. Is Isaac in?"

"Are you one of his school friends?"

"No, I'm..." He was on the verge of challenging her belief that he was only seventeen, but realised there was no point. "I'm from Filchers, and I'm here to talk to him about Jack Pickford."

She put the trowel and pot down on the ground, stood up, wiped her hands down the side of her dungarees and shook her head.

"What an awful business. That poor boy. I can't imagine how his parents are coping."

"No, it's terrible."

"How's Jack doing? Is he still in a coma?"

"As far as I know. Uh, is Isaac here?"

Josh had the feeling she would continue asking questions forever if he let her. She was inquisitive, almost prying, but he was keen to get on. Once he'd talked to her son, he could head home to Leanne. It was already gone six o'clock, and he was tired. Hungry too.

"Isaac did the same, you know."

"Is he inside the house or in the back garden?"

"He's…"

"Just a second. Did you say Isaac did the same as Jack?"

She nodded.

"It was just as well we got it out of him. Yesterday, he told us."

"That Isaac had attempted suicide?"

"Oh, no. My son didn't get that far, thank goodness, but he realised why Jack had done it and told us everything. Very brave of him it was to tell us, given, you know, the, uh…"

She formed her right hand into a fist, lowered it past her waist to her groin, extended the index finger and started wagging it backwards and forwards.

Josh didn't know where to look. It was an obscene gesture, and she followed it up with a lewd couple of words.

"Dick pics."

"Eh?" He swallowed. "Mrs Staples, I don't know what you're suggesting, but…"

"They both did it. Isaac and Jack. Isaac hasn't been blackmailed yet, but when they do, Ron's going to give them a right earful."

"Ron?"

"My husband, Isaac's dad."

"Isaac's dad. Right. Ah, would you mind explaining what you're talking about? I have to admit I'm more than a touch confused."

She did, and suddenly everything became clear.

Chapter 35

Emmanuel Mensah was whistling as he cycled through Victoriaborg.

Business was flourishing, and he wondered if he should recruit an additional employee. There was certainly the potential to expand further, but he was also conscious of the risks. He, Danso and Kwadwo had been friends since primary school, and he doubted there was anyone else he could trust as much.

He slowed to turn onto Thorpe Road, and wiped the sweat from his brow with the back of his left hand. It was close to 40 degrees, and his shirt was sticking to his skin. However, he was used to the high temperatures and humidity of Accra, and besides, in a few minutes he'd be able to cool down in the comfort of an air-conditioned environment.

They'd been in the rented office for nearly a month now, a major step up from working in the main room of his home. Not only was it more comfortable, it also prevented his wife from poking her nose in. Emmanuel had no problem with making a living this way, and the investment was proving more than worthwhile. However, if Shauntee knew the details, he knew she would disapprove, even though she was happy enough to spend the additional money he was bringing in.

And boy was he bringing in a lot more money. He was earning a lot more than when he had been an English Teacher at St Thomas Aquinas High School, even after you took off the cost of the rented premises and monthly software subscription.

His dream was to put enough funds away to be able to leave Ghana altogether, perhaps even move to England.

Emmanuel smiled at the irony.

The United Kingdom was far and away his biggest market, and here he was imagining himself living there.

He slowed as he turned into the parking lot of the three-storey building that housed Mensah Incorporated. The three of them had a small office on the second floor, with access to a shared kitchen and bathroom.

It was perfect.

He climbed off his bike, removed the chain and padlock from his backpack, and used them to secure the cycle to one of the iron railings.

No way was he going to let one of Accra's many criminals escape with his only mode of transport.

You couldn't trust anyone these days.

He took the stairs two at a time, and pushed open the office door to find Danso and Kwadwo hard at work.

It was Kwadwo who heard him first. He turned around, a broad smile on his face.

"I dey work plenty hard, Emmanuel. Plenty customers dey."

Emmanuel wagged his finger.

"No, Kwadwo. You must remember to speak proper English, not Pidgin English, when we are at work. It helps prevent slip-ups in our interactions with customers."

Kwadwo acknowledged this with a nod of his head.

"Sorry. I forgot. It is an excellent idea, and I remember in future."

"I *will* remember," Emmanuel corrected.

"Of course. I *will* remember in future."

Emmanuel tapped his other employee on the shoulder.

"How are you doing, Danso?"

"Very well. I have a new prospect. His name is Jamie Grant. That's him."

He pointed at the top left of his monitor, which contained an image of a forty-something man who had a broad smile but was otherwise unprepossessing, his thin

Mr Killjoy

brown hair combed across the top of his head in an attempt to hide his baldness.

The photo to the right was of a blonde girl in her late twenties. She was also smiling, but unlike the man was attractive, although not what you would call a classic beauty. She was wearing a low-cut, cream top which showed off her ample cleavage.

"How far have you got?"

"I'm still in the early stages, but he is already starting to be suggestive."

"That is excellent." Emmanuel indicated the image of the girl. "I see you have used Rosie."

"Yes. The system suggested her based on his search history and previous Instagram interactions." Danso grinned. "Jamie has a thing for blondes with big breasts."

It was the AI built into SexIt that had sold Emmanuel on the product, although he was equally impressed by its ability to suggest responses when a target made a comment. If there was anything even remotely sexual in a message, SexIt would recommend a reply that subtly upped the ante.

The person who designed it was a genius.

"A few minutes ago," Danso went on, "he told me that he liked what I was wearing, and I replied that I try to wear clothes that make the most of my assets. Hopefully, he'll take the hint."

A message popped up in the bottom half of the screen.

JAMIE
"That top you're wearing certainly looks lovely on you."

A second or two later, further text appeared below it.

RECOMMENDED RESPONSE
"That photo only shows part of my top. Do you want to see more?"

"Good work," Emmanuel said. "I'll leave you to it."

He returned his attention to Kwadwo.

"Have you heard from that boy, the one who went silent on you?"

"Not since he transferred the money last week and I asked for more. I've now threatened to send the images to his relatives as well as to his friends."

"Did you name his parents?"

"Yes, and his younger sister. The system was able to tell me who they were from his social media profiles, and it also gave me his parents' email addresses. He was quick to pay the first £500, so I'm surprised he hasn't come up with the second payment. Do you think it's time to send his mother and father the photos and videos?"

Emmanuel scratched at the stubble on his chin as he considered this.

On the one hand, it was important that they carried out their threats. If they started letting people off, word would get around and, before they knew it, people would be ignoring their demands for money.

On the other hand, once they sent the images to their loved ones or employer, that was it. The customer was lost to them.

He came to a decision.

"Let's give it a few more days. Keep sending the threats, at least once a day, and include his parents' email addresses."

A thought occurred to him.

"Do you have their photos?"

"Yes, they were on his Facebook account."

"Excellent. Include those as well, and ask him how he would feel if his mother received photos and videos of her son exposing himself and worse. Be explicit with the words you use."

"Okay. I'll do that."

"Good work, Kwadwo. This one's challenging but,

given we've already received £500, I'm sure we can squeeze more out of him. Remind me, what's the boy's name?"

"Pickford, Jack Pickford."

Chapter 36

Luke and Sam dropped Wilkins off with Marjorie, and then drove into the centre of Bath. It was still before 8 am when they parked in Charlotte Street car park, but Luke was keen to get to Ambrose's early to ensure he was fully prepared for the Project Static team meeting.

They had just rounded the end of Queen Square onto Gay Street when Sam reached for his arm and gave it a squeeze.

"It's Filcher," she hissed, gesturing up the street.

"Damn. I don't want him to know where we're going. Let's double back. We can cut through…"

He stopped when he realised his boss had spotted them and was marching down the street in their direction, his arms pumping backwards and forwards with each stride as if he were a sergeant major inspecting his battalion.

"Luke," he said as he drew close, his long nose twitching. "Good morning."

"I didn't expect to see you, Mr Filcher. You're not usually in this early."

"No. I… There's a reason."

"An early meeting?"

"Exactly. Early meeting. That's it. Early meeting."

He spotted Sam for the first time, tilted his head to one side as if debating what kind of rare beast she was, and then said, a note of pride in his voice for remembering her name,

"Good morning, Sal."

"Good morning," she replied. "It's Sam. My name's Sam."

He sniffed, looked at her for a split second, decided she'd already warranted enough of his time for one day, and returned his attention to Luke.

"I allocated you to number 25, Luke. You and your, ah…" He waved his right hand in Sam's general direction, but didn't deign to look at her again. "… underlings. You're on the first floor, sharing a room with Glen and James."

"I saw that."

"I will have my own office of course. Essential. Directors need their own office. Vital."

"Are you also at number 25?"

"Indeed. Yes. Number 25."

"Shall we grab a coffee, Luke?" Sam said.

Good on her, Luke thought. *That'll give us an excuse to avoid following him into the temporary accommodation.*

"We'll see you later, Mr Filcher," he said.

Luke turned to cross the road and almost collided with a man almost identically dressed to Filcher in a black pin-stripe suit and what looked to be the same old school tie. Unlike the Director of Internal Affairs, however, he was only about five feet six, had a significant paunch and sported a grey pencil moustache.

"Sorry," Luke said automatically.

The man twitched his lips a couple of times, looked up at the towering man above him and said, his voice plummy and reminiscent of many of Luke's father's cronies, "So you should be. Out of my way, you big oaf."

Luke moved to one side, and the man spotted Filcher.

"Ah, Teddy. Are you ready for action?"

Filcher glanced at Luke before replying.

"Hah! You mean our meeting, Willie. Our meeting, ah… that we're having. To discuss things. Work things. At our meeting."

Willie snorted.

"Work things? I'd hardly call breakfast at Boodles work things. Especially with Jemima and Alyson there. And if all goes well…" He winked and lowered his voice. "Willie's ready, eh, Teddy? Willie's ready."

*

To Luke's relief, there was no sign of Filcher or his friend when he and Sam emerged from the cafe, and they made their way quickly to the top of Gay Street, and around the left-hand side of The Circus to number 7, keen to avoid running into any other Filchers' employees.

It was Ambrose's personal assistant, Ellie, who answered the door.

"Hi, Luke. Hi, Sam." She smiled. "Ambrose thought you'd be early. Come on in."

She led them through an elegantly decorated hall to the kitchen at the back, and opened another door to reveal stairs down to the basement.

They followed her down and into a room that took up the entire footprint of the house. It was perhaps twenty feet wide by sixty feet long, with a projection screen along one of the shorter sides in front of navy blue velvet curtains. The panelled walls were also painted a dark blue, and the thick pile carpet was a russet brown.

Ambrose was seated in one of sixteen pale green, cushioned chairs that were arranged in a semicircle facing a large whiteboard.

"Good morning," Ambrose said as he got to his feet. "I hope this arrangement works for you."

"It's excellent, thank you," Luke said.

"You have Ellie to thank for the whiteboard, pens, Post-its and so on."

Luke turned to face her.

"Thanks, Ellie. Did you get my list of attendees?"

"Yes. I got it, thanks. There's one more coming. Rufus Brent."

Ambrose saw Luke's look of confusion.

"Jean Scarrott asked me to add him, Luke," he said. "I can't say I recognise the name, but I'm sure she knows what she's doing."

Mr Killjoy

"Please excuse me," Ellie said. "I need to sort a few things out."

She disappeared back upstairs.

"You'll have to excuse me as well, Luke," Ambrose said. "I see you've armed yourselves with coffees, but if you need anything else, I'll be in the front room."

Once he'd left, Sam took her phone out.

"I've got the photo Helen took of our..." She smiled as she decided to use one of Josh's favourite terms. "...crazy wall. Shall I transcribe it onto the whiteboard?"

"Yes, please."

Chapter 37

Almost everyone had arrived by 9:50, with the only people still to turn up being the assistant chief constable, her mysterious additional invitee, and Misty.

Luke was pleased to see that the others seemed relaxed.

Maj and Philip Angler were deep in conversation and, from the odd word Luke could pick up, seemed to be discussing neural networks and artificial cognition, whatever that was.

Sam, Helen and Pete were working their way through the shortlist of suspects and debating whether there was any chance that Mr Killjoy might be a woman.

Josh was the only person on his own, but he seemed happy enough. In fact, 'happy' was an understatement. The lad had let out an involuntary yelp of delight when Ellie had appeared with a tray of doughnuts, danish pastries and other sweet delights some ten minutes earlier, and hadn't moved from the table she'd placed it on.

Luke wandered over.

"You're not mixing with the others?"

Josh's answer was garbled due to the half of a toffee yum yum that he had just stuffed into his mouth.

"Kippin the pouter dye."

"I beg your pardon?"

Josh shook his head, pointed to his mouth to indicate his mouth was full, then decided to try again anyway.

"Pouter dye. Thick bits."

He shook his head, chewed faster, managed to swallow his mouthful, then grinned up at his boss.

"I want to keep my powder dry," he said. "About the dick pics."

"Did you say dick pics?"

Josh nodded. "I confirmed it yesterday evening."

Before Luke could probe further, he heard the door behind him open and turned to see the ACC accompanied by a slim, greying man in his late forties.

"Good morning," she said, and then gestured to the man beside her.

"Luke, this is Rufus Brent. Rufus, Luke Sackville."

Rufus smiled, and they shook hands.

"Pleased to meet you, Luke."

"Rufus is from the NCCU," Jean went on. "He is, or should I say was, Dominic's manager."

"I'm so sorry about what happened," Luke said.

Rufus sighed. "Yes. Dreadful business." He shook his head. "Awful, simply awful. I hope you don't mind me coming along today."

"Of course not. Please, both of you, help yourselves to coffee or tea, and to a pastry..." He glanced over to see Josh popping the tail end of a chocolate slice into his mouth, smiled and added, "...if there are any left. We'll get going in a couple of minutes."

"Is everyone here?" the ACC asked.

"Almost. The only person we're waiting for is Misty Mitchell."

As soon as he said these words, he spotted the PI behind Jean and Rufus, and watched her mouth gape open as she took in the splendour of the room.

"You said it was a cinema room," she said, "but bugger me senseless, and shake me 'til my melons drop, I wasn't expecting this."

"You must be Misty," Jean said, holding her hand out.

"That's me. Misty by name but sunny by nature." She grinned as they shook hands. "And you are?"

"Jean Scarrott."

"Pleased to meet you, Jeanie. Ah, pastries."

And with that she was gone.

*

Luke gave the three who had been the last to arrive a few minutes to get themselves a coffee and, in Misty's case, the remaining danish pastry, then clapped his hands together.

"Right, everyone. Can we make a start, please?"

They all shuffled into seats except for the ACC, who moved to stand beside him.

"Jean," he said and backed away slightly to give her the stage.

She stepped forward.

"Hi, everyone. For those of you who don't know me, I'm Jean Scarrott, assistant chief constable at Avon and Somerset Police. My portfolio includes cybercrime, which is how I first became involved in the hunt for the person behind ByteIt."

She gave a grim smile.

"It's odd to think that less than a week ago, I sat in Ambrose Filcher's office briefing Luke on Mr Killjoy's activities. At that time, we were looking at finding a criminal to bring charges under the Computer Misuse Act and the Fraud Act. However, as most of you are aware, the person calling themselves Mr Killjoy is now thought to have deliberately started the fire at Filchers' head office, a fire which resulted in the deaths of three people. Moreover, yesterday's post-mortem revealed that Dominic Watts had been deliberately knocked unconscious beforehand."

She paused to let this sink in.

"This is now a murder investigation, and I am grateful to each and every one of you for your part in helping to bring this evil person to justice. However, I urge you to be careful. He or she is extremely ruthless. Please don't take unnecessary risks."

She glanced around the room to ensure everyone

present was taking heed of her warning.

"One final point. If you need additional resources, or help of any kind, please let Luke know. The chief and I are prepared to do whatever is necessary to ensure this killer spends time at His Majesty's pleasure for many years to come." She smiled. "Now, if you'll excuse me, I need to return to HQ."

Chapter 38

Luke waited for Jean to leave and then gestured to the top half of the whiteboard.

"This summarises what we knew about ByteIt when The Ethics Team met only a couple of days ago."

<u>**PROJECT STATIC**</u>

ByteIt Components
FishIt (fake emails)
PayIt (fake invoices)
SexIt (sextortion)
FakeIt (deepfake)

"However," he went on, once he'd given everyone a couple of minutes to digest what was on the board, "things have moved on at pace since then. Helen, would you mind making changes and additions as we run through developments."

"Nae problem."

She stood up, walked over and picked up one of the marker pens and a pile of Post-its.

"Shall I start?"

"Yes, please do."

She turned to look at the team.

"One of our payments clerks, Harry Mullins, handled five invoices from different companies over the last month, transferring a total of £4,000. Each payment was to the same bank account. There was no beneficiary name, just a reference quoting the invoice number, but I've checked the Swift code and the account's with Scotiabank in the Bahamas."

"An offshore account is suspicious in itself."

"Yes, I thought that. However, I don't think Harry's involved in the scam itself. I talked to him yesterday, and I'm convinced he made the payments in good faith. Having spoken to his manager, I believe that ITSACAP, the IT system they use to manage workflow, was manipulated to pass them all to him because he was the most likely to miss the link between them."

She smiled.

"Apparently, it's the IT team who configure and optimise ITSACAP..." She tapped the list of suspects. "... which means it's most likely one of these five."

"Do you mind if I ask a question?" Philip Angler asked.

"Not at all."

"How do you know these invoices were generated by the PayIt service within ByteIt? Couldn't it be some completely unrelated criminal activity?"

"Let me take that," Luke said. "The truth is, Philip, that we can't be absolutely certain. However, we know, from the deepfake conference call on Wednesday, that someone, and it would be an unbelievable coincidence if that someone wasn't Mr Killjoy, is using Filchers as a test ground. On top of that, we also know that Mr Killjoy works in Filchers' IT department."

"Ah, but can you be certain? Maj told me how he and Dominic Watts pinpointed the location that Mr Killjoy's email was sent from, but couldn't it have been sent by someone who isn't based there? In other words, sent from one of those six cubicles deliberately, perhaps when the employee was at lunch, to make us look in the wrong direction."

"That's a good point, and you could be right, but

remember, it's only the staff in IT who are able to manipulate workflows, and that's what happened with the invoices sent to Harry Mullins."

As he finished speaking, Josh's hand shot up.

"Can I go next, guv?"

Luke smiled.

"Go ahead."

Josh walked to the front.

"I've been assigned to Project Move," he began, "trying to find the woman who broke up with Jack Pickford. It was as a result of that break-up that he tried to kill himself, or at least, that's what we thought."

"What do you mean?" Helen asked.

Josh tapped the third ByteIt component listed on the whiteboard.

"I don't think Jack had a girlfriend at all, or at least not a real one. Someone was blackmailing him, almost certainly using SexIt. I spoke to Isaac Staples, one of Jack's closest friends, yesterday, and he confirmed that both of them had developed relationships with women they met online, and had sent those women intimate photos and videos of themselves. It's my belief that those women don't exist, that their images, and their messages, are generated by the SexIt system to lay the seeds for blackmail."

"Do you think he attempted to commit suicide because they threatened to reveal what he'd done?" Maj asked.

Josh nodded.

"£500 disappeared out of his account last week, most likely transferred to the criminals. That brought the balance close to zero, and I think they demanded more, and I suspect that's what drove him over the edge."

Luke nodded.

"That's good work, Josh."

He walked over to the board.

"We now have evidence that these three…" He tapped the Post-its for PayIt, SexIt and FakeIt. "…have all been deployed within Filchers. "As for FishIt..." He tapped the top one. "...all we know about it is what Dominic told me, that a low-level criminal had been using it to send emails asking for charity donations. Aside from that..."

"It could be wider than that," Philip said. "More than just phishing."

"What do you mean?" Luke asked.

Philip turned to Josh.

"What about your girlfriend?"

"What about her?"

"That incident in Wandsworth."

"Eh?"

"The quishing. You were there when she told me about it. False QR codes in council car parks."

"Oh. You mean Mandy?"

Philip laughed. "Who else?" He raised one eyebrow. "Have you got more than one girlfriend?"

"I'm engaged to Leanne."

"Wow." He shook his head in astonishment. "I'd never have thought you were like that. Do they know about each other?"

Luke held his hand up before Josh could reply.

"You're right, Philip. The case Mandy's working on could well be someone who's subscribed to FishIt. Josh, perhaps you could talk to her, and see if she's got any further with catching the culprits."

"Will do, guv."

"You could ask her tonight when you get home," Philip suggested.

"What, when I'm at home with Leanne?"

"It's her night, is it? Perhaps tomorrow, then?"

Josh opened his mouth to say something, but Luke stepped in first before he could get any words out.

"Josh, when we've finished, perhaps you could explain your relationships to Philip to stop this confusion."

"Will do, guv."

"Misty, could you ask around and see if you can locate anyone who's used any of these services?"

"Be happy to. I know a few low-lifes who'd leap at this. Monty Rafferty for one. Not the fucking brightest by a long shot. If you ask me, he's got two brain cells, and both of them are fighting for third place." She paused. "Terry Lawson's another. If brains were chocolate, he wouldn't have enough to fill a smartie. Yeah, Monty and Terry are always on the lookout for new ways to scam people. I can think of a few others, too."

"Good. Thanks."

"I reckon you're missing a component," Pete said.

"What do you mean?"

"It didn't make sense to me before, but after everything that's been said about PayIt, SexIt and so on, the penny's dropped."

He paused to bring his thoughts together.

"As you can imagine, there were a few laptops left behind when the fire started. Most were damaged beyond repair, but one was still functioning. The screen was cracked but frozen, and it showed an image of a smiling woman. Beneath her were the words, *'Hi, I'm Fleur. How can I help you?'*. I could see it was a Chatbot, you know, one of those systems that simulate a human and pop up on websites to answer questions about products or services."

"So what?"

Pete grinned, opened his notebook, flicked forward a few pages and then passed it over.

Luke read from Pete's notes.

Customer:
'I'm having trouble signing in. What do I need to do?'

Fleur:
'I'm happy to help you with that. Please provide me with your email address and password, and I will initiate a reset.'

Fleur and others like her can provide you with many opportunities like this, and all for only £100 a month. Click below to learn more.

"I was confused by it at first," Pete said, as Luke passed his notes on for the others to read, "but having heard what the team has said this morning, it makes sense. This looks like a draft advert for a ByteIt component."

Luke nodded.

"And I wouldn't mind betting the service is called ChatIt. Do you know whose laptop it is?"

"No, I don't."

"Have you got the serial number?" Maj asked.

Pete turned to face him.

"Yes. Why?"

"If you send it to Jessica Moore, Filchers' Inventory Manager, she should be able to tell you who it belongs to."

Maj clicked on his phone a couple of times, then looked up again.

"I've sent you her contact details."

"Thanks. I'll text her now."

Chapter 39

"Okay, guys," Luke said, "let's move on to our suspects." He pointed to the bottom half of the whiteboard.

Mr Killjoy Suspects

Zara Opray (web developer)

Naomi Simmons (systems analyst)

Miles Barrington (software engineer)

Jordan Fellowes (software developer)

Charlie Wallace (database engineer)

"As Philip was saying, we can't be 100% certain that one of these five is Mr Killjoy, but they're the prime contenders. Sam, do you want to share what you told me about your meeting with Zara and Naomi?"

"Sure." She turned to face the rest of the team. "The main thing I came away with was the fact that Naomi's twenty-seven, and is frequently seen in the area where Jack Pickford works. That made me suspect her to be the woman he'd had a relationship with, but what Josh found out from Jack's friend has put the kibosh on that idea."

"Sorry, Sam," Josh said with a wry smile.

"There's something else, though. Zara's very quiet and withdrawn, but snapped at me when I asked whether she was full or part-time. It seemed very out of character."

"Have you changed your mind?" Luke asked. "Do you think she could be Mr Killjoy?"

She shook her head. "No. I can't see her knocking

Dominic out and then setting fire to the building, but I wish I'd probed a bit further. I have a feeling she knows more than she's letting on, and there's the chance she's seen one of our three male suspects doing something unusual or even suspicious. She doesn't live far from here, so I might pop to her house this afternoon after we've finished, and ask her a few more questions."

"That makes sense."

He turned to Maj.

"Maj, that's a neat link to Miles, Jordan and Charlie. How did you get on with them?"

"Not very far, if I'm honest. Charlie didn't say much. He seems laid-back, not introverted like Zara, but pretty chilled. Jordan's the opposite, and I can see why Sam thought he was arrogant. He's very full of himself, and he clearly hates the fact that Miles is his boss. I'd say he's got a real chip on his shoulder."

"And Miles?"

"Confident. Bright, too. When I asked if they'd seen any accelerants, he knew exactly what I meant and started talking about solvent-based liquids, turpentine, road flares and so on. That guy doesn't half like the sound of his own voice."

"What's your assessment? Could any of them be Mr Killjoy?"

"Yes. Any of the three. I'd probably put Charlie down as the least likely, but that's based on one brief conversation." He sighed. "I'm sorry. It doesn't get us much further, but I didn't want to push them too hard."

"Don't beat yourself up. You were right not to."

Luke considered everything that had been said.

"What worries me is that we're too reliant on Mr Killjoy making another mistake. Pete, can you speak to the fire brigade, and to SOCOs? See if they'd found anything that might help us identify the culprit."

"Will do, Luke."

Josh put his hand up.

"Yes, Josh?"

"Is there any chance of surveillance, guv?"

"That's a good idea. I'll speak to the ACC." He paused. "Anyone else got any ideas?" He looked over at the NCCU investigator. "Rufus?"

Rufus smiled.

"I've been listening to everything, and Josh's idea is an excellent one."

"Gucci," Josh said, a broad smile on his face.

"However, I think Philip's point was also valid when he said that it may not be one of these five at all, but someone who deliberately sent the intercepted email from that part of the building to mislead us."

Luke nodded. "You make a good point."

He turned back to Maj.

"Maj, you know exactly when that email was sent, don't you?"

"Yes. It's got a timestamp on it."

"Good. Can you look back through CCTV footage and see if anything pops up?"

"Sure. I'll get onto it as soon as we're done."

"That's great."

He addressed his next words to the whole group.

"I think we're finished now. Thanks for your time, everyone. If anyone makes progress today, let me know, but I advise you to finish as early as you can, and take a well-earned rest over the weekend. I want everyone back on Monday refreshed and ready for what's going to be an intensive week."

"Are we basing ourselves here, guv?" Josh asked.

"Yes. Ambrose has said this room's available until we've caught our villain and the case is closed."

Chapter 40

Mr Killjoy was pleased and furious at the same time.

Pleased because Dominic Watts was no more.

He was deceased.

Demised.

Departed.

Expired.

Terminated.

He smiled and shivered with delight.

There were so many words for death, so many delicious words.

The NCCU investigator had been perilously close to homing in on his operation, but was now out of the way, and good riddance. Without him, the police were nothing but headless chickens, their inability to find out more about ByteIt, let alone identify the man behind it, almost laughable.

That imbecile from the Ethics Team was no better. He had asked whether anything lying around could have helped to fuel the flames. Little did the idiot realise that this was no accidentally-placed accelerant.

He smiled as he recalled placing seven cylindrical tubes in a line on the server room floor, the base of each touching the top of the next one so that they would ignite in sequence.

All he'd had to do was strike the eighth tube against the floor, wait for it to emit its bright orange light, then place it on the ground in front of the others.

The beauty of it was that it had given him plenty of time to escape.

They'd been so easy to purchase too.

He was a genius, a certifiable genius.

His thoughts turned to his web designer.

This was where his fury stemmed from.

She still hadn't managed to recover her laptop, and was fast becoming an encumbrance.

Web designers were two-a-penny. They had to accept that what they were doing was illegal, but there were many unscrupulous individuals out there only too happy to break the law when they realised what they could earn.

It was a sad fact of life that people were greedy.

In Bellatrix's case, he knew that the money he paid her was being used to pay for her mother's care, but that didn't make her any more innocent.

Perhaps he should have locked her away with the NCCU investigator, and let the smoke and flames end her miserable life once and for all.

That would have been three birds with one stone!

He giggled.

Wouldn't that have been neat?

But hindsight was always twenty-twenty, wasn't it? He'd missed his opportunity, and now, given there was still no sign of her personal computer, he had to come up with a different way of dealing with her.

The worry was that the police might recognise the draft home page for ChatIt for what it was, and pull her in for questioning. Bellatrix didn't know his identity, but she was privy to the inner workings of his business, and knew the ins and outs of the product range.

With a shock, he recalled that she'd also prepared a provisional home page for FakeIt for him. It was a product he was hoping to launch in the next couple of months but, if she told the police about it, they might connect it to the AI-driven conference call that had netted him £200,000.

The more he thought about it, the more he realised that she had become a liability. He needed to deal with her, and deal with her quickly.

Chapter 41

"What did you think of Rufus Brent?" Sam asked.

Luke looked up from his laptop.

"He seemed okay, and that was a good point he made about us being too reliant on the location the email was sent from. I still believe that the five on the whiteboard have to be our principal suspects, but he's right, it could be someone else completely."

He looked over to Maj, the only other member of the team who had decided to continue working from Ambrose's house rather than head for home.

"Maj, getting anywhere with that CCTV footage?"

"Not yet, Luke. Still trying to log in. Filchers' IT systems are running from backup servers at our disaster recovery site, and it's making access more difficult. Hopefully, it won't take me too much longer."

"Okay. Let me know as soon as you get anywhere."

"I'm going to head off now," Sam said.

She stood up, walked over to him and lowered her voice.

"Are you sure you're all right with me being off with my mum all weekend?"

Luke smiled.

"Of course. I'll miss you, but Ben and Pippa are coming tomorrow morning, so it's not as if I'll be alone."

"It's not that. I feel guilty going away when Project Static has gathered momentum the way it has."

"Now you're being silly. I meant what I said this morning about everyone needing a rest over the weekend. Next week's going to be full on."

"If you're sure."

"Of course I'm sure."

She bent down, kissed him on the lips, then stood upright again and looked at her watch.

He saw what she was doing.

"Are you sure you've still got enough time to see Zara Opray?"

She nodded.

"Yes. Mum's not expecting me until five-thirty. I'll head for Zara's house first, and if I find out anything useful, I'll ring you straight away. Failing that, I'll go on to Mum's and call when we get to Summer Lodge."

She looked over at Maj.

"See you on Monday, Maj. Have a good weekend."

"Thanks. Have a great time, Sam."

*

It took Sam less than fifteen minutes to walk to St James's Park, which turned out to be a cul-de-sac. Number 21 was the last house on the right, a bland detached house dating from the 1950s.

The one difference from the other houses on the street was that, rather than having a front garden, the narrow strip of land running between the pavement and number 21 had been tarmacked to provide parking for one car. Currently occupying the space was a dark grey minivan. As Sam walked past it towards the front door, she noticed a sign in the rear window of the van saying, *'Disabled access needed - please allow 2 metres'*.

She rang the bell and waited.

Nothing happened, and she was about to press again when she heard a series of squeaks, clicks and rattles from inside. A few seconds later, the door opened to reveal a woman in her mid-fifties. She was in a wheelchair, and glared up at Sam, her brows furrowed.

"Bridget?"

She didn't wait for a response before adding, "You're early," in a tone of admonishment.

"My name's Sam. Sam Chambers."

"Oh, they've sent a replacement, have they?" She tutted and shook her head. "That agency is useless."

"Mrs Opray?"

"Of course I'm Mrs Opray. Are you useless, girl?"

"I'm not from… I'm here to see Zara."

The woman sighed in exasperation.

"Why didn't you say so?"

Sam smiled, but it was like smiling at a brick wall for all the reaction she got.

"Sorry, I…."

The woman didn't let her finish.

"My daughter's in the garage," she snapped

Sam hadn't seen a garage, and Mrs Opray saw the confused look on her face.

She sighed again, even more heavily this time.

"For goodness' sake. At the end, girl. The second garage from the left. At the end of the road."

"Oh. Thanks."

The door slammed closed.

Sam returned to the road and looked across at the four garages beyond the small turning area. They had up-and-over doors, all of which were closed.

She walked over to the second from the left, and rapped three times on the door.

"Who is it?"

"It's Sam. Sam Chambers."

She moved back a couple of paces, and the door opened to reveal a flustered-looking Zara. She had a manila folder under her left arm, and beyond her Sam could see various items of furniture, including a Welsh dresser against the right-hand wall on which there were five or six more folders.

"I don't understand," Zara said. "Why are you here?"

"I was passing, and there was something you said that I wanted to clarify. I hope you don't mind."

"Passing?"

"Yes. A friend of mine lives on Cavendish Road. At number six."

Zara seemed to accept this, though even to Sam's ears it sounded false.

"Okay, since you've come, you might as well ask away. What do you want to know?"

As she asked this, Sam heard the sound of an engine behind her as a car came to a stop.

"I was wondering…" she began, but Zara interrupted her before she could finish her sentence.

"Oh, it's you," she said, looking over Sam's shoulder as she spoke.

Sam turned around, and her eyes widened in horror as she saw the man standing there.

"Jordan?"

"That's me," he said as he looked her up and down. "I'm surprised you remember, given the fact that you dumped me."

He addressed his next comment to Zara.

"Why's she here?"

"She's been asking about the fire. She's in the Ethics Team…"

"The Ethics Team?" He looked back at Sam, sneering now. "You work with Maj, then?"

"Yes. I…"

"Well, well." He walked up to her and bent his head down so that his nose was almost touching hers. He was over six feet tall, and broadly built, an imposing and intimidating presence.

"He and you are in it together, are you?" he went on. "Both of you doing the rounds, asking stupid fucking questions about the fire."

"We were asked to by the fire marshal."

"Don't lie to me. What are you up to, Sam?"

"What do you want, Jordan?" Zara asked.

He backed away from Sam, and turned to address the other woman. He was grinning now, but there was no humour in it.

"I've got something to show you."

"I'll leave you to it," Sam said, and tried to edge past him, but he moved sideways so that he was blocking her path.

"No, darling." He was still grinning. "You need to see this as well. All those questions you've been asking deserve answers."

"Jordan," Zara said. "Leave her alone."

"Not a chance."

He pushed Zara so that she stumbled back into the garage, collided with the dresser and fell sideways onto the ground.

Before Sam could react, he grabbed her arm, twisted her round, and sent her stumbling after the other woman. She tried to retain her balance, but found herself tripping over Zara's outstretched leg and then past her, only managing to keep upright by raising both hands as she reached the back wall.

She turned to see Jordan pulling the garage door shut, the grin still plastered across his face.

The door slammed shut, and he reached into his pocket.

Chapter 42

Luke glanced at his watch to see that it was almost ten to six. Sam hadn't rung, which he assumed meant that she hadn't extracted any useful information from Zara Opray.

He wasn't surprised. The reaction to the question about whether she was full or part-time was doubtless something and nothing.

Which was just as well.

If Sam had found out something useful, she'd be wanting to work on it over the weekend, and she badly needed a couple of days off. She'd been working incredibly hard, and needed some spoiling.

In fact, going for a spa break with her mother would be good for both of them. Kate had had a rough time recently, suffering an acrimonious split from her partner of six months after finding out he'd been seeing someone else. She needed a couple of days of relaxation as much as her daughter did.

He was shaken out of his reverie by a yelp of triumph from Maj.

"Got it!"

Luke stood up and walked over to stand behind him.

The image on Maj's laptop was frozen. It showed three desks facing a second set of three, with shoulder-high dividers between each to create six cubicles.

"Have you watched it yet?"

"No. Just a second." Maj looked down at his notes. "The email was sent at 14:12 and twenty-eight seconds." He looked back up at the timestamp in the bottom right of the screen which showed 13:50. "I'll go forward twenty minutes to 14:10 and start it from there."

He pressed the fast-forward button, waited for a few

Mr Killjoy

seconds, and then hit play.

"That's Charlie," Maj said, pointing to the man nearest the camera on the left, "and Miles is opposite him. I can only see the top of the man's head on the far side of Miles, but I'm fairly sure it's Jordan."

As he said this, Jordan conveniently stood up and leaned over the partition.

"Yes, that's definitely him," Maj continued. "It looks like he said something to the woman, but I can't make out if it's Naomi or Zara."

As he said this, the woman turned to reply, and Zara's face came into view. Jordan nodded to her and then sat back down again.

A couple of seconds after that, the woman opposite Zara stood up.

"It's Naomi," Luke said, recognising her from the photo on the whiteboard.

They watched as she turned and walked away from the camera.

"Looks like she's going to the toilet, or possibly the canteen," Maj said. He checked the on-screen timestamp. "If she's not back in the next fifty seconds, we know she didn't send the email."

He had no sooner said this than a man appeared from the direction she'd gone in.

Luke and Maj caught their breath as they watched him walk to her cubicle and sit down at her desk.

"Is that who I think it is?" Maj said.

"It certainly is. I'd recognise him anywhere."

"That partition's a nuisance. I can't see if he's using her laptop."

They watched as the seconds ticked over on the screen.

All four men and Zara were still seated when it passed 14:12:28. Charlie and Miles were using their keyboards, but the camera's angle of view and the partitions made it impossible to see if that was the case for the other three.

Naomi returned at 14:15:36. She exchanged a few words with the man in her cubicle, after which he stood up and made his way back towards the corridor.

Maj pressed pause.

"It looks like we've got an additional suspect, Luke."

"It does indeed, although we're also one down. Naomi couldn't have sent the email, so we know it's not her." He paused. "That's good work, Maj."

"What do we do now he's in the frame, Luke?"

"Well, the first thing is to tell Ambrose. I think it's only fair, given our new suspect is one of the company's senior managers. I'll get a message out to the rest of the team as well, though I think doing anything further will have to wait until Monday. I suggest you head off home to your family."

"Thanks. Yes, I'll do that."

After Maj had left, Luke prepared an update for ACC Scarrott. Once he'd emailed it to her, he headed upstairs, where he found Ambrose and Ellie ensconced in the front room.

"Thanks for letting us use downstairs," he said.

Ambrose looked up from the report they'd been working on.

"Absolutely no problem, Luke. Did you make any progress?"

"Yes. Maj managed to access CCTV footage from…"

He stopped as his phone buzzed in his pocket.

"Do you need to get that?"

Luke looked at his phone and saw it was Kate.

"No, it's okay. It's Sam's mum. They're going to Dorset for a weekend spa break. She'll be ringing to tell me they've left. I can ring back when we're finished."

He rejected the call, and put the phone on silent.

"You were saying something about CCTV footage?" Ambrose prompted.

"Yes. At the time that the intercepted email was sent, Naomi Simmons was out of the room, so she can't be Mr

Killjoy."

"And? I sense there's more. Please feel free to talk in front of Ellie."

"Someone else took her seat, and was there when the email was sent." He paused. "I saw him clearly. It was Arwyn Thomas, our Head of IT."

"My, my. Arwyn, eh? I suppose that puts him in the frame for being Mr Killjoy?"

"It does indeed."

"What are your next steps?"

"To be honest, Ambrose, we've got very little to go on. We can't pull any of our suspects in for questioning, for fear that it would give the game away. We have to be sure who our villain is first."

He explained the various actions the extended team had been allocated.

"If that doesn't turn something up," he concluded when he'd finished, "We'll have to hope he makes a mistake." He gave a grim smile. "And that's not a position I like to be in."

"I understand, Luke, but don't beat yourself up about it. All you can do is your best. You need to have a relaxing weekend yourself."

"Thanks, Ambrose. I'll try to."

Chapter 43

Luke had almost reached his car when he remembered that he'd put his phone onto silent.

He pressed the button on the side to turn the sound back on, and saw that he had three missed calls, two from Pete and another from Kate.

He decided to ring the DI first.

"Hi, Pete. Has there been a development?"

"Yes. Jessica Moore from Property Services texted me back. That laptop, the one with the Chatbot on it. It belongs to Zara Opray."

"That's interesting, and it's got to be enough to warrant pulling her in. It's surprising, though. After what Sam said, I was convinced she couldn't be…"

His heart missed a beat, and he stopped mid-sentence.

"What is it, Luke?"

"Sam went to see Zara after she left Ambrose's." He swallowed. "Pete, can I ring you back?"

"Of course."

He hung up and called Sam's number.

It went straight to voicemail.

With a rising sense of panic, he rang Kate, who answered straight away.

"Hi, Luke. I'm still waiting for Sam. You don't know where she's got to, do you? She's not answering her phone, which isn't like her."

With an effort, he kept his voice steady as he replied, not wanting to frighten her.

"She said she was popping in on someone on the way to yours."

"Is this for one of your projects?"

"Yes. I suspect she turned her phone off to avoid being

interrupted, and the interview went on longer than she thought it would."

"Are you sure she's okay? She said she'd be here at five-thirty, and it's gone six now."

"There's nothing to worry about, Kate, but I know where she went, and it's not far from where I am now. I'll head there now and chivvy her along."

"Thanks, Luke."

He ended the call and sprinted the last fifty yards to the VW. Once inside, he accelerated away at speed, only buckling his seat belt when he reached the car park exit. By his reckoning, St James's Park was no more than a five-minute drive in normal circumstances, but he was intent on getting there inside three.

The tyres screeched, and the back of the car slid sideways for a split second, as he turned the car onto the A4. This earned him a middle finger and a banged horn from an angry motorist, but he didn't give it a second thought.

A few hundred yards further on, he swerved right again onto Marlborough Lane, this time squeezing through a convenient gap in the traffic.

As he accelerated past the Royal Crescent onto Marlborough Buildings, he depressed the steering wheel button twice to try Sam again.

Again, it went straight to voicemail.

He banged his fist on the steering wheel in frustration, and pressed still harder on the pedal, the immediate surge of power from the battery taking him from forty to sixty miles an hour in less than two seconds.

At the next junction he was forced to slow down for a bus. As soon as it had passed, he sped up the hill and took the first right onto St James's Park Mews.

Not far now.

He hoped Sam was okay.

She had to be okay.

He loved her with all his heart and wanted to spend the rest of his life with her.

Mr Killjoy had killed already, not once but three times.

If she'd been hurt…

He was hardly breathing as he reached the turning for St James's Park.

Sam had told him Zara lived at number 21.

He slammed on the brakes, lowered the passenger window and stretched over to peer at the first house on the left. The sign, almost hidden by a hanging basket, revealed that it was number 2.

Luke turned to the right and saw number 1, suggesting that on that side lay the odd-numbered houses, with number 21 a fair way up.

He was about to accelerate away, when he spotted a slight movement behind the bush in front of number 1, At first he thought it was a cat, then he saw something fluttering in the breeze.

Not just something.

Hair.

Strawberry-blonde hair.

Heart in his mouth, Luke charged out of the car and across the road.

Chapter 44

Sam was on her knees behind the hedge, pulling and tugging at the sticks and leaves that lay at its base.

Luke couldn't imagine what had happened to make her act this way. She was like a woman possessed.

"Sam! Sam! Are you okay?"

She looked up at him in surprise.

"Luke. God, it's good to see you."

He helped her to her feet and put his arms around her.

After a few seconds, she pulled away and looked into his eyes.

"How did you find me?"

"I was worried when you didn't turn up at your mother's. What happened?" He gestured to the base of the bush. "What were you doing down there?"

"I'm trying to find my phone. He threw it in there. I saw him do it."

"He? You've lost me. I thought you were seeing Zara Opray?"

"I was. I did." She shook her head. "It's a long story. Help me find my mobile, and then I'll explain everything."

They both bent to the task, and it was Luke who came up triumphant a minute or so later. He passed the phone to Sam and then took her by the hand.

"Come and sit in the car. You need to tell me everything, and then we need to call Pete."

He led her to the car, and they climbed into the front seats.

It was Sam who reached out for his hand this time.

"Why did you say we need to call Pete? I haven't even told you what happened."

"He needs to send a car to arrest Zara."

"Arrest her?"

"Yes." He squeezed her hand lightly, and looked into her eyes. "It wasn't just the fact that you were late that bothered me, Sam. You were seeing Zara, and that put you in danger."

"In danger? What on earth are you talking about? Zara wouldn't hurt a fly."

"That's not true. We now know that it was her laptop that had the Chatbot screen on it. She's Mr Killjoy."

Sam shook her head.

"No. I don't buy that. Someone else must have put it on there." She hesitated. "It could be Jordan Fellowes or even Arwyn Thomas."

"Arwyn Thomas? How did you come up with that name?"

He was confused. Jordan, he could understand, but the Head of IT hadn't been on their radar until he and Maj had seen the CCTV footage, and that was after Sam had left.

"Okay, Sam. Start from the beginning."

She took a deep breath to collect her thoughts.

"Zara was in the garage tidying things when I found her." She pointed through the front windscreen. "It's one of four around that next corner and up at the end. I was about to start questioning her, when a car pulled up and Jordan jumped out."

"Jordan? Why? What did he want?"

"He was acting kind of crazy. Really crazy." She shivered as the memory came back. "He's not a nice guy, as I told you, very arrogant and full of himself, but this was over and above the way I remember him. He was fidgety, and started saying he had something to show Zara, and that I ought to see it too. He's a big guy, and he was acting so aggressively that I decided to try and get away to call for help. I think that's what provoked him."

"Provoked him?" Luke caught his breath. "What did he do, Sam?"

"He shoved us into the garage and closed the door. I thought we were for it then. He snatched my phone from me, and he had this look on his face that made me think he might... that he might..." She stuttered to a stop and then swallowed. "I was scared, Luke, ever so scared."

He squeezed her hand again.

"What happened then?"

"Zara was thrown to the floor, and Jordan pulled a folded piece of paper out of his pocket and started waving it around. I was so focused on him, and what he might do, that I didn't realise she wasn't paying attention. The paper was proof, he said, proof of something he'd suspected. He unfolded it, and I saw that it was a handwritten note. There were six entries I think, all similar, although the numbers were different. The top line said 'Charlie 15,750', I remember that."

"Charlie 15,750?"

She nodded.

"The next line was similar, but the numbers were lower. I think it was 12,600, but I can't be certain and I didn't get the chance to read the whole thing because Jordan was waving it around triumphantly, almost as if he were Neville Chamberlain telling me this was peace for our time."

"Did he say anything at all?"

"Yes. He said, *This is Arwyn Thomas's handwriting which proves it wasn't me. It was Charlie. Fucking Miles. This'll show him.* That was it, word for word."

"What happened next?"

"It was then that he started worrying about what had happened to Zara. I don't know if she'd hit her head as she fell, or if she fainted, but either way, she was out for the count. He walked over to her, and saw she was on her back with her eyes closed. That was when he started to panic and decided to leg it. He shoved me again, then leapt into his car and was gone. I ran after him, saw him throw my phone out of the window, then returned to Zara. She sat up and put her hand to the side of her head, and I could see she'd cut herself. I told her to wait there while I fetched my phone, and then I'd call an ambulance."

She lifted her mobile up.

"I'd better do it now."

"Okay. You do that and I'll drive up so that we can see how she's faring."

Luke drove to the top of the road, and heard Sam say "Yes, she's breathing," as he climbed out of the car and walked to the second garage from the left.

The door was part open, and he pulled it all the way up.

As Sam had described, there was a mass of furniture inside.

What there wasn't, was any sign of Zara Opray.

Chapter 45

"I'm sorry," Sam said to the woman at the ambulance service call centre, "but she's, ah... she's feeling better. Sorry to have wasted your time."

She hung up the phone and turned to Luke.

"I don't think she was too happy with me. Probably thinks I'm a nuisance caller."

"You said Zara came to before you left?"

"Yes. She was groggy but seemed otherwise okay. Perhaps she went back to her house."

She pointed to number 21.

"It's that one."

They made their way across, and Luke pressed the doorbell.

Nothing happened for a few seconds, and he pressed it again, holding it down longer this time.

A few seconds later, they heard a noise from inside, a rattling, creaking noise that Sam recalled only too well from earlier.

"Shit," she said under her breath.

"What?"

"That sounds like her mother. She's not very..."

She stopped as the door opened to reveal a scowling Mrs Opray, who glared at her, then gave Luke a fleeting look up and down before grunting and turning her attention back to Sam, having seemingly decided he wasn't worth bothering with.

"What do you want now, girl? I'm an invalid, you know. I don't ride around in this for a joke."

"I appreciate that, Mrs Opray, and I'm sorry to bother you again. Can I speak to Zara?"

"I told you, she's not here, she's in the garage. Are you

deaf or stupid or both?"

"She was in the garage, but she's left. I wondered if she'd come back here."

"Didn't you see where she went?"

"No. I, ah… I had to look for something."

"She's probably gone to the shop. I'm not her minder, for heaven's sake." Her eyes flicked to one side so that she was looking over Sam's shoulder. "Ah, there you are, Bridget. You're late."

"Sorry, Mrs Opray."

Sam and Luke turned to see a woman standing behind them. She wore a navy blue tunic with the logo of a seagull over her breast pocket below the words 'Rest Assured'.

The woman smiled, and they turned back to see that this had earned her a scowl of her very own.

Mrs Opray waved her hands to signal that Sam and Luke needed to make room.

"Let her through, you two. I haven't got all day."

They stepped aside, and Bridget walked through the door and past Mrs Opray, who promptly slammed it closed without giving them another glance.

Sam turned to Luke.

"There's no way she's gone to the shops. I can only think that Jordan returned to fetch her while I was hunting around in that hedge."

"Wouldn't you have seen him?"

"No. I heard a few cars go past, but I was so focused on finding my phone, I didn't look up. This has to mean he's Mr Killjoy, doesn't it?"

"That doesn't make sense given what we found on Zara's laptop." He paused. "Unless he put the page there in an attempt to frame her, to make us think she's Mr Killjoy when in fact it's him."

He considered this for a moment before continuing.

"Another possibility is that Jordan and Zara are in cahoots, but if that's the case, how does Arwyn Thomas fit in? And Charlie Wallace for that matter. You said Jordan said '*this proves it wasn't me*' when he waved the piece of paper around."

"Yes, and then he mentioned Miles, which has to be Miles Barrington, his manager. It was as if Miles was the person he needed to prove his innocence to."

"But if Jordan's out to prove his innocence, why abduct Zara? Could it have been an act, Sam? Could the whole waving a sheet of paper around, and talking about Arwyn and Charlie, have been a ruse, a means of getting you out of the way so that he could grab her?"

"It's possible. What do we do now?"

"Jordan needs to be found. Something tells me Zara's life is in danger. What car was he driving?"

"A dark green Vauxhall Corsa."

"I'll call Pete now."

Chapter 46

Wilkins let out a series of high-pitched yelps, and Luke watched as a startled pheasant flew out of the long grass some twenty yards in front of the cocker. It squawked in fright as it flew away at forty-five degrees, its wings flapping wildly as it sought to escape.

Not that it should have worried.

Wilkins was a dismal failure when it came to the pursuit of birds. He'd retrieved a few dead ones, and even a rotting hedgehog on one occasion, and seemed to think he deserved a treat when he brought the carcass back to his master. But a live one?

No.

Not a chance.

The spaniel returned his nose to the ground, rushing hither and thither, his tail wagging excitedly every time he encountered an interesting smell or an intriguing object.

Luke found himself smiling, the first time that had happened since the events of the day before.

He sighed.

There was still no sign of either Jordan Fellowes or Zara Opray. Pete had been quick to act and, after checking with ACC Scarrott, an all-points bulletin had been issued to every officer in Avon and Somerset Police. It included photos of both the missing people, describing them only as 'persons of interest'.

The APB also included a description of Fellowes' car, including the registration number, meaning that it ought to be picked up by one of the many ANPR cameras dotted around the region.

And yet, there'd been nothing.

Fellowes had gone to ground, taking his captive with

him. The police were doing the best they could, sending officers to talk to families, hunting down close friends, visiting places both people were known to frequent, the works, but seemed no nearer to locating them.

He felt like calling in for an update, but he'd only rung thirty minutes earlier. Pete had promised to call if there was any progress, so he ought to leave him to it.

He checked his watch. It was just gone nine and Ben and Pippa were due to arrive at Bath Spa at ten, so he needed to leave soon to pick them up. It was a relief that they'd patched things up. She was a lovely girl, and they were well suited to each other.

As were he and Sam. They'd been a couple for nearly six months now, and their relationship was blossoming. He was already missing her, but was pleased he'd convinced her to travel to Dorset with her mum. She'd resisted at first, but agreed once he'd assured her that he would also be taking it easy over the weekend.

As for the other three members of the Ethics Team, he'd decided to leave them in the dark, for the time being at least. Maj, Helen and Josh deserved a rest, and there was nothing they could usefully contribute now that it was known that Jordan Fellowes was Mr Killjoy. It would be fine to bring them up to speed on Monday morning.

Not that it was a secret. In fact, he'd tell them everything if they were to contact him over the weekend. However, he knew that was unlikely. Maj, Asha and their daughter Sabrina were visiting friends in London, Helen had said that she and Bob were taking the narrowboat along the Kennet and Avon canal for the weekend, and Josh had mumbled something about taking Leanne to a festival in Cornwall and staying over on Saturday night.

His thoughts returned to Jordan Fellowes.

He was now their main suspect, and rightly so, given everything that had happened, but it was far from being a slam dunk. The evidence was circumstantial at best. Yes, he appeared to have taken Zara, but they had no proof of it.

Could there have been something in what he'd said about Arwyn Thomas and the financial relationship he had with Charlie Wallace? Might Fellowes have been telling the truth about being innocent? There was also the question about whether Zara Opray was blameless or not. Might she be a co-conspirator?

The more he thought about it, the more he was concerned that they'd leapt to the wrong conclusion.

He decided to ring Misty. There was always the chance she would turn something up that would help. She had many contacts among the criminal down-and-outs, the type of people who were ripe for Mr Killjoy's ByteIt offerings, and he needed to ensure she sounded them out as soon as possible.

He reached into his pocket for his phone, but it rang before he'd pulled it out.

He sighed with relief.

At last, there had been progress.

This had to be Pete with an update.

He accepted the call and put the phone to his ear.

"Pete, thank goodness. Have you located Fellowes?"

The response was squeaked out in a tone of surprise.

"Guv?"

"Oh."

Shit.

He swallowed.

"Josh. Hi."

"What was that, guv? You asked about Fellowes. Has something happened?"

Luke closed his eyes for a second.

"I was going to wait until next week before telling you, but since you rang."

"What, guv? What?"

Luke had to smile at the excitement in his voice.

"We think he's Mr Killjoy."

He went through everything that had happened the evening before.

"The only thing I'm confused about," Josh said when he'd finished, "is the whole Arwyn Thomas bit. What did you say was on that sheet of paper?"

"According to Sam, there were six lines of writing, which Fellowes told her were in Arwyn's handwriting. She could only remember what was on the top line, which was 'Charlie 15,750'. We think Jordan was trying to fool her into thinking Arwyn and Charlie Wallace were working together, that Arwyn was paying him thousands of pounds and keeping a record of it."

"I don't think that's what's going on, guv."

"What do you mean?"

"You said the first line said 'Charlie 15,750'. Did Sam remember what it said on the other lines?"

"Not all of them. They all referred to Charlie, but she said the numbers were different. She thought the second line said 12,600 but wasn't certain."

"That confirms it, guv. 600 divided by 12 is 50. It can't be a coincidence."

"What are you on about, son?"

"Philip Angler told us the going price is £50, so those numbers tally."

It suddenly dawned on Luke what Josh was getting at.

"My god. Those notes had nothing to do with Charlie Wallace, did they?"

"No, guv. We covered it on day 2 of the course. Philip ran through the street rates for drugs and talked about how they'd gone up over the past few years. The current price for cocaine is £50 a gram."

"Of course. Charlie." He shook his head, annoyed for not having realised earlier. "Well done, Josh."

"Thanks, guv. Do I need to do anything? Does this mean we have to work this weekend?"

"No, there's no need. I'll ring Pete and tell him what we

think that handwritten note was about, but it doesn't change much. Jordan Fellowes and Zara Opray still need to be found, and there's not much you or I can do to help."

"Won't Arwyn Thomas need to be pulled in for questioning?"

"Yes, but that can wait until Monday. You get on, Josh, and enjoy your weekend. You're off to a music festival in Cornwall, aren't you?"

"Ah... not as such. We're going to a fair."

"I hope you enjoy yourselves."

"Leanne will, guv. I'm not so sure it's my kind of thing, though. That's why I rang. I wanted some advice."

"Oh, come on, Josh. When I was your age, I used to love waltzers, bumper cars, and the rest. I'm sure you will as well."

"It's not a funfair, guv. I thought it was, that's why I was so keen to say yes, but it turns out it's more of a lack-of-fun-fair."

Luke laughed.

"A lack-of-fun-fair?"

"Yes. It's at Truro cathedral. Over 200 stands, and she wants to visit every one. Did Jess ever drag you along to something like that? It could cost us a packet. I can see Leanne wanting to sign up for everything. The photographers will be mega-expensivo, then there'll be extravagant multi-tiered cakes, live musicians for hire..."

"Hang on, Josh. Are you saying this is a wedding fair?"

"It certainly is. Billed as the largest in the South West. What should I do, guv?"

"How far are you on with your wedding planning?"

"Not very far. That's the problem. She's going to want to buy everything she sees. Everything." His voice went up an octave. "Everything!"

"Calm down, son. The cost of the wedding is down to the two of you, isn't it?"

"Yes. Leanne's parents and my Mum are each giving us

£2,000 to help, but we have to cough up the rest."

"Then I suggest you make sure you sit down with Leanne before you get to the fair and work through what you can afford. Build a budget and agree that you need to stick to it."

"Gotcha. Is that how you played it with Jess?"

Luke smiled. He'd never faced such a challenge with Jess.

And he didn't expect to with Sam, either, when they got married.

When?

Did he just think when?

Surely it was if? *If* they got married.

No, it was definitely when.

He wanted them to spend the rest of their lives together.

In that case, he ought to do something about it. He ought to propose.

Yes, that was it.

He should propose, and why hang around? When she returned from Dorset, he'd…

"Guv?"

"Oh. Sorry, Josh, I was daydreaming."

"I was asking if that's what you did with Jess. Built a budget together and then stuck to it."

Luke knew that this was what he wanted to hear, so he decided to go along with it.

"Yes, that was how I played it with Jess."

"Terrifico. Thanks for the advice, guv. I'll see you on Monday."

Chapter 47

Misty was pressing her back against the wall, trying to make herself as invisible as possible.

Fat fucking chance.

At six feet two, and broad with it, she was hardly ethereal.

Unlike her quarry, who was wispy as candy floss, with a wafer-thin body. The skinny scrote wouldn't be able to punch a hole through the skin on his custard.

Monty Rafferty was currently proving that he was also as thick as two short planks. He was standing on the edge of the pavement, in full view of passers-by, handing money to a teenager on a pushbike, and then taking the time to check the contents of the small bags passed to him before stuffing them in his pocket.

To be fair to the dealer, he was at least trying to keep an eye open for the police, and any moment now he was going to spot her.

She decided she'd seen enough and sprinted towards them, moving surprisingly quickly for a woman her size.

The teenager's eyes widened when he spotted her. In one swift move, he pulled his baseball cap down over his forehead, shoved the other man out of the way, mounted his bike and sped away.

Monty watched him disappear, then turned to face her.

"Whaddya do that for, Misty? He owed me one. I paid him thirty, and I only got two."

"He owed you one what?"

He blinked his eyes a few times.

"Uh?"

"He owed you one what?"

He hesitated for a second, then said, "A CD." She could

almost see the cogs turning as he added in a proud voice.
"Kenny Rogers."

"What do you mean a CD? They went into fucking freefall decades ago."

"A DVD, then."

"What, compressed into a green ball and packed into a clear bag? Oh, Monty! What am I going to do with you?"

She tapped her finger three times on the thin, straggly brown strands that stretched across the top of his head in an approximate simulation of hair.

"The wheel's still spinning, but the hamster's dead. Isn't that right, Monty?"

"I ain't got no hamster."

"That's exactly my point."

"What d'ya want, anyway?"

"I want some answers."

"Whazzit worth?"

"It's worth me not telling the police what you're carrying."

"I ain't got no knife. Just the weed."

It took him a second or two to register what he'd said, then he corrected himself.

"I mean the DVDs. Ah… of Kenny Rogers."

"I need to know what you know about ByteIt."

A confused look came over his face.

"Know what I know?"

"Yes. About ByteIt."

"Whazzat? A food product?"

"Don't act stupid with me. Oh, I forgot, it's not acting is it?"

He shook his head and grinned.

"Absolutely not."

"Well?"

"I don't know nothing about no ByteIt."

"That's a lot of negatives, Monty."

"Uh?"

She sighed. This was hard work.

"Okay. Let's try this. Have you heard of PayIt?"

"No."

"ChatIt?"

"No."

"What about SexIt?"

"Nah. You'd be too much for me."

"I'm not propositioning you, you arsehole."

Her phone rang.

"Don't move."

She answered the call, keeping her hand pressed down on his shoulder to ensure he didn't try to make a break for it.

"Misty, it's Luke."

"Hi, big guy." She kept her eyes on her captive as she continued. "I've caught up with one of the dumb pricks I was talking about."

To be fair to Monty, he didn't look affronted and nodded slightly as if acknowledging that this was a fair description.

"That's great. Can you ask him about drugs?"

"Drugs?"

"DVDs," Monty said.

She squeezed his shoulder, and he yelped in pain.

Luke heard this.

"What was that, Misty?"

"Nothing. I'm encouraging him to keep his fucking trap shut, that's all. What was that about drugs?"

"Can you ask if he's heard of a man called Arwyn Thomas? He's Welsh."

"No shit, Sherlock. With a name like that, I imagine he has leeks in his lugholes."

"We believe Arwyn's connected to the case but can't be sure. Something cropped up that indicates he might have been buying cocaine, and I know he lives in Bristol."

"Leave it with me."

She hung up.
"Did you catch what he said, Monty?"
He grinned.
"Problems with his John Thomas?"
She moved her hand from his shoulder and cupped it around his groin.
"You'll have problems with yours if you don't act smart. Oh, I forgot, that's not possible, is it?"
"Leave me alone!"
He started trying to wriggle away, but she was having none of it and started pressing her fingers towards each other.
"Ow! That hurts!"
He stared up at her, his eyes blinking again.
"Whaddya wanna know?"
She sighed.
"Okay. I'll take it slowly. First off, there are systems out there enabling low-lifes like you to send fake emails or invoices, obtain information through Chatbots, that kind of thing."
"Chatbots?"
"Yeah, they're... No. Never mind. These systems have names like PayIt, ChatIt, FishIt and SexIt."
"They all end in I-T."
"Fucking hell. You're turning into a proper Einstein, and before you say anything, he wasn't the guy who managed the Beatles."
"Uh?"
"Have you heard of any of them, or of anyone who's using them?"
"What were they called again?"
"Fuck's sake!"
She sighed again, and repeated the names, speaking more slowly this time.
"PayIt, ChatIt, FishIt and SexIt."
His grin returned.

"What was the last one?"

"Take that seedy smirk off your face. What are you, thirteen?"

She squeezed harder, and he let out another squeak.

"Ow! Stop it!"

"Well? Answer me."

"I'm forty-eight."

"Not your age, lardarse! Have you heard of any of them?"

"Nah."

"Okay. What about Arwyn Thomas? Have you come across him?"

"Might have done."

"Do you want to keep your ball bags intact or not?"

"Okay, okay. Yeah, I heard the name. He's a big spender on, you know…"

"DVDs?"

He shook his head, the sarcasm lost on him.

"Nah. Spends a lot on drugs, is what I heard."

"Now we're fucking getting somewhere. Where did you hear this?"

"From Oscar."

"Oscar Henderson?"

"I'm not saying. I ain't no snitch."

She didn't bother replying. The total number of Oscars in Bristol's criminal community was almost certainly one, so there was no need to push him further.

"You're hurting me," he went on. "Can I have me balls back now?"

She took her hand from his nether regions, and he immediately put his hand in its place and started rubbing.

Misty looked across at him in horror.

"What the fuck do you think you're doing?"

"Sore, ain't it?"

She closed her eyes for a second, started to walk away and then turned back.

"Do you know where I can find him?"

"Oscar Henderson?"

"Who else?"

"Oh. Right. Radcliffe Street. That's where he hangs out. Near the caff."

"Thanks."

Monty didn't respond, but looked down at the front of his jeans and reached for the zip. Misty grimaced and turned away again.

The last thing she needed at this time on a Saturday was a glimpse of the little scrote's little scrotes.

Chapter 48

Josh glanced across at Leanne to see that she was still buried in one of the bridal magazines she'd brought along for the journey. He couldn't read the words, but the photo showed several rows of covered chairs decorated with pink sashes.

Pricy pink sashes.

They looked like they were made of silk.

Super-pricy pink sashes.

"There's a turning for Okehampton coming up," he said. "Shall we find somewhere to have lunch?"

She turned the page, but didn't look up.

"Isn't it a bit early? It's only just gone eleven."

"Yes, but I'm starving, and it'll take a while."

She laughed, and this time she did raise her eyes from the page to look across at him.

"What do you mean? The way you eat, you'll have it finished within five minutes."

"Yes, but we need time to… ah…" He swallowed. "…to talk."

"Talk about what?"

"Um…"

He glanced down at her open magazine, not wanting to meet her eyes. It wouldn't be right to broach the subject until they were off the road and parked safely, plus he had to step carefully. She was so wildly enthusiastic about the wedding fair, and he didn't want to ruin her day.

On the other hand, Luke had been right. They had to budget, otherwise they'd be in serious financial pooey-poo.

"What is it, Joshy? You're got your serious face on."

"It *is* serious."

"What is? You've got me worried."

"It's nothing."

"You just said it's something serious?"

"Well, ah… That is… Ah… It's something, but…"

"Out with it."

"I can't. I'm driving, and I need to concentrate. I'll tell you when we get there."

A few minutes later, he saw the sign for Okehampton, indicated, and turned off.

He snatched a quick peek at Leanne, and saw that she had stopped reading her magazine, and was now staring fixedly ahead through the windscreen.

"This place will probably do," he said, when he spotted a sign about a quarter of a mile further on. "It's called 'Farmer Luxton's.'"

"Really?"

"Yes. And it says they've got a cafe."

"Really?"

Pissedy-piss-piss.

She was back to doing her 'really' thing. If it wasn't for the fact that she was sitting down, he knew she'd have her hands on her hips, giving him that look, the one with attitude.

The one that scared him.

He swallowed again, pulled into a parking space and heaved a big sigh.

It was important that he recover the situation, which meant coming right out with it.

He turned to face her.

"Leanne," he said, his voice flat. "We need to talk about our wedding."

She remained staring forwards, and raised her hand to wipe beneath her eye.

"I thought this was coming," she said, her voice soft and her bottom lip trembling. "I should have known. This stupid wedding fair's made you realise, hasn't it?"

He was relieved that she'd anticipated what he was

going to say, but hated to see her upset.

"There's no reason why we can't still go to the fair."

She turned to him then, and raised her voice.

"Still go? Why would we still go? Why would I *want* to go?"

"Well, because…"

His phone rang, the harsh tones startling both of them as it blared through the car's speakers.

Mandy's name came up on the screen.

"Well, doesn't that cap it all?" Leanne said.

"I'll ring her back later."

"No, speak to her now."

She reached over and tapped the button on the steering wheel before he could react.

"Ah…" He glanced across at Leanne, who was staring through the windscreen again. "Hi, Mandy."

"Hi, Josh. How are you?"

"Fine. I'm fine."

He was desperate to end the call. Leanne had shifted so that she was now turned away from him, her back stiff, and he hated seeing her like this. They needed to talk.

"Can I ring you back later?"

Mandy hesitated before replying.

"Are you sure you're okay, Josh? You sound tense. Is it Leanne? Have you told her?"

"Eh?"

"About the baby? Have you told her?"

Leanne turned around when she heard this.

"The baby?"

"Oh, Hi Leanne," Mandy said. "Sorry. I didn't realise you were there. Have I put my foot in it?"

Leanne was staring at him now, a horrified look on her face, and it dawned on him what she must think.

He held both hands up.

"No, no, Leanne. It's not what you think."

"Not what I think?"

"I want babies, that's all. You know I do."

"With me, yes, but not with..." She gestured to the screen and lowered her voice, "...with her."

"I..." he looked at the screen, then back at Leanne. "What? No... You've got it all wrong. Her baby... The pregnancy... It's..."

"Yes?" Her voice was raised again now. "It's what?"

"It's Leo's."

"And who the fuck is Leo?"

"I'm still here," Mandy said.

"I'll ring you back," Josh said, and put his finger on the button to end the call.

He turned to his fiancée.

"Leanne, I told Mandy I'm keen to have a baby, that's all. With you, with the person I want to spend the rest of my life with. The father of her baby is her partner, Leo."

She hesitated for a second as she took this in.

"Then you don't want to finish with me?"

"Of course I don't. Whatever made you think that?"

"The way you've been acting. I could see you didn't like me bringing these magazines along, then when you said you had something serious to tell me."

"Budgets."

"What?"

"We can't afford to spend a lot, that's all. I wanted the two of us to agree how much we can afford."

"Is that it? That's what you wanted to talk about?"

"Yes."

She smiled.

"Oh, Joshy. I do love you, but I'm not stupid. I wanted to come to this wedding fair because it'll be fun, but I'm not expecting to order anything. I want to get ideas, that's all."

"Oh. Right."

"You'd better ring Mandy back. I'll go inside and check the menu out."

She bent forward to give him a kiss, then left.

He watched as she disappeared into the building, then rang Mandy back.

She answered straight away.

"Is everything okay, Josh?"

He smiled. "It was a misunderstanding, but it's sorted now. I guess you weren't ringing simply to ask how I was?"

"No, I wondered if there'd be the chance to meet for a coffee. I'm heading your way next week."

"Is that for work?"

"Yes. I think I've identified the man running that QR code scam in Wandsworth. He lives in Bristol, and I want to confront him with what I've found."

"Was he using FishIt?"

"What?"

"I forgot. You don't know, do you?"

He explained about Mr Killjoy and the ByteIt subscription service.

"Wow!" she said when he'd finished. "You could well be right."

"About what?"

"About my guy using Mr Killjoy's FishIt service. I caught him on CCTV covering the council's QR codes with his own in another car park, and used my police contacts to identify him from his fingerprints. He's not the brightest by all accounts, so it's unlikely he'd be able to set up a false website without help."

"Terrifico. What's his name?"

"Lawson. Terry Lawson."

Chapter 49

Luke was pleased to see that Ben and Pippa seemed as close as ever.

They were sitting side by side on the sofa and holding hands. Every now and then, they'd look at each other in a way that made it only too clear how they felt.

He sat back in what the twins always referred to as his 'Dad-chair', absent-mindedly stroked Wilkins, who had climbed onto his lap, and took a sip of his espresso.

"How are your courses going?"

"We've both dropped out," Ben said.

"Pull the other one."

Ben smiled.

"I'm loving it. I'm thinking that in my third year I might specialise in…"

He stopped speaking when the doorbell rang, causing Wilkins to leap to the ground and start barking excitedly.

"Are you expecting anyone, Dad?"

"No. It's probably a delivery."

He stood up and left the room, the cocker at his side, his yelping subsided now that his master was going to deal with the monster interrupting their weekend.

Luke was surprised to open the front door and find his sister-in-law standing there. As ever, she was immaculately dressed, on this occasion in a pink linen midi-dress with a flattering neckline, but her beauty was spoiled by the hard-faced expression on her face.

The Range Rover was parked on the driveway behind her, but there was no sign of his brother, nor of Marion, his niece.

"Hi, Erica. Are you on your own?"

"Can I come in?"

It was typical of her to avoid answering his question, but there was something in her manner that told him she was distressed.

"Of course you can. Ben and Pippa are here."

He tried smiling to no avail.

"Fine."

She pushed past him and into the lounge.

Ben stood up when she entered.

"Hi, Erica. We weren't expecting you."

"I need to speak to your father. Would you mind?"

She nodded her head towards the door, the message abundantly clear.

"Of course not. Come on, Pippa, let's go into the kitchen."

They left, and Erica promptly planted herself in the centre of the sofa.

"Has something happened?" Luke asked.

She looked up at him.

"Sit!"

This was delivered forcefully, resulting in Wilkins immediately dropping onto his haunches. Not that Erica noticed, so focused was she on Luke as he descended into his chair.

He reflected on the fact that she had come into his house and commandeered it without a second's thought. But then, that was the way she was. How Mark had lived with her for so long was beyond him.

She glared at him for a few seconds before speaking, then her first words took him aback.

"Your mother's dead."

He waited.

This was a prelude to something, but to what, he had absolutely no idea.

"Aren't you going to say something, Luke?"

"What is there to say? I know she's dead. What's your point?"

"Hugo. That's my point. He's become intolerable."

Pot calling the kettle black was the first thing that occurred to Luke, but he managed to restrain himself from saying it out loud.

"In what way is he intolerable?"

"In every way. And Mark does nothing. Nothing!" She shook her head. "Your father walks around Borrowham Hall as if it's... well, as if he..."

"As if he owns it?"

"I know it's his, but *we* live there now. I manage everything, but the demands he puts on me... they're..."

"Intolerable?"

"Yes. And *you* need to do something about it."

"Why me?"

"Because you're the eldest son and, well..." She paused. "Unlike Mark, you've got gumption."

This was the nearest she'd ever come to paying him a compliment, but it pained him to hear the inherent criticism of his brother.

"What exactly is my father doing that's so intolerable?"

"Many things."

"For instance?"

"Yesterday, for example, I asked him whether he wanted lamb or beef for dinner. He said he wanted lamb, then came up to me three more times and told me to ensure he had lamb for dinner. He seems to think I'm useless."

"What else?"

"He did the same when I told him I was going into Dorchester on Thursday to see some friends. Asked me to get him a tie, then asked me twice more before I left. The man treats me as if I were stupid."

A chill shot down Luke's spine as he heard this.

"Have you noticed anything else, Erica?"

"Like what? Isn't that enough?"

"Is my father becoming repetitive in any other way?"

"He's boring, that's for certain. Tells the same stories over and over again. If I hear once more about his drunken escapade with the Duke of Harrogate…"

Luke held his hand up, and she stopped mid-sentence.

"I've heard enough, Erica. I need to speak to Mark."

"I told you. He won't do anything."

"I think I know what's wrong." He shook his head. "I'd noticed some things myself, but hadn't put two and two together."

"What do you mean?"

He didn't bother answering, but pulled out his phone and called his brother.

"Hi, Luke."

"Mark, Erica's here."

"Oh. I knew she was heading your way, but I thought she was going to see her friend in Bath."

"How's Father?"

"Okay. Why?"

"Erica's been telling me he repeats himself a lot."

"A bit, yes." He chuckled. "He and I laugh about it, actually."

"Is it becoming worse?"

"Possibly, but he's not far off eighty, and…" He stopped speaking as the penny dropped. "Oh. I see what you're getting at."

"We need to decide what to do. If it's Alzheimer's, there are drugs that can ease the symptoms. It's not urgent, but let's talk once Ben and Pippa have headed back to Uni tomorrow."

He hung up and turned to Erica, whose face had by some miracle turned even more sour.

"That's it, is it?" she said. "I should have known you'd side with Hugo over me."

He didn't bother to reply

"You're as weak as your brother, Luke. I wish I hadn't bothered coming. Now excuse me, I'm due at Helena's."

Mr Killjoy

She pushed past him for the second time, slamming the front door behind her as she made her exit.

Ben and Pippa heard her leave and returned to the lounge.

"What was that all about, Dad?"

"Your Grandpa's not well. He's been forgetting things and repeating himself, and it's most likely early signs of dementia."

"Oh, no!"

"Should we go down there this weekend?" Pippa asked.

"No. I don't think there's any need. You'll be at Borrowham for Mark's birthday in a few weeks, and there won't be much change in that time."

His phone rang.

"Is that Mark?" Ben asked.

Luke looked down at his phone.

"No, it's Josh, but do you mind if I get it?"

"Not at all. Come on Pippa, let's rustle together some brunch. The works for you, Dad?"

"Yes, please."

They left for the kitchen, and he answered the phone.

"Hi, Josh."

"Hi, guv. Having a lovely weekend?"

His voice was light and airy, and Luke didn't want to puncture his mood.

"Lovely, thanks. What's up?"

"I took your advice."

"Advice?"

"About the budget. You know, for the wedding spend."

"Ah, right. It all went well, then?"

"Ah… Kind of. I got in a pickle, but we're fine now."

"Is that why you're calling?"

"Not entirely. Mandy rang me. That's what caused the baby business."

Luke wasn't in the mood to ask what he meant by 'the baby business', so let this pass.

"And?"

"She's found the criminal behind the quishing scam at Wandsworth's car parks. His name's Terry Lawson."

"That was one of the names Misty gave."

"Has to be the same man, guv, because according to Mandy he lives in Bristol."

"You're right. I'll ring Misty and tell her. Good work, Josh."

"Thanks, guv."

Chapter 50

Luke sighed.

He had anticipated a relaxing weekend with Ben and Pippa, and now not only did he have his father to worry about, but the hunt for Mr Killjoy was heating up.

There was still no news on Jordan Fellowes or Zara Opray. It was as if they'd vanished off the face of the earth. Zara only had access to one vehicle, which remained outside her house, suggesting that she'd gone with Jordan, either voluntarily or because he'd abducted her.

But his car hadn't pinged any of the many ANPR cameras in the region, nor had he been spotted by any of the beat or traffic officers. Did that mean that he'd gone to ground locally, taking Zara with him? If so, where? The police had contacted their families and friends, but they had claimed not to have seen or heard from them.

However, there were four people who hadn't yet been asked if they knew where Jordan and Zara were. Those four were the other main suspects: Arwyn Thomas, Miles Barrington, Charlie Wallace and Naomi Simmons. He and Pete had agreed it would be sensible to wait until Monday before questioning them. They were sure that Jordan and Zara would have been located by then, and once they had been interviewed, the picture would become a whole lot clearer. They didn't want to spook Mr Killjoy before they were ready to pounce.

But at present, their disappearance was a mystery.

Why would the two flee?

What were they planning?

Could Jordan have planted the ChatIt screen on Zara's laptop, knowing that it would be found? If that was the case, he had to be Mr Killjoy, and it meant that Zara was an innocent woman.

But if he'd framed her, then why take her into hiding? Why not let her be arrested by the police?

Or were they a couple?

Yes, that was a possibility. They could be in a relationship. If that was the case, could that relationship have extended to the creation of Mr Killjoy? Was the ByteIt operation a joint enterprise?

There were too many ifs and buts for his liking.

"Black pudding?" Pippa asked.

"What?" Luke looked up, momentarily confused by the interruption. "Ah. Yes, two slices, please."

"Are you thinking about Grandpa?" Ben asked.

"I have to admit that I wasn't. We're working on a case that I can't get off my mind."

"Is this connected to the fire?"

Luke nodded and gave a wry smile.

"It's also linked to one of our employees who attempted suicide, to a scam with QR codes in London, to a series of false invoices, to a deepfake conference call, and to the purchase of crack cocaine."

"Three pieces of bacon?" Pippa asked.

"Yes, please."

Ben helped Pippa to dish the food out, and then brought his and Luke's plates over to the kitchen table. Pippa sat down beside her boyfriend with her own breakfast, a much slimmed-down version of what the two men were having.

There was silence as they tucked into their food.

"This is great," Luke said after a couple of minutes. "Thanks, guys."

"No problem," Ben and Pippa said in unison.

Pippa finished her meal first, put her knife and fork down on her plate, and stared sideways through the window into the back garden.

"Are you okay?" Ben asked.

"I'm fine, but… I was thinking… Luke, do you mind if I ask something about this case you're working on?"

"Of course not. Fire away."

"Why did the employee attempt suicide?"

"We think it was sextortion, that he befriended a woman on social media, sent her intimate photos and videos and was then blackmailed."

"And was this woman real?"

He shook his head.

"No, we don't think so. Whoever's behind these crimes is very technology savvy, and she was most likely created using artificial intelligence."

"He's a cybercriminal?"

"Yes."

"What are you thinking, Pips?" Ben asked.

"It might just be me, but that list doesn't make sense." She looked across at Luke. "One of those crimes doesn't fit with the others."

"What do you mean?"

"You said someone bought drugs, but that's not a cybercrime."

"No, but…"

Luke stopped speaking as he thought this through.

The piece of paper Jordan Fellowes had waved in front of Sam suggested that Arwyn Thomas had bought crack cocaine, large amounts of it, too much for personal use.

They'd also seen Arwyn on CCTV at the time the intercepted email from Mr Killjoy was sent.

But Pippa was right. Buying, and potentially dealing, class A drugs was not a cybercrime.

He smiled across at her.

"You're brilliant, Pippa. Brilliant!"

She smiled back.

"That's very kind of you, but it's only a fried breakfast."

He grinned, finished the last of his meal and stood up.

"After that piece of super-sleuthing, I've got a couple

of calls to make. Please excuse me."

Chapter 51

Misty had checked the length of Radcliffe Street and most of the side roads, but had so far drawn a blank. She decided to try the greasy spoon itself, to see if they knew where Oscar Henderson might be.

The middle-aged man behind the counter was leaning down and writing on a piece of paper when she approached.

"What can I get you, sir?" he said without looking up.

"SIR!" she exclaimed, her voice loud enough to be heard throughout the room. "What do you fucking mean, 'sir'?"

He looked up and swallowed when he took in her size and the expression on her face.

"Oh! Ah... Sorry. It was the shadow. The large shadow."

"The large shadow?"

He nodded.

"Yeah. You're, ah..."

"Are you saying I'm big?"

"Well..."

"Okay. I know I'm big, but do I look like a man?"

He started to speak, but she held a hand up to stop him.

"No. Don't answer that. I'll be deeply fucking upset if you say anything other than I'm the most gorgeous thing to ever enter your life, and you weren't about to say that, were you?"

"Ah..."

He swallowed again, then his next words came out in a squeak.

"What do you want, ah..." He paused for a second

before concluding in a higher pitched voice with a questioning, "…Miss?"

"That's better. I don't mind Miss or Ms. Either will fucking do. Just not Mister. I may be big, but cast your eyes on these babies." She gestured to her substantial breasts. "These don't come with men, well, not with most men, anyway. I've got chesticles, not testicles. A pair of titties, not a pair of little bitties. Got that straight?"

"Ah… Got it."

"Good. I'm glad we've got that out of the way. Now, I'm looking for an arsewipe by the name of Oscar Henderson. Know where I can find him?"

"Oscar Henderson?"

Misty recognised this immediately as buying for time. Not only that, but he'd raised his voice as he said it, and she knew what that meant.

She whipped around to see a slim man in his late thirties tiptoeing down the centre of the room towards the exit. He was completely bald, and had two birds tattooed on the back of his neck. She recognised him instantly.

He hadn't managed more than a step further when she grabbed his right ear, twisted, and pulled him lughole-first towards the nearest vacant table.

"You going to be a good boy, Oscar?"

"Ow! Leggo!"

She grinned.

"Well? All I want is to talk."

"Okay, okay. Just let go of me ear."

She released her grip, and he started massaging his earlobe as he descended into the nearest chair.

"That hurt, that did."

She ignored him, and called over to the man at the counter.

"Can you get us two lattes?"

"Not for me," Oscar said. "I'd rather have a mocha."

"Oh, would you? And do you want chocolate sprinkles

on top?"

Oscar considered this for a second.

"Yeah, that'd be nice."

Misty sighed and turned back to the waiter.

"Did you hear that? A mocha for my little drug-dealing amigo."

"Shh," Oscar said.

"Why's that, Oscar? Don't you want people to know that your secret fucking pleasure is coffee and chocolate?"

"No, I meant… You know what I meant. What do you want, Misty?"

Her phone started ringing, and she looked down at the screen and then back up.

"Our friendly little chat will have to wait, Oscar. The Incredible Hulk is calling."

She accepted the call.

"Twice in one morning, Luke. What have I done to fucking deserve it? And both times you've caught me when I'm talking to one of Bristol's finest."

"Finest?"

"Yeah. Finest turds. How can I help?"

"We've found out that Terry Lawson is the one behind the Wandsworth QR code scam. Have you spoken to him yet?"

"Not yet, no. However, your timing is im-fucking-peccable. My current turd-in-residence may be able to help with that piece of paper issue we discussed. Hang on, and I'll put you on speaker."

She pressed the speaker button, and placed the phone face up on the table.

"Ah, thanks," she said as their drinks were placed in front of them.

"Sugar?" The waiter asked.

"No. I'm sweet enough. What about you, Oscar?"

He shook his head.

"Nah. Too many additives."

"What are you? The first in a line of environmentally-conscious drug dealers?"

He shrugged and lifted the mug to his lips.

"The man I'm with is Oscar," she went on for Luke's benefit, "and I think he may know our Welsh friend."

She watched the other man closely as she continued.

"What do you know about Arwyn Thomas, Oscar?"

"Never heard of him."

"Is that right? You've never supplied him with cocaine?"

"I don't deal no drugs no more."

She wasn't sure if that was a double negative or a triple negative. Either way, the toerag was lying.

"I don't believe you, numbnuts, but I'm going to do you a favour." She grinned. "In fact, I'm going to do you two favours."

"What?"

"First…" She pointed to his ear, which was still red where she had squeezed it. "…I'm going to let you keep that. And second, I'm not going to shop you to the powers-that-be."

"You ain't got nothing on me."

"I've got plenty on you. I've got film of you taking a delivery from Badger Mattinson for starters."

This made him stop in his tracks.

"How did you know about Badger?"

She ignored the question.

"Well, are you going to spill the beans on Arwyn Thomas?"

He shrugged.

"Not much to say. He's a client, ain't he?"

"Not a dealer?" Luke asked.

Oscar looked down at the phone and laughed.

"What, him? Nah. He's a punter who likes to spread joy, that's all."

"You mean, he buys enough to feed the nostrils of his

mates?" Misty asked.

"Yeah."

"How do you know that's what he's doing?"

"I challenged him, didn't I? He bought 15 G of light, then came back the next week and bought 12 G, then 20 G the week after. I mean, it's good business, but too much for one person. I shoved him against the wall and showed him my blade, told him what I'd do if he was moving in on my patch. That's when he told me it was for his friends." He grinned at the memory. "Proper snivelling, he was."

"Have you heard enough, Luke?" Misty said.

"Yes, that's useful, Misty. Thanks. Let me know when you've spoken to Lawson."

"Will do."

Chapter 52

Luke was now ninety per cent certain that Arwyn Thomas wasn't Mr Killjoy.

He couldn't rule him out completely, but if the person behind ByteIt was a user, he didn't see how buying it on the street would be his style. Mr Killjoy would have made a whole string of connections in the criminal underworld through promoting and selling ChatIt, PayIt and the rest. One of those contacts would be the obvious way to fuel his addiction, not a blatant exchange of money for drugs in one of the murkier areas of Bristol.

However, Arwyn was believed to have been the author of the note that Jordan Fellowes had waved around. And Jordan was suspect number one, which might mean that Arwyn had useful information that could help them locate and apprehend him.

Luke decided he ought to discuss developments with Pete. It might be worth questioning Arwyn sooner rather than later.

He was pleased when his call was answered straight away, and even more pleased at Pete's first words.

"We've got him."

"Jordan Fellowes?"

"The very same."

"That's great news. Where was he?"

"At a mate's house. In a wardrobe, to be precise."

"What about Zara Opray?"

"No sign of her, and Fellowes claims not to know where she is. He hasn't been properly interviewed, though. I was hoping…"

Luke knew exactly what he was hoping for, and didn't wait for him to finish.

"Where is he?"

"Still en route to Portishead. This is hot off the press, Luke. He's only been in custody for twenty minutes."

"Okay. I'll see you there in about an hour."

*

Luke made record time to Avon and Somerset headquarters, aided by the fact that it was a low-traffic weekend, and was halfway through a disappointingly weak, machine-made coffee when Pete turned up.

They headed for the interview suite, where Pete had booked room 2. A few minutes later, Jordan Fellowes was brought in by a uniformed officer.

"Please take a seat, Mr Fellowes," Pete said, once the officer had left. "I believe you've been read your rights, and you've declined your right to a solicitor."

"I don't need one. I've done nothing wrong."

"Good, then this won't take long. Please…"

He gestured to the seat opposite, and Fellowes sat down, though it was clear from his body language that he would rather do anything but.

Once seated, he seemed to notice Luke for the first time.

"Who are you?"

Luke smiled.

"I'm Luke Sackville."

"Luke Sackville? Don't I know your name? Aren't you Head of Security at Filchers?"

"No, but I do work at Filchers."

Fellowes looked at Luke again, then at Pete, then back at Luke.

"Then what the fuck are you doing here if you're not police?"

"Please calm down, Mr Fellowes. All will become clear

in a moment. Pete, would you mind…"

Pete clicked the button on the recording device.

"Interview with Jordan Fellowes in interview room 2 at Avon and Somerset headquarters in Portishead. The time is 13:42, and also present are Detective Inspector Pete Gilmore and ex-DCI Luke Sackville in his capacity as police consultant."

"Can we get on with it now?" Fellowes said impatiently. "All I've been told is that I've been arrested on suspicion of kidnapping, which is crap. I haven't done anything with Zara, and I don't know where she is."

"How did you know this concerns Zara Opray, Mr Fellowes?" Luke asked.

"I don't, but who else could it be?"

"Why do you say that? Were you aware that she had disappeared?"

"No."

"Then why would you think she's been abducted?"

"I don't know. I suppose because we argued."

"You argued?"

"Yes."

"When was this?"

"Friday afternoon. It was between five and six. I can't remember the exact time."

"And were you and Zara on your own at the time?"

"No. An ex-girlfriend of mine was there as well."

Luke knew this to be grossly overstating the nature of the relationship between him and Sam, but decided to let it pass.

"I see. And what's the name of this ex-girlfriend?"

"Sam Chambers."

Luke leaned forward on the desk and steepled his hands together.

"The problem I've got, Jordan… May I call you Jordan?"

"Sure."

"The problem I have, Jordan, is that you were the last person to see Zara before she disappeared. According to her mother, she never returned to the house from the garage. That was where the two of you argued, wasn't it? The garage?"

"Yes, but you've got it wrong. I wasn't the last person to see her. Sam was there when I left."

"Are you saying that you and Zara argued in front of her?"

He nodded.

"Please can you say 'yes' for the tape?" Pete said.

Jordan sighed.

"Yes, we argued in front of Sam."

"Okay," Luke said. "Can you tell us exactly what happened?"

"I told you. We argued."

Jordan crossed his arms and sat back in the chair, as if suggesting that was the end of it.

"You do realise the seriousness of what you've been accused of, don't you, Jordan?"

Jordan shrugged his shoulders, but said nothing.

"Pete, what sentence are we looking at?"

"Eight years minimum. Life if violence was used."

Luke waited for this to sink in.

"Did you use violence when you abducted Miss Opray, Jordan?"

"No, and I told you, I didn't take her. I don't know where the fuck she is."

"Isn't it true that you shoved her hard, causing her to bang her head and fall unconscious?"

Jordan sat forward at this.

"Where did you hear that? It was fucking Sam, wasn't it? Sour-faced bitch."

"Well? Did you push her?"

"Yeah, but she was fine. A bit groggy, but fine."

Jordan sat back in his chair and re-folded his arms.

"It sounds to me like Jordan just admitted using violence, DI Gilmore."

"Yes. As I said, that means a life sentence."

Luke looked across at Jordan and shook his head.

"It's not looking good, Jordan. Are you sure you don't want us to call a solicitor."

Jordan swallowed and sat forward again.

"I told you! I didn't kidnap her. I don't know where the fuck she is!"

"In that case, tell us everything. It's in your best interests. Unless you're lying, of course."

"I'm not…"

Jordan gulped and looked from one man to another.

Luke could see he was on the verge of speaking, of telling them what happened, but whether that was going to be the truth was another thing altogether. If Jordan was Mr Killjoy, he'd hold something back to protect himself.

"It was Miles."

"Miles?" Luke prompted, feigning ignorance.

"Miles Barrington is my manager."

"What do you mean when you say, 'It was Miles'?"

"He took her. Miles kidnapped Zara."

Chapter 53

Luke looked carefully at the man opposite.

"Did you see him take her, Jordan?"

"No, but it has to be him. He's out to get me. Always has been."

"This sounds like guesswork to me. Either that, or a story to cover what you've done, to try to throw us off the scent."

"No, I…"

"What have you done with her, Jordan? Think carefully before you answer. There's a possibility of a reduced sentence if you co-operate and lead us to her."

"I didn't take her. I've already told you."

"Then tell us exactly what happened in that garage between you and Zara. What have you got to lose?"

"Everything," Jordan mumbled under his breath. "Everything."

Luke waited, and this time the words did come, and once he'd started Jordan kept going, the story tumbling out of his mouth as if he'd lost control of what he was saying.

"I was angry. Angry with Miles more than anything, but not just him. Arwyn was at the root of it."

"Are you talking about Arwyn Thomas, Filchers' Head of IT?"

"Yes. He gave Miles the ammunition, not that he knew it, but Arwyn's probably so hooked on what he sucks up his nose he wouldn't have realised what he'd done."

He sighed.

"Last Tuesday, Miles called me into an office and said my career was over, that he'd found a bag in my desk drawer with traces of white powder in it, and that the sensible option was to resign. He was delighted, I could tell he was. He's always had it in for me."

"What did you say?"

"I told him to fuck off, that he was talking bollocks, and that if there was a bag he must have planted it. He said he'd give me until the weekend to think it over, that if he didn't have my resignation by next Monday, he'd go to the police."

Jordan swallowed again before continuing.

"I was furious and confided in Zara, asked what she thought I should do. She suggested that the bag might have been put there by Arwyn, not Miles, that she'd noticed he'd been moody lately, and on other occasions full of energy, both signs of a regular drug-taker. I didn't know if she was right, but I went into Arwyn's office when he was out at a meeting, and I struck lucky."

"In what way?"

"The top drawer of his desk was locked, but I forced it open, and found a note in his handwriting. It was a list of numbers, each preceded by 'Charlie'. At first, I thought it was a reference to Charlie Wallace, who sits next to me in IT, then I realised it was a record of Arwyn's cocaine purchases."

"When was it you found this note?"

"On Wednesday. I didn't have the chance to speak to Zara about it because of the fire, so I thought I'd catch her at home. I wanted her advice on what to do next. That's why I was at the garage, but I didn't get the chance to ask her because that bitch was there."

"That would be Sam Chambers."

"Yeah. I took the note out of my pocket and asked her to leave because I wanted a private word with Zara, and she went berserk. She pushed Zara out of the way and leapt at me. I thought she was going to scratch my eyes out."

"Have you any idea why she did that?"

"It's cos I dumped her."

Luke tried to keep his face emotionless.

"You dumped her?"

"Yeah. She was really into me, but it got too intense, and I'd had enough. She took it badly, but I didn't realise she'd wanted me that much."

"I see. Now you're saying Sam pushed Zara over and then attacked you. Earlier, you said that you'd done it."

"Yeah, but I was trying to protect her. We used to go out, and I've still got a soft spot for her."

"For Sam Chambers?"

"Yeah."

"And was Sam's attack on you the reason you fled the scene?"

"I wasn't frightened of her, if that's what you mean. I thought I'd come back later, that's all. Once she'd left."

"And did you? Did you go back to the garage?"

"Yeah. I gave it ten minutes, then I went back."

"And that's when you abducted Zara?"

"No! She wasn't there. I assumed she'd gone off with Sam somewhere, so I thought I'd try again later in the evening. But I rang to check first, and her mother told me she'd vanished, and that the police were looking for her. That was when I kind of panicked and went to Vern's house."

"Didn't you tell us earlier that you didn't know Zara was missing?"

"Yeah, I guess."

Luke sighed.

"Okay, Jordan. I think we all need a break."

"Aren't we done? I've told you everything I know."

"I'm afraid not. We have a few more questions. Pete, would you mind?"

"Interview paused at 14:14."

Pete clicked the button to stop recording.

"We'll take ten minutes," Luke said. "Do you want a tea or coffee, Jordan, or do you need to use the toilet?"

"No, I'm fine."

Pete went outside to ask the uniformed constable to

return to the room, and then he and Luke headed for the drinks machine.

"Well," Luke said, as he waited for his espresso, "what do you think?"

"He wasn't telling the truth about his relationship with Sam, that much is clear. Didn't you tell me that they went out twice, and that she dumped him rather than the other way around?"

"Yes, but I put that down to his vanity and narcissism. The big question is whether he's lying about taking Zara. Can you ring her mother to check his story about ringing her?"

"Will do."

Luke took his cup from the machine, and Pete pressed the buttons for a flat white.

"I'm wondering if we should change tack," Luke went on."

"What do you mean?"

"A draft ChatIt home page was found on Zara's laptop, and it would be an unbelievable coincidence if her disappearance isn't linked to the operations of Mr Killjoy. I think we should start to probe Jordan on cybercrime and see how he reacts."

Pete pulled his coffee from the dispenser, took a sip, pulled a foul face, and then poured it away.

"That's disgusting."

Luke took a sip of his own drink and grimaced.

"You're right, but it's warm and wet, and that'll do me." He took another sip. "Well, what do you think?"

Pete considered this for a few seconds.

"My worry is that we haven't got enough to charge him. If we spook him, and he is Mr Killjoy, who knows what he'll do when we let him go? What's to say he won't take it out on Zara Opray?"

'That's a good point. Mr Killjoy is ignorant of the fact that we've narrowed our list of suspects to five, and we need to keep it that way. I'll ask about his technical abilities, which will play to his high opinion of himself, and take it from there."

Pete nodded.

"Yes, that might work."

He gave a wry smile.

"Whether it'll get us anywhere is another matter altogether."

Chapter 54

"Interview resumed at 14:23," Pete said and pressed record.

Luke looked across at Jordan.

"Only a few more questions, Jordan, and then you can be on your way."

"You're letting me go, then?"

Luke smiled.

"There's no reason to keep you. You've given us comprehensive answers, and we value your honesty, don't we, DI Gilmore?"

"Absolutely, Luke."

"However, before we finish, I'd like to ask you a few questions about your colleagues in IT."

Jordan sat up and shuffled in his chair, happy to be talking about something other than Zara's disappearance.

"Sure. I'll do anything I can to help."

"Thank you. I appreciate it. Tell me, what exactly is your role in the IT department?"

"I'm a senior software engineer."

"That must require significant technical skills."

Jordan nodded, pleased to be given the opportunity to show off about his abilities.

"I'm proficient in Javascript and PHP, as well as the latest software development methodologies such as Agile and DevOps."

"That's impressive. And your colleagues?"

"In a word, useless. Miles is a jumped-up software developer, and as for Charlie..." He laughed and shook his head. "Charlie's understanding of data structures and algorithms is extremely basic for a database engineer."

"Charlie?"

"Charlie Wallace. He's in the cubicle next to mine."

"I see. And what about Zara herself? I believe she's the team's web designer. Is she good at her job?"

"Not as woeful as some of the others. She's creative, but..." He stopped speaking. "Why are you asking me all this?"

"Purely to get a sense of the people that Zara shares office space with. You've made it clear that you had nothing to do with her disappearance, but it looks like someone took her, and that someone could well be a person in the IT department. Who else does she work closely with?"

"Naomi, that's Naomi Simmons. She's a systems analyst, but an awful one if you ask me." He grinned. "I can see her doing well, though."

"Why's that, if she's not very good?"

"Because Arwyn will see she's promoted. All she has to do is say yes, if you know what I mean."

"Are you saying he's propositioned her?"

"Of course he has. And who can blame him? Fucking gorgeous, she is. I wouldn't kick her out of bed."

His grin grew wider, and Luke found himself feeling more than a little nauseous.

It was time to change the subject.

"That was a very useful insight," he lied. "You said Zara is creative. What did you mean by that?"

"She designed a lot of Filchers' internet pages, and did a half-decent job. She hasn't got my deep technical skills, but she's got a fairly good grasp of HTML."

"I see. And what do you know about Zara's relationships with Miles, Charlie, Naomi and Arwyn? Does she get on with them? Is she particularly close to anyone?"

"She's quite close to Naomi."

"They're friends?"

"Yeah, I'd say that. I've heard them arranging to meet in the evening."

"What about the others?"

"She doesn't like Miles, but then, who would?"

"Any reason why?"

"He micro-manages. So fucking proud of his own skills, he seems to think everyone else is useless."

He sounds exactly like you, Luke thought, but said, "What do you mean by micro-manages?"

"He's always leaning over her shoulder, pointing out where a screen could be improved or her code could be optimised. Does it to all of us, the wanker."

"And Arwyn? How does she get on with him?"

"Doesn't see much of him. None of us do." He laughed. "Too busy with a straw up his nose to be bothered with us lot." His lascivious grin returned. "Unless you look like Naomi, that is. He's got plenty of time for her."

"That brings us to Charlie. How would you describe Zara's relationship with him?"

"More or less non-existent. Charlie keeps himself to himself. Whenever he does talk, he's rubbishing the place. Don't know why he doesn't just leave. It's not as if he needs the money."

"What do you mean?"

"He's stinking rich. Don't know where he got it from, but he drives a top-of-the-range Merc, and lives in a house that has to be worth a couple of million. Must have inherited it, or else he's smarter than he makes out and is moonlighting somewhere."

"Interesting."

Luke turned to Pete.

"Any other questions, DI Gilmore?"

"No, I think that's everything. Interview ended at 14:33."

He clicked the stop button.

"Can I go?" Jordan asked.

"Certainly," Luke said. "Thanks for your time."

Pete stood up, went to the door, called the uniformed constable over and then turned back to their interviewee.

"PC Bell will show you out, Jordan."

"Ah, right."

He seemed unsure whether to offer to shake hands or not.

"Thanks," he said, after a few seconds' consideration, then stood up and left the interview room.

*

Luke was the first to reach The Globe, a pub on both men's way home, and he ordered their coffees and found a quiet corner.

"Good call," Pete said, when he dropped into the chair opposite.

Their drinks arrived, and both men sighed when they had a first taste of drinks that were a million times better than the liquids dished out by the interview suite's machine.

"Well," Luke began, "what did you make of our friend Jordan Fellowes?"

"Mmm." Pete took another sip of his flat white. "He lied about his relationship with Sam, which begs the question, how much of everything else he told us was true?"

"I think it's important to separate his opinions and boasting from the rest of what he said. He bigs himself up at every opportunity, and that's what he was doing when he was talking about Sam, and when he was showing off about his technical skills. However, I find it hard to believe the stuff about Arwyn Thomas was invented. There's a possibility he created that handwritten note, but why?"

"To put us off the scent?"

"I don't know. If that was the case, surely he'd have come up with something simpler." He paused. "There's also the fact that Fellowes was hiding in the wardrobe at a friend's house. That doesn't make sense if it was him who abducted Zara Opray."

"No, you're right. What next?"

"With luck, she'll turn up and we'll find she went to a friend's house as well. On Monday, can you look into what he said about Charlie Wallace, about him being rich?"

"Will do."

"Great. I'm going to have a word with Arwyn, but I want to do it without alerting him as to why. I'll catch up with him at work. As to Naomi Simmons and Miles Barrington, I didn't pick up anything useful. If Zara doesn't turn up soon, we may have to find a way of questioning them further without raising suspicions."

Chapter 55

Mr Killjoy locked the door, slid the bolts across at both top and bottom, then turned and walked down the corridor to the room he had ploughed so much time, effort and money into.

The nerve-centre of his operation.

He retrieved his spare laptop and returned to the other room, sliding down the panel that covered the observation window to check that his prisoner was seated on the bed.

"Don't move. I've got something for you."

Zara looked up, still shocked that he was Mr Killjoy.

And no wonder.

The stupid girl had thought he was based in Yorkshire, a belief he'd courted carefully through comments he'd made when they'd communicated over Telegram.

He slid the bolts back, turned the key, and dragged open the heavy wooden door. Pale blue and faded, it was reinforced with battens and metal studs, and had seen service in Shepton Mallet before the prison closed a few years earlier. He'd seen it at an architectural antiques yard and bought it on the spot.

The door had kept people secure for well over a hundred years, and was now continuing to serve its purpose well. He was pleased he'd had the foresight to ready the room in case it was needed. The bolts were probably overkill, but it was better to be safe than sorry.

He passed her the laptop.

"It's already connected to wifi."

She took it from him, a confused look on her face.

"What's this for?"

"What do you think? I haven't brought you here to idle your time away. First off, I need you to work on that FakeIt home page. Your first attempt was pathetic. It needs more pizzazz, more oomph, if people are going to be drawn in."

She looked up at him, her mouth open.

"Well, get on with it."

"What…" She swallowed. "What are you going to do with me?"

"Do with you?" He laughed. "Nothing. I'm not going to do anything with you. You'll continue to work on ByteIt, but you won't have the distraction of Filchers to worry about. You're now my full-time employee, and I'll pay you accordingly."

"But, but…you're locking me in."

"It's to be safe, that's all. The police are on to you, because of that idiotic mistake you made, but I'll release you when it's all blown over."

"You'll let me go?"

"Of course I will."

"It doesn't matter that I know who you are?"

"No, Zara, it doesn't matter. In a week or two, you'll be free to leave. All this…" He waved his hand to the bare stone-walled room, and the prison door. "…is a precaution." He smiled. "Try not to worry. I'm not a monster, but I need to be careful, that's all."

She looked doubtful, but nodded.

"Okay."

He didn't trust her, never would, but she needed to believe she had a future, otherwise she was useless to him.

"What about my mother? What about the money for her carers?"

"As I said, I'll continue to transfer money to pay for them." He bent his head to one side. "You must learn to listen, Zara, you really must."

"Do you want me to work on the FakeIt home page?"

He took a step towards her, hands formed into fists but held tight to his side as he fought the urge to strike out.

"Didn't I already tell you that?" he hissed, his voice low

and menacing.

She shrunk backwards on the bed.

"Yes. Sorry." She swallowed again. "I'll start on it now."

He shook his head.

"No. I want a Zoom call with the team first, and you, as Bellatrix, need to be on it."

"Ah... Okay."

"Don't say anything out of the ordinary. Understand?"

She nodded several times.

"Good."

He left the room, locking and bolting it as before, and returned to his den.

Once inside, he allowed himself a smile.

She had agreed to do as he asked, and he was relieved that he didn't have to go through with her 'accidental' death so soon after the fire at Filchers.

Not that she had much option. He'd made it clear what he would do if she didn't comply.

He was proud of the idea he had come up with. It meant that he wouldn't have to recruit and train a replacement web designer, and wouldn't have to explain to Draco and Gilderoy what had happened to their teammate.

And as for Zara.

She got to live.

For the time being, at least.

Plus, her mother's care would continue to be funded. After all, as he'd told her, he wasn't a monster.

He grinned and rubbed his hands together.

It pleased him to think that, even in her last days, Zara would add value to his business.

He sat down at his desk, scanned the monitors to ensure everything was running smoothly, and then logged in.

Draco was already online, and Gilderoy's face appeared a few seconds later, followed shortly afterwards, to his relief, by Bellatrix.

"Good afternoon, everyone," he typed. "I want to run through our normal agenda."

Voldemort delivered these words, and he had almost finished typing his next statement when Bellatrix started to speak.

"I have something to say," she began, and Mr Killjoy's eyebrows furrowed.

Was that idiotic girl about to go back on her word? If she said anything, anything at all, that gave away his identity, or the fact that she was now his prisoner, she'd have to pay.

"I'm working hard on the FakeIt home page," she went on, and he breathed a sigh of relief. "I hope to send a new version through today."

"Thank you, Bellatrix. That's good to hear. Now, Draco, perhaps you could bring us up to date on the latest sales figures?"

Chapter 56

Luke called the team together as soon as he and Sam walked into the basement room of Ambrose's house.

"I hope you had a relaxing weekend, everyone. This week is going to be hard work, and intense for all of us."

He brought them up to speed on what had happened over the weekend, though the only real progress had been pulling Jordan Fellowes in, and even that had been pretty much a non-event.

"No news of Zara Opray?" Josh asked when he'd finished.

He shook his head.

"None. We're going to give it another twenty-four hours, and if there's no sign of her by tomorrow morning, we're going to have to make waves, even though it might mean Mr Killjoy picking up on what we're up to. Pete's working out of Portishead today, looking into Charlie Wallace's rumoured wealth, and has promised to let me know if there are any developments concerning Zara."

"Is there anything we can do in the meantime?" Helen asked.

"Most definitely." He turned to Maj. "Maj, please can you head over to Portishead? Philip Angler's there and I want the two of you to see if you can find anything more on Zara Opray's laptop. Also, please work with him to research ByteIt. I want to know about the component services, how they're marketed and sold, and, if possible, details of any subscribers you can track down. Speak to Rufus Brent. It could be that we need him to use his contacts at GCHQ."

"Will do."

Luke turned to the two female members of the team.

"Helen and Sam, I want you to find a reason to speak to Naomi Simmons, both of you together if possible. It doesn't look like she's our culprit, but if Fellowes was telling the truth, she and Zara are close friends. Try to assess what she thinks might have happened, and get her views on her male colleagues while you're at it."

Both women agreed to this.

Josh's arm shot up.

"What about me, guv?"

Luke smiled.

"I was coming to that. You're a vital member of the team, Josh, and I want you to ensure the rest of us have refreshments when we need them. Doughnuts mid-morning would be good as well."

Josh's eyes widened, and his mouth started to open and close. This made him resemble nothing less than a whale searching for plankton.

"Ach, you're a gullible wee soul," Helen said with a smile.

Luke grinned.

"I want you to speak to the Pickfords again, Josh. Sam managed to find out a lot from Jack's younger sister, but there may be something she omitted to mention, so you need to probe as much as you can. When you've done that, see if you can get any more out of Jack's friend, the one who also fell for the AI-generated woman. Isaac wasn't it?"

"That's right. Isaac Staples."

"Ask him more about her, and the nature of their conversations. It might give us a clue as to who these sextortionists are."

"Gotcha, guv."

"Good. As for me, I'm going to speak to Arwyn. He'll be at Filcher's Monday morning meeting, so it's an ideal opportunity. I believe that Fellowes was telling the truth about his cocaine use, and I'm going to use that to try and suss whether there's any chance he's Mr Killjoy. I'll also try to get his views on Naomi, Miles, Jordan, Charlie and, for that matter, Zara."

Chapter 57

Luke was pleased to see Leanne sitting behind the reception desk in the small atrium at 25, Gay Street.

"Morning, Leanne. How was the wedding fair?"

She smiled.

"It was good, thanks. Gave me lots of ideas." She lowered her voice. "How come you're here? Josh told me you were basing yourselves at Ambrose's."

"We are, but I'm here for my boss's Monday meeting. Is he in?"

She laughed.

"What is it?"

"He's in, but he's not a happy bunny."

Before Luke could ask why, the man in question appeared at the bottom of the stairs.

"Ah, Luke. What time do you call this?"

Luke glanced at the clock behind Leanne's desk.

"9:20, Mr Filcher."

This earned him a scowl and a harrumph, and then Filcher turned his attention to Leanne.

"Have you sorted it out, Rheanne?"

"It's Leanne," Luke corrected.

"Is it?" Filcher shot his head left, then right. "Where?"

"My name's Leanne," Leanne said.

"I'm sure it is, but that's irrelevant. I need an office. My own office. I can't share. Much of my work is private and personal. Confidential." He tapped the side of his nose. "Secret."

"We're strapped for space, Mr Filcher, and Ambrose has insisted that an office isn't needed for anyone."

"Has he? Has he, indeed? Well, of course. He's right. Always right. No. I shall be noble and make do. In the interests of... " He looked like he was going to bow as he added, "...of our eminent chief executive."

"Mornin', Luke."

Luke turned to see Fred Tanner and Arwyn Thomas.

"Hi, Fred. Hi, Arwyn."

Filcher tapped his watch and glared at Fred.

"What time do you call this?"

"Probably needs a battery," Fred replied, nodding his head towards Filcher's wrist. "Or winding. Depends how old it is."

"Eh?"

"Good morning, Mr Filcher," Arwyn said. "I'm looking forward to this morning's meeting with great enthusiasm. Are we holding it in your office?"

"My office! Hah!"

"Sore point," Luke said.

Filcher grunted.

"We're in an 'open area'." He said these last two words as if there was a bad smell associated with them. "And no lift! Did you hear me? Not even a lift!"

"It's only on the first floor, in't it?" Fred said.

This earned him another grunt, followed by an immediate about-face as Filcher marched towards the stairs.

Fred and Luke exchanged a look, and then the three men followed their boss to the first floor.

The 'open area' he'd referred to had only four desks, two of which were occupied by James and Glen, while Gloria had the third, opposite a fourth on which was a brass sign reading 'Edward Filcher MA (Oxon)'.

"I see you rescued t't sign," Fred said, pointing to it.

"Gloria," Filcher said, ignoring this. "Arrangement!"

"Arrangement?"

"Yes. There are six of us. We need an arrangement. Me at the head. Subordinates..." He waved his hand in the general direction of Luke and the others. "...at my feet."

"As if you were a Maharishi?" Fred suggested.

"Yes. We need chairs. And an arrangement."

"I'll get right on it, Mr Filcher," Gloria said

"I'll help," James said. "I think there are some spare chairs on the floor above."

Luke saw this as his opportunity.

"Arwyn, while they're doing that, could I have a word?"

"Of course."

Glen overheard this.

"You're welcome to sit here. I'll help James and Gloria with the chairs."

"Thanks," Luke said.

He took Glen's seat, and Arwyn sat opposite. Filcher and Fred were in the corner of the room, deep in discussion, but Luke knew this was as private as it was going to get. He also knew that he wouldn't have much time before Gloria and the others returned.

"What is it?" Arwyn said, and sniffed then brushed his knuckle against the bottom of his nose. He was fidgeting in his seat, and somehow it suddenly seemed all too obvious why he was doing these things. Luke was surprised and disappointed that he hadn't put two and two together before.

He decided to go straight for the jugular, and leaned forward across the desk.

"Arwyn," he whispered, "I know."

The Head of IT feigned ignorance, but Luke could see in his eyes that he was worried.

"Know what? I don't understand."

"I know you buy cocaine in large quantities, too much for personal use."

"No…" He swallowed. "That's not true."

"That makes you a dealer, Arwyn. Supplying others with a class A drug could earn you a life sentence."

Arwyn's eyes widened. He didn't say a word, but his expression told Luke that Jordan Fellowes had been telling the truth, or at least that he had been when it came to

Arwyn's drug use.

He decided to push home while he had the advantage.

"ByteIt," he whispered, watching the other man carefully as he said it.

The only reaction was one of surprise and confusion. The term meant nothing to him, Luke was sure of it, but he wanted to be doubly certain.

"ByteIt," he repeated.

Arwyn frowned.

"What?"

There it was again. Complete ignorance of what was meant by the term.

Luke had heard enough.

"It's what the wolves will say to you inside."

"The wolves?"

"The hard men, the prisoners who hold power through intimidation and violence. That's what they'll say when they threaten to rape you."

"How's it going, guys?" Glen said, all teeth and bonhomie.

"Can you leave us for a moment please, Glen?" Luke asked. "We're having a private conversation."

Glen held both hands up.

"Sure." He grinned. "If you're having intimate relations, I'll get out of your way."

He headed off towards the stairs.

"How did you know?" Arwyn hissed, once Glen was out of earshot.

"That doesn't matter."

"I don't deal. I buy it for my friends."

"And they don't pay you for it?"

"Of course they pay me for it, but I don't make anything. I pass on the costs, that's all. That's the truth. I swear on my mother's grave."

Luke didn't say anything.

"You're ex-police, aren't you?"

"Yes."

Arwyn swallowed.

"Are you going to turn me in?"

"Arwyn, do you admit you have an addiction?"

"No. It's recreational, that's all."

Luke looked the other man in the eyes.

"Is it?"

Arwyn sighed, and Luke saw this as a good sign. The man knew he was having problems, and that was always the first step.

"I want you to do two things for me, Arwyn. If you do, I won't take this any further."

"Anything."

"First, I want you to sign up for rehab. I can provide you with contacts to help with that."

"Okay."

"And second, I want you to tell me everything you know about five people in your department."

"What? I don't understand. Why?"

"It's for a case I'm working on, but the fact that I've asked you about them has to remain between the two of us. If word of this conversation gets out, I won't hesitate to take what I know about you to the police. Is that clear?"

"Abundantly."

"Good. The five people in question are Naomi Simmons, Zara Opray, Jordan Fellowes, Miles Barrington and Charlie Wallace."

"Ho, ho, I'm back," Glen said. "Have you completed intercourse?"

He was carrying a chair, and James was behind him with a second.

"Let's continue this discussion after the meeting, Arwyn," Luke said. "We need somewhere with more privacy."

Chapter 58

Josh headed straight for the intensive care unit when he arrived at the Royal United Hospital, but when he turned off the main corridor, he almost collided with Larry Pickford.

Jack's father was pacing backwards and forwards, and mumbling to himself.

"Larry, are you okay?"

The other man glanced up, and Josh was shocked to see how pale he was. If anything, he was even more wretched-looking than he had been the week before.

"It's Jack." Larry shook his head. "It's not looking good. He's…"

"Dad! Dad!"

Both Josh and Larry turned as Amelia emerged from the side corridor that led to the ICU.

She was smiling.

"He's coming around."

Larry looked shocked.

"But I thought…"

"Come quickly. See for yourself."

She turned and returned the way she had come. Larry ran after her and, after a moment's hesitation, Josh followed.

Amelia pushed open the door to Jack's room, and they went inside to find a nurse checking one of the drips, while a female doctor was making notes on a clipboard. Jack's eyes were closed, but a second later they slowly opened, and a glimmer of a smile appeared on his lips as he saw his father.

The doctor looked up.

"What's happened, Dr Khan?" Larry asked. "He was

shaking. I thought…"

"When coma patients regain consciousness, they are often agitated. Jack's shaking was temporary, and it lasted for less than a minute."

"Is he…" He swallowed. "Is he going to make a full recovery?"

"It's too early to be absolutely certain, and you may find he's confused initially. However, he asked after you and his mother while your daughter was fetching you, and that's a good sign."

Larry moved to his son's side, grasped his hand and gave it a gentle squeeze.

"It's good to have you back, son."

Jack's voice was weak and croaky, but he managed to whisper, "Sorry, Dad."

"Don't talk nonsense."

"You're welcome to stay, Mr Pickford," Dr Khan said, "but please be careful not to tire Jack out."

"What happens next?"

"We'll continue to monitor him for the time being but, all being well, he'll be transferred to a ward later today."

"Thank you, Doctor."

Larry pulled up a chair, and Josh saw his opportunity.

He tapped Amelia on the shoulder.

"Could we have a word?"

She seemed to spot him for the first time and narrowed her eyebrows.

"Who are you? Are you one of Jack's school friends?"

"No, I work with Sam Chambers. I've got a few more questions…" He smiled. "…and I believe you like coffee and walnut cake."

She turned to her father.

"Do you mind if I leave you, Dad?"

He answered without looking up.

"No. You go."

Josh led the way to the Atrium Cafe where he bought a

slice of coffee and walnut cake for each of them, a Diet Coke for Amelia, and a luxury hot chocolate for himself.

"I told Sam everything I know," Amelia said, once they'd found a table.

"You think you did, but did you?" He raised one eyebrow as he said this, but all he succeeded in doing was make Amelia laugh.

"What is it?" he said, his voice slightly higher-pitched than normal.

"You trying to be serious, when you've got cream all over your top lip."

"Have I?"

He picked up a paper napkin and cleaned himself up.

"Dad told me about Matilda."

Josh shivered as the memory came back to him.

"He said it was your pet. That thing! A pet!"

"Before I had Matilda, there was Bruce."

"What was he? A tarantula?"

She nodded, held both hands up and curved her index fingers and thumbs to form a circle about seven inches in diameter.

"He was this big."

"Please tell me you're joking?"

She shook her head. "And before him…"

He held his hand up to stop her.

"No. I don't want to know."

He pushed his coffee and walnut cake away, looked at it for a moment, then his stomach's desire outweighed his brain's distress, and he pulled it back towards him and stuck his fork in.

"Kwame Nkrumah," Amelia said.

"Bless you."

She smiled.

"I wasn't sneezing."

"What then?"

"It's a place." She hesitated. "Or a name. It might even

be both. Dad was beginning to tell me about it when Jack started waving his arms around like a mad thing. The doctors were rushing around, and we thought it was bad news. We didn't realise it was actually a good sign. It's such a relief. Oh!"

"What?"

"I need to ring Mum and tell her. She's staying with my Aunty, because she's been finding it all too much."

She pulled her phone out and started keying a number in.

"But what about this Kwame N-whatsit?"

Amelia hit the green button on her phone.

"Dad knows the… Oh, Mum, good news…"

Josh continued with his cake, successfully blocking thoughts of green insects and over-sized arachnids from ruining his enjoyment, while Amelia told her mother about Jack recovering consciousness.

After a couple of minutes, she said goodbye and ended the call.

"Kwame N- thingy?" he prompted.

"Kwame Nkrumah. Dad knows the details. I'll take his place and ask him to come out and explain." She stood up, then turned back again. "There's something else you ought to know."

"What's that?"

"My dad also likes coffee and walnut cake."

*

Josh was halfway through a slice of lemon cheesecake when Larry appeared.

He looked ten years younger and was smiling.

"How is he, Larry?"

"Sleepy, but gradually getting more and more with it." He sighed, but the sigh was accompanied by the glimmer of a smile. "It's a massive relief."

Josh gestured to the table.

"I bought you some coffee and walnut cake."

"Coffee and walnut cake? That's good of you, but I can't, I'm afraid. I'm allergic to nuts. I can take it for Amelia, though."

Crafty little madam, Josh thought.

"Larry, Amelia mentioned a Kwame something-or-other. What is it?"

"Ah, she told you that, did she? Kwame Nkrumah was Prime Minister of Ghana back in the 1950s."

"I don't get it. What's that got to do with anything?"

"I'm not sure it helps you much, but I did what you suggested and spoke to the bank about the £500 that Jack transferred. They were very helpful, and provided me with the beneficiary's sort code and account number. They couldn't tell me whose name the account is in, though, and said that the Republic Bank wouldn't reveal it either because of data privacy regulations."

"The Republic Bank?"

"Yes, the account is with the Central Branch of the Republic Bank. The address is 31 Kwame Nkrumah Avenue in Accra, the capital of Ghana."

Chapter 59

Maj entered his details into the visitor's book at Avon and Somerset Police HQ, and the receptionist rang through to Pete Gilmore, who came down a couple of minutes later.

"I've booked a meeting room," he said, as they made their way to the lift. "It's not a formal incident room, but it's better than nothing."

Philip Angler looked up when they walked in.

"Good news, guys. I may have found something useful on Zara Opray's laptop."

"What is it?" Pete asked.

"It's a zip file and it's called '*drafts-for-bit*'. With any luck, 'bit' is her way of referencing ByteIt. The only problem is that it's password-protected."

"Can you use Python to unlock it?" Maj asked.

"Hopefully, yes. I've already downloaded tqdm, and I've located a document with the top 10,000 passwords."

"Do you need my help to create a script with true-false clauses?"

"No. I should be fine."

"Great."

Maj pulled his laptop out of his briefcase and sat at the table opposite Philip.

"I'm going to use Tor to see if I can access ByteIt on the dark web. Luke asked me to try to find out as much as I can about ChatIt, PayIt and the rest."

Pete, whose head had been switching left and right, and who was now in a state of total confusion, held one hand up.

"Is it okay if I leave you two to it. I don't think I can add anything." He smiled. "Especially since I didn't understand a word of that conversation about pythons and clauses. I'll head back upstairs and give Rufus a call at the NCCU. He may be able to give me a hand finding details of ByteIt subscribers."

"Okay," Maj said. "We'll ring if we find anything useful."

He opened his laptop, connected to wifi, loaded the Tor browser and entered his first search parameters.

*

Pete managed to find a hot desk on the second floor, and was about to call the NCCU investigator when his phone rang.

It was Josh.

"Hi, Josh."

"Hi, Pete. Luke said I should ring you. Do you remember that Jack Pickford transferred £500, which we think was to the sextortionists?"

"Yes, I remember."

"I've got the destination sort code and account number. It's an account with the Republic Bank in Ghana."

"Ghana!"

"Uh-huh. Can you try to get the bank to reveal the name on the account?"

"I'll give it my best shot. What are the details?"

Pete wrote the account details in his notebook as Josh read them out.

He hung up, and considered his best course of action. After a few moments thought, he rang Rufus Brent, who picked up straight away."

"Hi, Rufus. It's Pete here, Pete Gilmore."

"Hi, Pete."

"I'm ringing for two reasons. First, the Interpol National Crime Bureau for the UK is also part of the National Crime Agency, isn't it?"

"Yes, the NCB is a sister organisation and it's based in Manchester. Why?"

"We believe the people who blackmailed Jack Pickford are operating out of Ghana, and I need Interpol's help to track them down."

"Okay, the best person for you to speak to is Crystal Haney, whose main focus is cybercrime. I've dealt with her a couple of times, and she's very responsive. I'll text you her contact details."

"Thanks."

"What was the other thing?"

"I'm not sure whether you can help, but we're trying to find out the names of any subscribers to ByteIt's component services. I've had no joy looking on the PNC."

"We've got an internal database which I can search. I'll ask around the team too."

"Great. Cheers, Rufus."

Pete hung up, and a few seconds later his phone pinged as Rufus's text came through.

He rang the NCB investigator.

"Hello. This is Crystal Haney."

"Hi, Crystal. I was given your details by Rufus Brent in the NCCU. I'm DI Pete Gilmore, and I'm hoping you can help."

He explained about Jack Pickford's attempted suicide, and what was needed.

"I'll do what I can," she said when he'd finished. "It's the first time I've worked with the Ghana NCB, but I've worked with the police in Nigeria a few times, and they've been very helpful."

"On similar cases?"

"Simple phishing scams in the main, although one a couple of months ago was much like yours. The criminal was working out of his apartment in Lagos, and blackmailed a man in Scunthorpe. However, the idiot somehow managed to insert his home address into one of his messages, and that's when the victim went to the police." She laughed. "Not the brightest by all accounts, but he'd managed to obtain money from at least a dozen people, a few in the UK but the majority in the States. There was no way he could have done it without help, but we haven't been able to trace the person who developed the software for him, and he's staying quiet on it."

"That's interesting. What I didn't tell you is that there's a possibility that these cybercriminals in Ghana are using a subscription service, a service that's part of a wider offering created by a person calling themselves Mr Killjoy. That's what I'm working on with Rufus."

He gave her the full details on ByteIT, and told her that they believed Mr Killjoy to be one of five, possibly six, Filcher employees, and that he or she was likely to have started the fire that killed three people.

"I see what you're getting at," she said when he'd finished. "The sextortionist is on remand in a prison in Lagos awaiting trial. I'll speak to the Nigerian NCB and see if the police can ask him a few pertinent questions."

"Thanks, Crystal."

Chapter 60

Misty watched as a young man pointed at her, before nudging the girl beside him.

He was laughing, but she gave him a look that would have made Hannibal Lecter back off, and he swallowed, turned, and practically sprinted away, dragging his confused friend with him.

She checked that the pink carnation was still secure over the top of her left ear, though she knew it had to be given the guy's reaction, and watched as the London train pulled into platform 2.

A few seconds later, a mass of people descended from the carriages and made their way in her direction. She'd never met Mandy, hence the flower, and found herself looking closely at every young woman she saw.

She was trying to catch the eye of a likely-looking executive-type, who was dipping her hands into an open briefcase, when she felt a tap on her shoulder, and swung around to find a woman in her early twenties with long brown hair staring up at her and smiling.

"Are you Misty?"

Misty looked her in the eyes, then up and down.

"Fucking Nora, Josh didn't say you were harbouring a fugitive."

"A what?"

Misty pointed to Mandy's belly.

"I'm not a private detective for nothing. You've got a Joey in the pouch, and one that's close to fucking escape by the look of it."

Mandy laughed.

"I'm nearly seven months."

"Well, good on you. Wait there a second."

She walked to a nearby bin, dropped the flower in, and then returned and offered her hand.

"Pleased to get rid of that. Flora isn't my style. Great to meet you, Mandy."

They shook hands.

"Good to meet you, too. I gather you caught up with Terry Lawson."

"Too fucking right. He's in The Cornubia, and I told him what I'd do to his knackers if he wasn't there when I got back. It's a great pub, if a little rough, but then, rough pretty much describes Terry, so it's a good fit. They have a mean range of real ales too, but I guess with being up the duff, you're not drinking?"

"No. Not at present."

"Very fucking sensible. Let's head there now. It's less than a five-minute walk."

True to her word, five minutes later, Misty pushed open the door of the pub, and led the way to a secluded table on the right, where her quarry was chewing on gum, a half-drunk pint of beer on the table in front of him.

He looked up and grinned, displaying four or five browny-yellow teeth on the bottom row, and only two on the top, with a good inch or more between them.

"All right, Misty?" he said, his accent pure Bristol. "Who's your friend?"

"This is Mandy."

He lifted a nicotine-stained hand in acknowledgement.

"Hi, Mandy." He pointed to her stomach, then turned back to Misty. "Is she pregnant?"

"What sort of stupid fucking comment is that, Terry?"

"I'm being polite, that's all. She might be fat, for all I know."

"Fucks' sake." She sighed. "Mandy, grab a seat opposite the brain of Britain here, and I'll get us some drinks. What will you have?"

"Another IPA for me," Terry said.

"I wasn't asking you, numbnuts."

"I'll have a sparkling water, please," Mandy said.

Misty fetched the drinks, and returned to find Terry staring at Mandy's belly as if The Alien was about to tear through it and go for his throat.

"What's up?" Misty said. "You never seen a pregnant woman before?"

"Course I have, but I'd forgotten how big they get."

"I've still got two months to go," Mandy said.

"Buggering hell."

"Terry, watch your fucking language."

"Sorry, Misty." He took a sip of his beer. "What's this all about, then?"

"You haven't told him?" Mandy asked.

"No. I thought it would be more fun to do it when you were here."

"You after some intel," Terry said, and grinned again. "Cos it's gonna cost ya."

"No, Terry," Misty said. "It's gonna cost *you*. Five years would be my guess."

His grin vanished and was replaced by a vacant look.

"Five years of what?"

"Prison, Terry."

"What? But…"

"How much do you know about QR codes?"

His eyes widened, and he started to open and close his mouth. After a few seconds, he shut it tight, swallowed, looked at Mandy and then back at Misty.

"Well, Terry?" Misty prompted. "What have you got to say for yourself?"

He turned to Mandy.

"Are you in the police?"

"No, but I found out all about your scam with the fake QR codes in the car parks."

He shook his head violently.

"Wasn't me. You've got the wrong man. I've never been

to Wandsworth."

"Wandsworth?" Misty said.

"Yeah." He hesitated as he realised what he'd said. "Or wherever it is. I've never been there." He swallowed again. "Wherever it is."

"I've got CCTV footage," Mandy said. "It shows you sticking the fake QR codes over the real ones."

He bent forward and started banging his forehead against the top of the table.

"Fuck! Fuck! Fuck!"

"Language!" Misty said. "What did I tell you?"

He lifted his head.

"What do you want?"

"We want to help you, Terry. Five years is a long time, but it could be a lot worse."

She turned to Mandy.

"What's the sentence for accessory to murder, Mandy?"

"Life, with a minimum term of thirty years."

Terry looked at her in shock.

"Thirty years! That'd mean when I got out, I'd be sixty, ah…. Or is it seventy, ah…"

"How old are you?" Misty asked.

"Fifty-two."

"Then you'd be eighty-two."

"Eighty-two!"

"Or dead. More likely dead."

"F…"

She wagged a finger and he stopped mid-expletive, then a thought occurred to him.

"Hang on. I stuck some codes up, but no one got killed. I haven't accessorised anyone."

"This isn't about you giving anyone a fucking handbag and jewellery to go with their designer dress, Terry."

"What?"

Misty sighed.

"I'll take this slowly, and even then I can see it's going

to be hard work."

"What is?"

"Shut up and listen. If you help us, we can help you, possibly even keep the police out of it…"

"You can?"

"Possibly, I said, but you have to be honest with us. You're nothing but plankton, and we've got much bigger fish to fry."

He furrowed his brows.

"Fish?"

She ignored this.

"Are you going to tell the truth?"

He nodded.

"Yeah. Definitely."

"Okay. First question. How did you obtain the QR codes?"

"Through something called ByteIt. It's got a load of services in it, but the one I used is PhishIt. He hesitated. "Oh, is that what you meant by 'bigger fish to fry'?"

"No, Terry, it fucking isn't. Now, pay attention. How did you hear about ByteIT?"

"A mate told me. He and I have done things together before. You know, ah… things. Anyway, he said it was easy money. He installed this thing called Tor on my PC."

"That's the browser?"

He shrugged.

"Could be. This Tor thing allows me to access the black web, and…"

"You mean the dark web."

"Yeah, that's it. The dark web. And he showed me how to get to ByteIt and, after they'd checked me out, I was able to sign up for PhishIt."

"Checked you out?"

"Yeah. I had to provide details of my convictions. Get this, though. PhishIt isn't free. I have to pay."

He was evidently appalled by the unfairness of this.

"How does it work?"

"It's easy. Even an idiot could use it."

"You're living proof of that, Terry."

"Thanks." He took a sip of his beer. "I had to provide my bank account details, then answer questions about the target. Stuff like the name of the business, the nature of the operation, and the value of the payments. All I had to do after that was print the QR thingies and stick 'em up, then wait for the money to arrive."

"Smooth as silk, then?"

"Yeah, apart from the ads."

"The ads?"

"Yeah. I'd be trying to key something in, and this little purple cartoon devil would pop up, congratulate me on my purchase, and ask if I'd considered other ByteIt services. And I couldn't turn it off, or continue what I was doing, until he'd finished speaking."

"He?"

"Yeah. The devil called himself Mr Killjoy."

Chapter 61

Luke was on his own in Ambrose's cinema room, staring at the whiteboard, trying to take everything in.

Had he missed something vital?

Was the answer up there somewhere, staring him in the face?

After a few minutes thought, he stood up, put a red 'X' through Arwyn's name, then sat back down again.

His conversation with the Head of IT had been something and nothing. He'd enjoyed rubbishing his team, that much was clear, but hadn't said anything that implicated any one of them more than the others. They'd already known Charlie was wealthy, Miles was full of himself, and Jordan had a chip on his shoulder. As for Naomi, Arwyn had said that he'd resisted her advances, but Luke strongly suspected it had been the other way around.

As far as he was concerned, there were now three main suspects: Charlie Wallace, Miles Barrington and Jordan Fellowes. He wasn't ready to completely rule out Naomi Simmons or Zara Opray as being Mr Killjoy, but in his mind they were a long shot.

And if Zara wasn't the main villain, she had to have been working alongside him or her. She was close to Naomi, but was Naomi really the stuff that arch cybercriminals were made of? He thought not, but Sam and Helen had arranged to see her and, with any luck, that meeting would confirm it one way or the other.

Hopefully, that meeting would also throw up some clues as to where Zara might have gone, if she'd done so voluntarily. That was still the most likely scenario, he felt. She must have realised that she'd left incriminating evidence on her laptop, which had been left behind after the fire, and decided to make a run for it.

The alternative was more scary.

If Mr Killjoy had discovered what she'd done, and feared that she might give him away, he may well have taken her. If that was the case, it was unlikely she was a prisoner. He'd already proved himself to be cold and ruthless with what he had done to Dominic Watts, not to mention the two others who had died in the fire. No, if Mr Killjoy had taken her, she would be in a shallow grave or at the bottom of a river now, he was sure of it.

His phone rang, and he looked down to see it was Pete.

"Hi, Pete."

"Hi. No sign of Zara Opray, but I have got a couple of updates for you."

"Good news or bad news?"

"A bit of both."

"Go on, then. Hit me with the good news first."

"There's been progress with the guys who extorted money from Jack Pickford. Josh rang me to say that Jack's father had found out their bank account details. They're based in Ghana. I spoke to Crystal Haney at Interpol, and she's on the case to try to find the name of the account holder. She also said that they'd had a similar case with a Nigerian extortionist who's on remand awaiting trial, so she's going to see if the local police can question him to see if he was using ByteIt."

"That's good work. Did she say how quickly she'd be able to get answers?"

"She's hoping in a day or so."

"Okay. What's the bad news?"

"I've done everything I can to try to find out where Charlie Wallace's wealth has come from, but so far I've drawn a blank. There are regular large payments into his personal account, but they're from a Swiss bank, and you know what that means."

"I do indeed. Getting information from the Swiss is like

getting blood from a stone." He paused. "The fact that he's being transferred money from a Swiss bank account is telling in itself, though."

"That's what I thought. Do you think we should get him in for questioning?"

"Not yet. We said we'd give it until the end of today, to allow more time for Zara Opray to be found. Let's leave it at that. Sam and Helen are seeing Naomi Simmons this afternoon. That might throw up some clues as to her whereabouts."

"Fair enough. Excuse me a moment, Luke."

After a few seconds, Pete came back on the line.

"Maj is here. He and Philip have found something on Zara Opray's laptop. I'll ring you back in a couple of minutes."

True to his word, he rang back two or three minutes later.

"You're on speaker, Luke. I'm back in the meeting room with Maj and Philip."

"I gather you've found something, guys."

"We found a zip file called '*drafts-for-bit*,'" Maj said, "and managed to crack the password. It contains two files. One is a draft home page for ChatIt, which doesn't tell us much, but the other one is a video, and it's very revealing. Do you want to read what's written at the bottom, Philip?"

"Sure. The words scroll across as the video runs. Hang on, and I'll press play."

Philip went silent for a couple of seconds, then started reading from the screen.

"Do you want to earn thousands from a simple conference call? FakeIt is the latest product from the people who brought you PayIt and SexIt. Click below to find out more."

"It's the video itself that's particularly interesting, Luke," Maj said. "It shows a Zoom call between three AI-generated people, and they're talking about a funds transfer.

Mr Killjoy

In the bottom right of each of the participants' video feeds, it says 'Hugger'."

"Wasn't that the name of Stairway's product?"

"That's what I thought."

"What's Stairway?" Pete asked.

"It's a high-tech company, one of Filchers' clients. Hugger is one of their products, and creates videos of real people using artificial intelligence."

"Do you think that's the company behind ByteIt?"

"No, I suspect that Mr Killjoy is using it without Stairway knowing. My team, or more precisely Sam, helped the Chief Executive, a man called Sebastian Thatcher, when he became embroiled in something a couple of months ago. From what she's told me, I don't imagine for a moment that he's involved in anything criminal. I'll give her a ring and get her to talk to him. Good work, guys."

He ended the call, but his phone rang again before he had the chance to retrieve Sam's number.

It was Misty.

"Hi there, Goliath. I've got sign-in details for you."

"For ByteIt?"

"No, for Tinder. Of course, for fucking ByteIT."

"I take it this is from Terry Lawson."

"It is indeed."

"Great. Can you text them to me, please? I'll pass them on to Maj and Philip and see if they can find out anything useful."

"Will do."

He hung up, forwarded Misty's text as soon as it came through, then called Sam.

"Hi, Sam."

"Hi. I'm with Helen. We're on our way to Walcot House to meet Naomi."

"When you get a chance, can you ring Sebastian at Stairway? Maj and Philip managed to access a mock-up FakeIt ad on Zara Opray's laptop, and the videos had

'Hugger' in the corner."

"That's intriguing. It suggests they're using his code, but I wonder how they got hold of it. I'll call him as soon as we leave the cafe."

"Thanks. Good luck with Naomi."

Chapter 62

Luke sighed.

On the face of it, they were making progress, and it was good to have new avenues of enquiry too. In many ways, it seemed like they were close to a breakthrough, yet he had the feeling that Mr Killjoy was running rings around them.

Had he missed something obvious?

Was the answer already staring him in the face?

He stood up and walked over to the whiteboard. Most of it was covered in names, events, dates, and any number of connecting lines, but there was a portion at the bottom left that still hadn't been written on.

Using a red marker, he started to list the primary pieces of evidence. His gut told him that one of these was key to solving the mystery.

One, Charlie Wallace had large amounts transferred to him from a Swiss bank account.

Two, the sextortionists were based in Ghana.

Three, Hugger was used in an advert for FakeIt.

Four, Zara Opray, now missing, had ByteIt software on her laptop.

He stood back and shook his head.

Was that really all they had?

Aside from Zara Opray, the only other person implicated by those pieces of evidence was Charlie Wallace, and that was circumstantial at best.

He decided that a blast of fresh air would do him good. Walking helped him to think more creatively, and that was what was needed. He needed to clear his head and consider every little detail. Experience had taught him that the answer might well be hidden in the minutiae of the investigation.

Luke took one last look at the whiteboard, and then headed outside, deciding he'd walk from The Circus to The Royal Crescent, then make his way down Marlborough Buildings before returning to Ambrose's through Victoria Park.

He might even stop at the Royal Crescent Hotel and grab an espresso.

Make that a double espresso.

As he left the Circus and turned onto Brock Street, he found his mind turning to the primary suspects.

It was unfortunate that they hadn't yet been able to formally question them, but they'd had to delay it for fear of what might happen to Zara. There had been those brief discussions that Maj had had with the three men, and Sam with the two women, but they hadn't been able to cover much ground.

He stopped in his tracks.

There was one area which *had* been discussed.

That was it.

It had to be.

He pulled out his phone and resumed walking as he called Pete.

"Pete, did we ever get the report back from the Chief Fire Officer?"

"Yes, it came in a couple of hours ago, but I haven't had the chance to look at it yet."

"Could you email it to me, please? There's something I want to check."

"Sure. I'll send it now."

Luke kept his phone in his hand, tapping his fingers impatiently on the screen, and almost jumped when two short beeps announced the email's arrival.

He stepped to one side of the pavement, opened the attachment, quickly read the summary, then dived into the detail.

It was illuminating in more ways than one.

He nodded to himself.

Yes!

They'd got him, he was sure of it. There was a chance it was a coincidence, that what had been said was an off-the-cuff remark that meant nothing, but he didn't believe for one moment that that was the case.

Mr Killjoy had given himself away.

There was no need now to wait until the end of the day. The cybercriminal had to be arrested as soon as possible and brought in for questioning. He had Zara Opray, and they needed to find out where he was keeping her as soon as possible.

He was about to ring Pete when he felt something jab into the base of his spine, and he knew instantly what it was.

The next hissed words confirmed it.

"Get in the van or you're dead."

Chapter 63

Sam and Helen reached Walcot House ten minutes before the time they had arranged to meet Naomi Simmons, and Sam was surprised to see that she had arrived before them.

"She's over there," she whispered, indicating a table near the window as she turned her phone to silent.

"I'll get the drinks. Do you want to go over and say hello?"

"Will do."

Sam walked to the table where Naomi was busy touching up her lips, using a small mirror to ensure it was being applied perfectly, and pursing her lips together every now and then to prevent it from smudging.

"Hi, Naomi," Sam said. "Is it all right if I join you?"

"Yeah."

She didn't look up as she said this, and continued applying the lip gloss for a few seconds more before nodding in approval, folding the mirror up, and dropping it and the stick of gloss into her handbag.

She looked at Sam for the first time.

"I thought you were coming with someone?"

"I am. She's getting drinks."

"Good. Lemonade for me."

She said this just as Helen arrived.

"Naomi wouldn't mind a lemonade, if that's okay, Helen?" Sam said.

"Slimline," Naomi said, then glanced at Sam's midriff before adding, "Some of us are careful what we have."

Sam was startled by the blatant rudeness of this. She wasn't personally offended and knew that she wasn't carrying any extra weight, but acting in that way spoke volumes about the woman's nasty nature.

She decided it was best to ignore what she had said and smiled.

"Thanks for seeing us."

Naomi shrugged, but didn't say anything.

"Ah, here's your drink."

Helen passed the lemonade to Naomi, who took the glass in her hand and stared at it for a moment.

"Are you sure this is slimline?"

"Yes. I watched her pour it."

Naomi sniffed haughtily, and took a sip as Helen sat down.

"Naomi, this is Helen," Sam said. "She and I work together."

Naomi looked over at Helen.

"I'm surprised you're not retired. Must be tiring working at your age."

Helen took the same approach as Sam and simply smiled.

"As I said on the phone," Sam said, "we're becoming increasingly worried about Zara."

"Yeah, but I don't understand why it's you asking me questions, and not the police. You're in support services, aren't you? It doesn't make sense, asking admin assistants to look for a missing person."

That was three jibes already.

She really was the most unpleasant woman.

Sam smiled again, even though she knew it wouldn't be returned.

"It's a special favour. Our boss used to be in the police, who are working like mad to find her, but they're short of resources with all the budget cutbacks. They asked Luke if he could do anything to help, and he roped us in."

"Right."

"I gather you and Zara are close friends."

"We go out together from time to time. Not bosom buddies, but she's okay." She raised one eyebrow. "Did you say your boss's name is Luke?"

"That's right."

"Luke Sackville, from Essex?"

"Ethics. He heads up the Ethics Team."

"Whatever. Yeah, Arwyn was telling us about him, sticking his nose in and all."

"Sticking his nose in?"

"Yeah, although it might just be Arwyn talking crap as usual, and showing off that he knows more than we do."

"What do you mean?"

"He called us together, me, Miles, Charlie and Jordan. Started off talking about Zara, like you just did, acting worried and all, then he starts saying how we all want to be careful, because your boss is on the warpath, asking all sorts of questions."

"What sort of questions?"

"Where we were from, what our experience is, how skilled we are, that kind of thing. It didn't bother me, but I could see Charlie was getting irritated. Miles too. Then Jordan asked an odd question. He asked if your boss had been questioning Arwyn because of Charlie, and he had this odd, kind-of knowing, look on his face. Arwyn went a bit red, then said, *'No. Of course not.'*, but Charlie was furious. You should have seen him."

She smiled then, the first time this had happened. It seemed to Sam that, for Naomi, pleasure came from other people's discomfort.

"He turned on Arwyn and shouted at him, which isn't like Charlie at all. He demanded to know what he'd been asked, and was it about his financial situation, because that was his own business and no one else's. Furious, he was. I've never seen him like that."

"How did Jordan react?"

"He was watching everything pan out and seemed to be enjoying it."

As were you, I suspect, Sam thought.

"What about Miles?"

"He didn't say anything, which is unusual. He's very full of himself, and not usually short of something to say, but he was dead quiet."

"What did Arwyn say when Charlie challenged him?"

"He started backing down, saying he valued his staff and had refused to answer the questions. Started getting all creepy, like he does, telling Charlie what a valued member of the team he is. But we all know what he's like. He'll have told that Ethics guy anything to suck up."

Sam was becoming increasingly concerned about what Arwyn had done, and decided she needed to warn Luke.

"Please excuse me. I need to pop to the loo."

Naomi sniffed again, but didn't say anything, making it clear she didn't care either way.

"It would be useful," Helen said, "if you could tell me a little about Zara's interests. Her other friends, places she frequents, that kind of thing."

Sam left them to it.

She headed towards the ladies, checked Naomi wasn't watching, then veered off to the exit.

Once outside, she walked around the corner and pulled out her phone.

Unusually for Luke, his phone went straight to voicemail. She left a message asking him to ring her as soon as possible, then decided now was a good opportunity to ring Sebastian.

It was his personal assistant who answered.

"Hello, this is Jenny in Sebastian Thatcher's office. How may I help?"

"Jenny, hi. It's Sam, Sam Chambers."

"Hi, Sam. How are you?"

"I'm fine, thanks. Is Sebastian available?"

"He's in a board meeting. Shall I ask him to ring you when it's finished?"

"Yes, please."

She turned her phone off silent, not wanting to miss a call back from either Luke or Sebastian, then returned to Helen and Naomi.

Chapter 64

"WAKE UP!"

The shouted command was followed by a deluge as the bucket was emptied over Luke's head, and it was this that brought him back to consciousness. As he came to, the pain hit, and he instinctively put his hand to his left temple.

It came away covered in a mix of blood and water.

He sat upright and looked between blinking eyes at his captor, the man who had forced him into the van at gunpoint before knocking him out with a swipe of his pistol butt.

His head was throbbing, but he knew that he had to ignore the pain, had to fight through it, had to focus, had to find an inner strength.

His very survival depended on it.

It gave him little satisfaction that he had been right about the identity of Mr Killjoy. Five minutes more, and he would have been able to tell Pete. As it was, he was the only person who knew, and he had doubtless been driven to a remote location, somewhere where shouts couldn't be heard, where no one would come to his rescue.

A place where a person could readily be murdered and disposed of.

His captor had moved to the rear of the van. He was silhouetted by the light streaming in through the open doors, but his smile was visible, and it was clear that he was enjoying himself, gaining satisfaction from being in control, and from the power he had over his prisoner.

The gun was in his hand and pointed at Luke's face.

After a few seconds, he put the empty bucket down and picked up a set of handcuffs, and what looked to Luke like two heavy-duty bike chains.

"Shuffle round on your backside, put your arms behind your back and interlock your fingers."

He had a determined look on his face as he said this. There was also a coldness there, and a ruthlessness too. Luke needed to find a way to delay, to make the man believe he was making a mistake.

If he failed to do so, he didn't give much for his chances of making it through the day.

"We need to talk," he croaked, squeezing his eyes together in an attempt to put the agony of his head wound to the back of his mind.

"Are you attempting to delay the inevitable?"

"Where's…" Luke swallowed as he tried to force the words out. "Where's Zara?"

"Zara's at my house, in the basement to be precise. She's working hard, but not for long." He grinned. "Her days, like yours, are numbered."

"There's no need to…"

"SHUT IT! The time for talking is over." This was followed by an obscenely inappropriate wink, then he added, "It's action time, baby."

Mr Killjoy lowered his arm so that the gun was pointed at Luke's left knee.

"Any more delaying tactics, and I'll shoot. Do I make myself clear?"

He pulled back the slide on his semi-automatic and then released it to load a round into the chamber.

"Last chance, amigo."

Mr Killjoy's smile broadened, and there was something undeniably chilling about it.

Luke was left in no doubt that he would be shot in the leg if he didn't comply. He shuffled around as ordered, then interlaced his fingers behind his back.

As he did so, it dawned on him that this could be his only chance to get one over on the other man.

He had surprise on his side.

Mr Killjoy

Whether he had the strength to act was another thing, but he had to try.

He braced himself and drew in a deep breath.

It required two hands to cuff someone's wrists, which meant Mr Killjoy would have to put the gun down. If Luke timed his move right, he'd be able to swing around, raise his leg and kick out.

This was his opportunity to take the man by surprise, but he'd have to move quickly, and fight through his grogginess, through the pain in his head.

He held his breath and waited.

As anticipated, Mr Killjoy did put the gun down.

With force.

Into the back of Luke's skull.

Chapter 65

Pete wondered what it was in the Chief Fire Officer's report that Luke wanted to check.

He decided he had to find time to read it in the next hour, but the issue was finding time. This was a complex investigation, and he had several officers making discrete enquiries, trying to find out more about their suspects, and each one seemed to need to check back with him regularly.

Rufus Brent at the NCCU was also on the case, using his links at GCHQ to see if there was anything more that could be discovered from the intercepted email.

Meanwhile, Maj and Philip were focused on the ByteIt site itself. Thanks to Misty, they now had Terry Lawson's login details. Both men had been excited to receive them, having struggled to find a way past the website's identity checks which demanded proof of previous criminality.

Then there was Crystal Haney at Interpol, trying to find out more about the people in Ghana who were behind the blackmail of Jack Pickford, and also attempting to arrange to interview the extortionist who may have been using SexIt.

He was considering ringing her to see if she was making any progress, when one of his detectives called him over.

"What is it, Danny?"

"I found this, guv."

The young officer pointed to the screen.

"Charlie Wallace changed his name in 2016. Before that, he was Christopher Wendell."

"Mmm. He's kept the same initials, which is interesting. See if you can find out anything more. There's a possibility he has a criminal record."

"Will do."

Pete returned to his desk and rang Crystal.

"Crystal Haney."

"Hi, Crystal, it's Pete Gilmore."

"Pete, hi. I have to apologise. I'm snowed under, and I haven't had the opportunity to speak to anyone in Accra yet."

"Is there any chance you can do it today?"

"It's next on my list, so yes, definitely. Remember, though, that when I do get through to them, they'll have to contact the bank and then the local police regarding your extortionists, as well as arrange a time to interview the man on remand. It's not going to be a quick turnaround, and there's always the chance the bank won't reveal the account holder's name. We don't have a TIEA with Ghana, which doesn't help."

"TIEA?"

"A tax information exchange agreement. The UK has TIEAs in place with twenty-one countries, but they tend to be those used as tax havens."

A thought occurred to him.

"Such as the Bahamas?"

"Yes, that's a good example."

"Crystal, is the Bahamas a member of Interpol?"

"Yes." She paused. "Do I sense another request coming my way?"

"You do. Sorry, it's only just dawned on me that there's something else you may be able to help with."

"Is this a separate case?"

"No, we believe it's linked. There have been a series of fraudulent invoices within Filchers, which we know is the company that employs Mr Killjoy, and we suspect he's using it as a testing ground for a new subscription service."

"Is this another one where you want me to try to find the name on the beneficiary account?"

"You guessed it."

She laughed.

"You don't ask for much."

"Sorry, Crystal."

"Email me the account details and I'll add it to my to-do list."

"Thanks."

He hung up, and his thoughts returned to the Chief Officer's Report. Perhaps this was a good time to read it, now that the rest of the team were otherwise engaged.

He logged into his computer, opened the document, and was halfway through the summary when his phone rang.

It was Maj.

"Pete, can you come down. We've found something."

He sighed as he closed his laptop. The report would have to wait, but there was no urgency. Luke had doubtless read it by now, and if he'd found anything of value, he'd have been straight back in touch.

And besides, Maj had sounded animated on the phone. Perhaps whatever they had found would be the breakthrough that was so badly needed.

Chapter 66

Mr Killjoy lifted the observation window, and the noise it made caused Zara to twist around in her seat.

She had dark circles under her eyes, and her face was pale and expressionless. However, it was clear that she'd been working on her laptop, and that was all he cared about. The more he got out of her before they parted ways, the better. It was going to take time to recruit a replacement, and there had been several tweaks needed to the website, not to mention new home pages for his up-and-coming products.

As he slid back the bolts, he reflected that it was a shame the current arrangement wasn't working out. Yes, she was delivering, but there was too much risk in keeping her here, especially with the too-smart Luke Sackville on the case.

He smiled.

Not that he was on the case any more.

He was out of the way, and good riddance.

However, the fact that he had been asking Arwyn those questions in the first place highlighted how near Sackville had been to exposing him and his operation.

That was why he had decided to act now, before anyone else caught on.

He turned the key and pulled the door open. As expected, she didn't move a muscle. His captive was now full and truly house-trained.

"How are you getting on, Zara?"

She swallowed.

"I've made progress with those two screens you asked for. It was difficult without access to the internet, though."

He bent his head to one side.

"Zara, Zara. What have I told you?"

He moved one step forward, and she instinctively sat back in her seat.

"Ah… To work harder?"

"Yes, but also to bring me solutions, not problems. I don't want to hear you whining."

He raised his voice, enjoying the power he had over her.

"DO YOU UNDERSTAND?"

She nodded.

"SAY IT!"

"Yes, yes. Sorry."

He lowered his voice.

"Good. That's better."

His smile returned.

"This isn't working as well as I hoped, so I've decided on a change of location."

She didn't say anything.

"Aren't you curious? Don't you want to know where I'm taking you?"

"Ah… Yes, I suppose so."

"I think ahead, Zara, and make sure not to miss a trick. That's why I'm so successful. I've considered every eventuality, including that it might come to this."

"Come to…" She gulped. "Come to what?"

"Didn't you wonder why I made you retrieve your passport from that dresser in your garage? It was foresight, Zara. I stay one step ahead, and that's what's made me what I am."

He paused, then grinned.

"Mendoza."

Her face remained blank.

"You do disappoint me. Haven't you heard of Mendoza?"

Her head swung slowly from left to right and back again.

"No," she whispered.

Mr Killjoy

"My, my, you're ignorant. Mendoza is a beautiful colonial city in Argentina. You'll love it there."

She didn't say a word, but started breathing more heavily.

He waved his phone in front of her face.

"I've bought us tickets, Zara. First class tickets." His grin became almost Joker-like in its intensity. "We leave today."

"Today?" She gulped again. "Argentina?"

He nodded and gestured to the laptop.

"When will you complete the two draft homepages?"

"An hour more, and they'll be ready."

"Good. There's time for you to complete them, then we need to leave."

"Leave for where?"

"For Heathrow, of course. We have a plane to catch. Oh, and when we leave, I have something else for you."

"What?"

He produced the gun from his back pocket and, in one swift movement, lifted it and pressed the nozzle to her forehead.

"BAM!"

She screamed, and her head shot back as if she'd genuinely been shot.

He laughed.

"You're so easily scared, Zara. So easily scared."

He waved the gun in front of her face, and her eyes widened in horror as she shrank back away from it.

"This is for our journey. It's a precaution, but don't be mistaken. If you give me cause to use it, I won't hesitate."

Chapter 67

Pete was back in the meeting room, and felt like he was side-on to a long and confusing tennis rally, his head flicking from one man to another as they attempted to explain what they'd found.

"It's a worm," Maj said.

"More of a trojan," Philip said.

"I don't think so. It's self-replicating."

"But it relies on social engineering."

"Mmm. I suppose it could be a rootkit trojan."

"Yes, although we can't rule out a downloader."

Pete held both hands up.

"Woah, guys. Can one of you explain what on earth you're talking about? In plain English, please."

Maj smiled.

"Sorry, Pete. Philip, you tell him."

Philip took a deep breath, and Pete could sense he was finding it a battle to make his explanation jargon-free.

"We've found the home page for a new service, but we don't think we were meant to. We identified it using Tor, but to access it we had to download a different anonymising browser, use daunt.link and then access a hidden Wiki."

"You call that plain English?"

"Ah…"

"Philip," Maj said. "May I?"

"Sure."

"We found a draft homepage for something called RansomIt, Pete. It looks like it's yet another offering that Mr Killjoy is going to offer the criminal community. Are you familiar with ransomware?"

"Wasn't that what caused problems for Marks and

Spencer?"

"Yes, and for Co-op too. M&S was the worst hit. The ransomware scrambled their servers, rendering their computer systems useless. As a result, they struggled to keep shelves stocked and had to halt online shopping for weeks."

"What did the RansomIt homepage tell you?"

"It listed a few benefits for subscribers, such as guaranteed anonymity and low subscription costs, and some brief details of how it would work, but no more than you'd find on a simple Google search."

"It doesn't appear to move us forward any."

"It might do. The page said to click for more details. Although the link wasn't active, we suspect the page with more information is there somewhere. There are a number of ways we could try to find it."

"We could use Dirstalk to brute-force the subdirectories," Philip suggested.

Pete held his hands up again.

"I'll leave you two to it. Good work. Let me know if you find anything useful."

He left the meeting room and was halfway up the stairs when his phone rang.

"Pete, it's Crystal."

He mentally crossed his fingers.

"Hi, Crystal. I don't suppose you're ringing with the name on the sextortionists' account in Accra?"

"Sorry, Pete. No. I haven't had the chance to ring the Ghana NCB yet."

"Ah." He tried to hide the disappointment in his voice. "I see."

"No, I thought I'd try the Bahamas first, and they moved quickly, very quickly."

"You've got a name for me?"

"I have indeed. I'm not sure if it'll be any use, though. It's probably invented, created using falsified identity papers. That's what's usually done. The name will probably mean nothing to you."

"What is it?"

"Christopher Wendell."

Chapter 68

Pete took the final stairs two at a time and rushed over to PC Anderton.

"Danny, you did say Charlie Wallace's original name was Christopher Wendell, didn't you?"

"That's right, guv."

"Found anything on the PNC?"

"Not yet."

"Keep looking. If you find anything, anything at all, let me know straight away. If I'm on the phone, text me. Okay?"

"Will do. Is he our man?"

Pete nodded.

"Yes. Have we got his address?"

"It's 18 Somerset Place in Bath."

"Thanks."

Pete rang Luke's phone, but it went straight to voicemail. He waited for the beep, then left a message.

"Luke, we've got him. Charlie Wallace is Mr Killjoy. Ring me as soon as you get this."

He hung up and called the assistant chief constable's office.

"Good afternoon. ACC Scarrott's office."

"Hi, it's DI Gilmore. Is she there? I need to speak to her urgently."

"Just a second."

After a couple of clicks, Jean Scarrott came on the line."

"Hi, Pete. Have there been developments?"

"We've identified Charlie Wallace as being Mr Killjoy, Ma'am. He used his birth name for an invoicing scam, and we believe he's holding Zara Opray captive, most likely at his home address. He could be armed."

"You want to use AFOs?"

"Yes, Ma'am. Two. With firearms as well as tasers."

"That's okay by me. Where's Luke?"

"I haven't been able to contact him. I've left a message, but I think we should move now. There's a risk Wallace may harm her, which means we can't afford to wait for a search warrant."

"Very well. You have my authority to do so. Let me know how it goes."

"I will do, Ma'am."

He hung up and called over to Detective Sergeant Morris.

"Cliff, we need two authorised firearms officers. Sort that out pdq, and then the four of us will head to Bath to arrest him."

He turned to PC Anderton.

"Danny, anything?"

"He's not in the PNC under either name."

"Okay. Do some googling, see if his original name turns anything up."

"Will do, guv."

*

Fifteen minutes later, lights flashing and sirens wailing, Pete pulled out his phone as DS Morris screamed past a container lorry on the Keynsham by-pass. They were almost halfway to Wallace's house.

He tried Luke for the third time.

Again, it went straight to voicemail.

What on earth had happened? It wasn't like him to turn his phone off. Could there have been a family tragedy? Luke had mentioned that his father wasn't well, but not the specifics. Perhaps he'd had a heart attack, or a stroke, and

Mr Killjoy

Luke had had to rush to Dorset.

But if that was the case, he'd ring. He knew he would.

He didn't want to frighten Sam, but decided he needed to call her. She needed to know about Charlie Wallace in any case, and she would almost certainly have an explanation for Luke's radio silence.

She answered straight away.

"Luke?"

The name came out in a rush. It was clear that she was worried as well.

"No, it's Pete."

"Is he with you, Pete. I can't get hold of him."

"No. I was hoping you'd know where he was."

"What's that noise?"

"We've got blues and twos on. Charlie Wallace is Mr Killjoy, and I'm en route to his house to arrest him."

"How do you know it's Wallace?"

"I haven't got time to explain. Please can you tell Luke to call as soon as you get hold of him?"

"Will do."

Chapter 69

Sam turned to Helen, who was in the passenger seat of the Volkswagen.

"Pete doesn't know where he is either."

"What was that about Wallace?"

"He's Mr Killjoy. Pete's on his way to arrest him."

She looked down at her phone, as if by doing so she could will Luke's name to come up on the screen.

"I'm worried about him, Helen. What if Wallace has got him? Do you think we should head there, head to his house?"

Helen put her hand on the younger woman's arm.

"Try not to worry, pet. I don't see why he'd grab Luke. It's not as if any of us had a clue he was Mr Killjoy. Ach, if anything, he was bottom of my suspects list. In any case, we don't know where he lives."

"I've got to do something."

She retrieved Luke's number and called again.

Yet again, it went straight to voicemail, and she left her fourth message.

"Luke, I'm really worried now. Please ring."

She hung up, then a thought occurred to her.

"I could ring Pete back. Ask him where Charlie Wallace lives."

"He's not stupid, Sam. He'd know why you're asking, and he'd be worried you'd get there before him. He wouldn't tell you."

"You're right." She paused. "HR! Filchers HR! They'd know. I'll call *them*."

She rang the main number for Filchers. It was answered immediately.

"Hello. You're through to Filchers, providing business

consultancy and outsourcing services to companies across the United Kingdom. Please listen carefully to the following, and make your selection using your numeric keypad. Press 1 for Marketing. Press 2 for Sales. Press 3 for Human Resources. Press…"

Sam pressed 3.

There was a pause, and then the voice came back on the line.

"Please wait for all the options before making a selection."

There was a click, another short pause, and then,

"Please listen carefully to the following, and make your selection using your numeric keypad. Press 1 for Marketing…"

She closed her eyes and gave a deep sigh. The woman's calm, slow delivery was driving her up the wall. How long was she going to whitter on for?

"…Press 2 for Sales. Press 3 for Human Resources. Press 4 for Information Technology. Press 5 for Support Services. Press 6 for Security. For all other calls, please press 7."

She waited for a moment to ensure she didn't add an eighth option for the sheer hell of doing so, then jabbed 3 on the screen. There was a short pause.

"Thank you. Please wait a moment while you are connected."

Sam sighed again as there were several clicks, then, finally, a second female voice spoke.

"Hello, this is Filchers' Human…"

"Hi, I need to…"

But the voice droned on, ignoring her interruption.

"…Resources Department. Due to a fire at our Head Office, we are working limited hours. Please call back between 9 am and 11 am, Monday to Friday."

"For fucks' sake!"

She turned to Helen as another thought occurred to

her.

"Naomi. She might know."

She retrieved the number and called, hoping Naomi would answer quickly.

She didn't.

It rang several times, and Sam was preparing herself to leave a message when a voice came on the line.

"Hello."

"Naomi, it's Sam."

"What do you want now?"

Sam gritted her teeth. She had to continue being polite to get what she wanted out of the woman, ignoring any barbs or digs, but it was hard.

"Is there any chance you've got Charlie Wallace's address?"

"I might have guessed."

"What?"

"He's a lot older than you but, I suppose, when you're desperate…"

"I'm not after a fu…"

Sam gritted her teeth and forced herself to start again.

"I don't want to date him, Naomi. I need to see him as soon as possible about the…" She paused, trying to think what it could be.

Naomi laughed.

"You trying to think of an excuse?"

"The fire," Helen mouthed.

"About the fire, Naomi. I need to talk to him urgently about the fire."

"Yeah. Like I'm going to believe you."

"Let me," Helen said, recognising Sam was close to blowing a gasket.

Sam bit her tongue, forcing herself to stop from shouting out the two words that had been forming in her mind, the first beginning with 'F' and the second with 'O'.

"Naomi, it's Helen. This is important, a matter of life

and death."

"Pull the other one."

"I'm being deadly serious, I assure you. I thought you were Zara's friend. Do you care about her at all?"

Naomi hesitated before replying.

"Yeah. Course I do."

"Then, do you have Charlie Wallace's address?"

"No."

"You don't?"

"No, sorry." She paused. "Are you still in Walcot?"

"Yes. We're in Sam's car in the Cattle Market car park. Why?"

"You could ask Miles. He's only round the corner, and I remember him saying once that Charlie lived in one of the posher Bath crescents. He might know."

"Okay. We'll try him. What's his address?"

"5 Chatham Row."

"Thanks."

She hung up, and Sam keyed the address into her maps app.

"It's less than half a mile from here. Let's drive, though. I'm happy to risk a speeding fine if it means we can get to Charlie's house more quickly."

"I hope Barrington is at home," she went on, as she manoeuvred out of the car park. "It'd be just our luck if he's popped to the shops."

Chapter 70

Pete turned the lights and sirens off as Cliff screeched around the corner onto Sion Hill.

They were now less than half a mile from Somerset Place, and he wanted surprise on their side.

The two AFOs in the rear had introduced themselves as PC Ivor Gunn and PC Hugo Furst when they'd met him and DS Morris beside the police Volvo.

This had made Pete smile.

Finding ways to lighten the mood was a good thing, he felt. They were heading out to arrest someone suspected of kidnapping and murder, and to be armed came with considerable responsibility, especially when you were still in your twenties, as these two officers clearly were. A small amount of levity helped to lighten the load bearing down on their shoulders.

Cliff, however, hadn't been amused.

"This is a serious business, lads," he'd said, then pointed at the taller of the two. "And you can wipe that smirk off your face, too."

The smirk vanished.

"Now, what are your names?"

"I'm PC Parrish, sarge," the officer who'd smirked said. "Warren Parrish."

"PC Alec Tate," the other man added.

"I'm Detective Sergeant Cliff Morris, and this is Detective Inspector Pete Gilmore."

Pete had briefed them while Cliff drove, and both officers had impressed him. They'd listened carefully to everything he said and asked questions in the right places.

He turned around to face them.

"Are either of you trained to use the big red key?"

"I am, sir," PC Tate said.

"Good. You grab it out of the boot when we park. I'll knock first, but if there isn't a quick response, you ram the door. Okay?"

"Got it."

"I'll take the lead, but if I suspect our man is in a room, I may signal for one of you to go in first. Understood?"

They both nodded.

"I want you to have your Tasers at the ready, but be prepared to draw your pistols if I ask you to."

Again, they nodded their agreement.

Cliff slowed when they reached Somerset Place, a Georgian crescent of elegant townhouses. He drove past the lawn that fronted it, then turned left onto the road itself.

"This first one's number twenty," PC Parrish said from behind him. "The next is nineteen."

Cliff drove forward, stopped outside number 15, and all four officers climbed out.

Pete led the way to the front door, knocked hard three times, then raised his voice.

"ANSWER THE DOOR! THIS IS THE POLICE!"

There was no response.

He knocked again.

"OPEN THE DOOR!" He paused. "OPEN IT NOW!"

Again, there was nothing, and he moved to one side.

PC Tate took his place, swung the battering ram back and then into the door.

It creaked but didn't give way.

He swung again.

Still no luck.

The third time he put everything he had into it, and the door was torn off its hinges, collapsing onto the tiled floor of the house.

Pete stepped onto the open door and through to the

hallway.

"COME OUT!"

He held his arm out to quieten the others and listened.

No one responded, but he realised there was a sound, a click-click-click, almost metronomic in its regularity. It appeared to be coming from the room at the far end of the hall.

He signalled that he was heading that way, and for the others to follow, and walked quickly but silently to the end of the hall. Once there, he pushed the door open to reveal a very modern, undeniably high-end, and totally deserted kitchen.

The click-click-click was still there. Slightly louder now.

"There," PC Parrish hissed, pointing to a door at the far end of the room beside a large American-style fridge.

He was right. The sound did appear to be coming from behind the door.

Pete walked over to it, twisted the knob and pulled, revealing steps down into a cellar.

The noise was louder still.

He briefly debated sending one of the armed officers first, but decided he'd prefer to take the lead.

After putting his finger to his lips to indicate that he wanted complete silence, he started to tiptoe down the steps.

The click-click-click continued, but he realised there were other sounds too. He heard birds twittering, then a woman's voice, but she wasn't distressed. She was speaking very quietly, something about delays.

He emerged at the bottom of the stairs, and almost collided with a man facing the other way. He was wearing black headphones, and twiddling knobs on a hand-held device about the size of a laptop.

On the other side of him was the most sophisticated model railway system that Pete had ever seen. There were at least three locomotives on the move, each with rolling stock and weaving under bridges and beside buildings. The layout even incorporated a hill, with a railway tunnel through it, and there were model cars, bicycles and figures dotted everywhere.

He tapped the man on the shoulder, causing him to jump into the air, before twisting around, his mouth forming an 'O' of horror as he took in the four men, two of whom wore full body armour and were extending their tasers in his direction.

"OFF!" Pete shouted and gestured to the man's ears.

The man pulled the headphones off.

"Are you Charlie Wallace?"

"Yes."

He gulped and risked a second look at the tasers.

"What's going on? What is this?"

"Charlie Wallace, you are under arrest on suspicion of kidnapping and murder. You do not have to say anything, but it may harm your defence if you do not mention when questioned something which you later rely on in court. Do you understand?"

Wallace nodded.

"Sergeant, can you cuff him, please?"

Chapter 71

Sam banged both hands on the top of the steering wheel in frustration.

"What's that idiot doing now?"

It should have been a two-minute drive to Chatham Row. Instead, they'd been stuck in traffic for ten, maybe fifteen, minutes as a massive lorry attempted to turn around. On the side of the juggernaut was an image of boxes of washing powder, accompanied by words in a language Sam didn't recognise. However, one of those words was 'magyar', which suggested it might be Hungarian.

The driver, presumably also Hungarian, had climbed out of his cab and was offering his hands up in apology to the people stuck in their vehicles.

"Why doesn't he just get on with it? One or two more manoeuvres and he could be out of here."

"Are you sure you don't want me to walk to Miles Barrington's house?" Helen asked.

"No. We might as well wait now. Oh, thank goodness. He's getting back in the cab."

The lorry reversed back, then forward, then frustratingly back again. Each movement was turning him no more than five degrees in the right direction.

As Sam watched him go forward again, her phone rang. She pressed the button to answer the call, hoping against hope that it was Luke.

"Luke?"

"Sorry to disappoint you, Sam. It's Sebastian."

"Oh. Not at all," she lied, and took a deep breath in an effort to compose herself. "Thanks for ringing back."

"No problem. How can I help?"

"It's about Hugger."

As she said this, the lorry finally found enough space to turn, straightened up and headed away towards Batheaston. Sam engaged drive and waited for the queue of cars in front to move forward.

"Hugger?"

"Yes, we've been investigating someone who's using deepfake technology to create fake Zoom call participants."

The vehicles ahead started moving, and Sam followed.

"So far," she went on, "we know he's stolen £200,000, and we believe he's using your software."

She put the brakes on as the car ahead stopped, his indicator on showing that he too intended to turn onto Chatham Row.

Sebastian sounded doubtful as he replied.

"That's hard to believe. We have strong encryption on our source code. Unless you were one of my employees, it would be nigh on impossible."

"Does the name…"

She stopped as Helen nudged her in the arm and pointed down Chatham Row.

She followed her gaze.

Bugger.

She'd been worried they might miss Miles, that he might leave the house for some reason, and there he was. Two minutes earlier, and she could have stopped him.

"You were saying?"

"Sorry, Sebastian. I was distracted by something. Does the name Charlie Wallace mean anything to you?"

"No, I've never heard of him."

"Oh. I was hoping you would have done."

"If you'd said Miles' name," Sebastian said, "that would have made more sense. Stealing source code is exactly the sort of thing he'd do."

Sam didn't take this in as she focused on trying to identify the person in the passenger seat. He or she was wearing a hoodie and facing forwards.

"Who's that beside him, Helen?" she said, as the driver in front waved his hand to let Miles out. "I wish they'd turn around."

She hesitated as it suddenly dawned on her what Sebastian had said.

"What was that you said, Sebastian?"

"I said that if you'd mentioned Miles, I'd have understood."

She swallowed.

"I don't suppose that's Miles Barrington by any chance?"

"Yes. How did you know? Miles worked for me, but I was forced to fire him."

As he said this, Miles pulled into the gap in traffic, and the hooded figure turned left for an instant.

"It's Zara," Helen hissed, as the car turned right and followed in the direction the juggernaut had taken.

Chapter 72

Luke had felt rough when he'd woken after the first of Mr Killjoy's blows to his head, but this was a million times worse.

His eyes were closed, his chin resting against his chest. How long he'd been out, he didn't know. It could have been minutes, hours, or even days.

He raised his head slowly, ever so slowly, trying to fight the urge to collapse back into unconsciousness.

Once his head was upright, he squeezed his eyelids together, then opened them as wide as he could.

It was then that the pain hit him, a sharp, searing pain that seemed to be at once inside his brain, and also stretched across the back of his head. It was as if the blade of a sharp knife had been dragged across his skull, then plunged inside again and again.

Instinctively, his head jerked up, and that made the agony worse.

It was torture.

Pure and simple torture.

He realised he was gasping for air, and tried to slow his breathing down, taking deep breaths then counting to three before slowly exhaling.

He needed to regain control.

Of himself.

Of the situation.

Slowly, he managed to steady his breathing.

He opened his eyes.

It was dark but not pitch black. He was still seated, his hands handcuffed together behind his back. In addition, he could feel something constraining both elbows.

After a minute or two, his eyes adapted to the low level

of light, and he saw that his arms had been secured to metal handles bolted to the floor of the van. This had been done using bike locks wrapped around each elbow.

He tried tugging, but there was no give. These were strong enough to protect a half-tonne motor-bike from theft, and there was no way he'd be able to break through them.

His breathing was back to normal now, but the pain was still blindingly intense.

He tried to think.

His hands were cuffed.

His elbows were secured to the floor.

His legs and feet were free, but there was insufficient give in the bike locks to enable him to stand up.

He wasn't gagged, so he could shout out at the top of his voice. Barrington knew that, though, so he was bound to be somewhere remote, somewhere no one ever visited.

There had to be a way, had to be. If he…

He stopped as he realised he could hear a soft ticking, and turned his head to look over his left shoulder. He managed to make out several thin cylinders on the ground, each perhaps eighteen inches long. They were laid end to end, and shaped like fluorescent tubes, but the light was too poor to make out whether they were white or not.

He turned his head the other way, and that was when he saw the clock. It was facing him and had been placed that way deliberately, he was sure. Barrington had done it to demonstrate the power he had, knowing that there was nothing Luke could do.

The clock was counting down in minutes and seconds, and he watched as it flicked from 9:00 to 8:59. It was perched on a cardboard box, into which the first of the tubes was inserted.

He realised what they were now.

They were road flares, doubtless the same make as the ones used to start the fire at Filchers, and the cardboard box had to contain an improvised detonator.

Road flares burned at 800 degrees Celsius and, once lit, it would only take seconds for the fire to take hold.

In this confined space, he wouldn't stand a chance.

He had little more than eight minutes to find a way out.

Chapter 73

There were three cars between the Volkswagen and Miles Barrington's Audi, and Sam wanted to keep it that way if she could. He had no reason to believe anyone was following him, but it was best to be cautious.

They were on the London Road, and in half a mile they would reach the roundabout where the A4 met the A46. She was worried that he might turn left, which could indicate he was heading for the motorway, and possibly for London.

She checked the console.

As feared, the car had only eighty-five miles before it would run out of charge. Not enough to get to Reading, let alone London.

"Any luck yet, Helen?"

Helen looked up from her phone.

"Ach, no. I cannae get through. It's not even ringing."

"What about 999? Is it worth trying that?"

"Hang on, it's finally connecting."

A few seconds later, Pete's voice came through the car's speakers.

"Hi. Sorry, I couldn't talk earlier. We were waiting to load Wallace into the police van."

"You tell him," Sam said. "I need to concentrate."

"Tell me what?" Pete said.

"It's not Charlie Wallace," Helen said. "He's not Mr Killjoy."

Pete laughed.

"Of course he is. We know he changed his name, and his name was on the…"

Helen didn't let him finish.

"It's Miles Barrington, Pete. He used to work for

Mr Killjoy

Stairway, the company behind Hugger. The CEO told Sam that he'd had to fire him. It must have been him who stole the code."

"No. That's circumstantial at best. We've got our man."

Sam was annoyed and trying to bite her tongue.

She failed.

"For fuck's sake, Pete!"

"Calm down, Sam."

"Look, I'm sorry, but…" She sighed. "We're following him now, and he's got Zara Opray in the passenger seat. Doesn't that prove he's Mr Killjoy?"

"It means she's been staying with him, that's all. They work together and must have developed a friendship. They might even be in a relationship. He's helping her out, but it doesn't mean he's a cybercriminal."

"What about Luke, Pete? He's not answering the phone. What if Barrington's taken him somewhere? What if he's…"

She couldn't bring herself to finish the sentence.

"I had a long chat with Naomi Simmons, Pete," Helen said. "She'd have known if Zara and Miles were in a relationship, and she said the opposite. Zara can't stand him."

"Bugger," Sam said. "He's turning left. I hope he's not heading for London."

"The wool!" Helen exclaimed.

Sam flicked her head sideways.

"Pardon?"

"What did you say, Helen?" Pete asked. "It sounded like 'the wool'."

"It was." She paused. "Sam, Barrington's CV said he went to school in Chester, didn't it?"

"Yes."

"And Charlie Wallace is from Southampton?"

"That's right, but how's that relevant?"

"Naomi's from Liverpool, and Harry Mullins said

something that I thought I'd check with her. He's an out-and-out scouser, and he told me that it was always the same person who configures ITSACAP, the invoicing system, one of the IT team he called 'the wool'. According to Naomi, it's a term used by scousers to describe someone who's not from Liverpool, but from nearby. Chester's near Liverpool, and Southampton's hundreds of miles away."

"Don't you think you're grasping at straws?" Pete said.

Sam could tell his mind was fixed and decided to take a different tack.

"Zara needs to be arrested, doesn't she, Pete?"

"Yes."

"Then, shouldn't Barrington's car be stopped? What if he's taking her to the airport? This might be the police's only chance to apprehend her."

He hesitated before replying, and she could tell he was mulling this over.

"You're right. Have you got the registration number?"

"It's a black Audi Q5," Helen said. "Registration number PZ63 PWO."

"Got it. I'll put in a request for a stop and search. If he continues driving, it won't be long before ANPR picks the car up."

"Thanks, Pete," Sam said.

"You two need to back off. Don't continue following the car. You're not trained, and it's dangerous. Understand?"

"Of course. We'll pull over now."

She ended the call.

"We're not pulling over, are we?" Helen asked.

"No way. We're not letting that bastard out of our sight."

Chapter 74

The theme from the Harry Potter films started to play, causing Zara to twist sideways in the passenger seat to look at Miles.

"What's that? What's that music?"

He didn't look across at her, but allowed himself a smile of cold satisfaction.

"It's the timer on my phone. Goodness me, you need to stop panicking. Don't you like the tune, Zara? Doesn't it remind you of our delightful team meetings?"

"Why's it going off? What's it for?"

He placed the gun on his right thigh, pulled the phone from his pocket, pressed the button to stop the alarm, and then lifted the gun again and pointed it back towards her.

"It was a reminder to leave the house. I wanted to ensure we were at Heathrow in plenty of time, but we're ahead of schedule."

It was nothing of the sort, of course. There was no plane, well, not for her, and his flight didn't leave for another six hours.

No, he'd set it for an hour when he'd set the timer in the van for an hour.

That way, he'd know.

And what was the point of setting something that elaborate up, if he couldn't relish the moment?

He sighed with pleasure.

The thought of Luke Sackville's face in those last few seconds gave him a joyful thrill. He'd have been struggling against the chains, shaking, his eyes wide and staring, his last thoughts of his loved ones.

It was pathetic really.

The man thought he was so brilliant, that he had

thwarted Mr Killjoy, and yet there he was, bound and shackled and completely powerless. He'd have been a trembling wreck as he watched the last few seconds count down, his fate outside his control.

Miles realised they had almost reached the roundabout and glanced across at his captive.

She was still on edge, and her head was turned away.

Would she notice him turn left, and realise what it meant?

He smiled inwardly.

It wouldn't matter if she did.

There was nothing she could do. The doors were locked, and his pistol was directed at her stomach.

And if she did try to do something, if she tried to reach for the gun…

BOOM!

Chapter 75

"He's turning left," Sam said.

"And without his indicator on," Helen said, "but then, I suppose a wee traffic violation is the least of his worries."

Fortunately, a Mini followed the Audi onto Chippenham Road, meaning they weren't immediately behind their quarry.

"I hope he doesn't turn onto an even more minor road," Sam said. "If he does, it might become obvious we're following."

"Ach, we'll face that hurdle when we reach it. And if he does spot us, I'll beat him to the ground with my handbag."

Sam loved Helen's eternal optimism, but she was concerned on several fronts.

Extremely concerned.

Most of all, she was worried about Luke. He wasn't in the car, that was clear, but what did that mean? Was it possible that he was safe somewhere, had simply gone for a long walk to think through the case, and forgotten to take his phone?

No, that didn't stand up to scrutiny. It had been almost two hours since she'd first tried to call him, and it wasn't in Luke's nature to go off radar, especially when an investigation was heating up the way this one had been.

Which meant what?

They knew now that Miles was Mr Killjoy, and had been responsible for three deaths in the fire. While two might have been unintended, the NCCU investigator, Dominic Watts, had been knocked out and then left to the ravages of the fire.

Murdered.

Dominic Watts had been murdered.

Mr Killjoy was ruthless. That much was clear.

But had he killed Luke?

She gulped.

No, she couldn't allow herself to think that way. She had to believe he was safe somewhere. A prisoner perhaps, but unharmed.

And what about Zara? Was she still working alongside him? Naomi had told Helen that Zara and Miles didn't get on, but that could have been an act. They could be laughing together right now, confident that they were safe.

Alternatively, she might be his prisoner.

"Helen, I didn't get a good look at Zara. How did she seem to you?"

"I think the technical term is scared shitless."

"There's no chance she's with him willingly?"

"Absolutely none."

She *was* his prisoner, then, which could only mean one thing.

"He's got a weapon, and that's why she's not trying to escape or to overpower him."

Helen sighed.

"You're right. It could be a knife, but my money would be on a gun."

"What are we going to do? He's got to stop, but it's going to be a secluded location, bound to be. That means he'll see us, know we're following."

"Aye, and we're unarmed."

"There's only one thing for it."

Sam slammed her foot down on the accelerator.

Chapter 76

The Volkswagen's power took Sam by surprise, and she was forced to swerve out to pass the Mini, narrowly avoiding clipping his rear light, only to see a lorry coming straight for them, its headlights on full beam as the gap closed.

The driver slammed on his horn, and she swung the steering wheel back, tyres screeching as she straightened the car to slide into the gap between the Mini and Barrington's Audi.

The truck shot past, a hair's breadth away, horn still blaring.

"Miles knows we're following now," Helen said, in typically understated fashion.

Sam saw their quarry's eyes flick to his rear-view mirror, then Zara swung around to face them, before jerking back again.

"Hold on."

She swung the car out again, then immediately back so that the nearside front of the Volkswagen crashed into the rear side of the Audi.

There was a sickening crunch as metal connected with metal, and she slammed the brakes on, gripping the steering wheel tightly with both hands to stop the car from swinging back into oncoming traffic.

The impact caused the Audi to enter into a clockwise spin, its forward velocity continuing to take it down the road as more horns blared, and drivers swerved away to avoid collision.

Sam had regained control of the VW, and she accelerated again to ensure she kept pace with the other car.

The Audi continued to spin for the fourth time, then the fifth, but it was slowing and would come to a halt soon.

When it did, she knew they had to move quickly, while surprise was on their side.

She waited until it was almost stationary, then slammed the brakes on, opening her door before the Audi had come to a complete stop, and rushed to the driver's door, pulling it open to reveal a grinning Miles Barrington.

Before she could react, he lifted the gun, directed it at her forehead and started to squeeze the trigger.

The next few seconds were a blur.

A sixty-year-old tornado connected with the side of his body, causing his gun arm to swing to one side. There was a loud explosion as he fired, and a bullet whistled past Sam's ear.

He gasped in shock as he tried to push Helen away, but managed to retain control of the pistol and started to pull it back towards Sam. Not for the first time, she was grateful for her karate skills as she reached out and grabbed his wrist, using a well-practised technique to maximise her grip.

Miles yelped in pain as she slammed his hand into the bare metal of the car's door frame, but he wasn't done yet. He twisted in his seat, his face a mask of anger, and threw himself to his feet, pushing Helen away with his free hand as he did so.

Sam stepped back, but not because she was defeated.

She stepped back to ready herself.

There was no time for a spinning back kick, which would have generated the maximum force, so she contented herself with a simple front kick.

His gun arm came up again, his grin returned, and she struck, lifting her right knee then extending her leg so that the ball of her foot struck his hand.

The pistol flew away, and she struck again before he could react, this time using a brachial stun, chopping him on the neck with the edge of her hand.

He swayed and fell back into the driver's seat, disoriented but still conscious.

Mr Killjoy

Sam was trying to decide what to do next when Helen spoke.

"Make one move, Miles," she said, as she pointed the gun at his solar plexus, "and I will kill your joy once and for all."

Chapter 77

Sam knew that one, if not several, of the drivers who'd been forced to pull over would have rung the police, so she didn't have much time.

"Get out of the car and lie on the ground."

Miles looked at Helen, who had backed out of his reach but was still directing the gun at his stomach.

"You wouldn't shoot."

She glared at him.

"Try me, ya wee bawbag."

He shook his head.

"No. I…"

She fired into the air, and he shot down to his knees as if he'd been hit by the bullet.

"Lie flat, on your front," Sam said.

He did as he was told.

"Where's Luke Sackville?"

"Dead."

She gasped, and Miles picked up on it.

"He means something to you, doesn't he?"

There was something akin to pleasure in his voice. He was on his front, a gun trained on him, but he was acting as though he was in control.

She didn't speak, thoughts spinning around her head. He'd said Luke was dead, and yet something made her think he wasn't telling the truth, that he was playing the power game by keeping something back.

Then she realised.

He'd used the present tense, '*he means something to you*', not '*he meant something to you*'.

Or was she reading too much into it?

No.

Luke had to be alive.

He had to be.

And this bastard was going to tell her where he was.

She thought of threatening him, of taking the gun from Helen and putting it to his head but, no, that wasn't her, and he'd see through it.

The way to find out the truth was to play to his narcissism, to his belief that he was the centre of everything, the most important person in the universe, an all-conquering genius.

She sighed in a way she hoped he would recognise as a woman defeated.

"You had us all fooled," she said. "The police arrested Charlie Wallace this afternoon. The evidence seemed overwhelming."

"And yet it was so simple. His father was Weaving Wendell, the rock and roll superstar from back in the 1980s. That's where Charlie's money came from, and that's why he changed his name."

She wanted to tell him to hurry up, so that she could obtain the answer she needed before the police arrived, but knew that would be foolish. She had to let his boasting continue in the hope he'd slip up.

"Obtaining false identity papers in the name of Christopher Wendell was easy," he went on. "All my accounts were in his name. All of them."

He giggled, which came across as ridiculous given the position he was in, prone on the floor, a gun pointed at his midriff.

"The Audi's in his name, the van too. Even the farm. It's derelict, but I knew it would come in handy. I plan ahead, always have done. I'm meticulous."

He was on a roll now, and loving it.

"I'm a genuine genius, too. Did you know that my IQ is 160? That's the same as Albert Einstein's."

"That's amazing, Miles. What you did with Zara must

have taken a lot of preparation."

"Thinking more than preparation. She believed she was on her way to Mendoza, which she was…"

He giggled again.

"…just not the Mendoza she was thinking of, not the city in Argentina. Oh no, a long, long way from there."

Sirens sounded in the distance, but Sam had heard enough.

"Helen, keep your gun on him until the police arrive."

"Where are you going?"

"To find Luke."

"But you heard what he said, Sam."

"Yes. I heard every word."

She smiled.

"For someone with that high an IQ, he really is incredibly stupid."

Chapter 78

Sam climbed into the Volkswagen and continued along the road towards Bristol, relieved that the car was still drivable.

She slowed down as a police Range Rover passed, lights on and siren blaring. To her relief, the officer driving was focused on reaching the accident, and didn't notice the badly damaged VW driving away from the scene.

She pulled into the side of the road and searched on Google for 'Mendoza farm UK'.

Nothing useful came back.

She tried 'Argentina farm UK', then 'Mendoza ranch UK'.

Still nothing.

She was sure she'd been right.

She had to be right.

Sighing, she opened the maps app, traced the road she was on through Wick and to the other side, where it became Homeapple Hill.

There were several properties with the potential to fit the bill, but it was impossible to tell whether they were working farms or derelict farms, and the app only showed the names of the larger ones.

Frustrated, she decided to continue driving and keep her eyes peeled.

As she did so, Miles' words replayed in her mind.

"He means something to you, doesn't he?"

Was she reading too much into the tense he'd used?

Had she lost Luke forever?

She wiped a tear away.

Come on, Sam. Be strong.

She slowed whenever she saw a possible opening, or track, or even gap in a hedge. After a mile, there was a turning off to the left, a minor road.

What if it was down there?

She decided to carry straight on, and return to the side road if she drew a blank.

She slowed yet again when she saw another small opening, and was startled by the blast of a horn as an angry motorist sped past her, his fist waving through the window as he glared in her direction.

She turned away from him, continued, still hoping.

Then she saw it.

The sign was almost concealed by the branches of a hedge, but she caught the word 'Granja'.

She pulled over, climbed out and pulled back the offending branches to reveal 'Granja de Mendoza'.

This was it.

Next to it was a five-barred gate, pulled closed but not locked. She lifted it and pushed it wide open, then returned to the car, reversed back and then forwards through the opening onto a rough track.

A hundred yards ahead she could see a derelict farmhouse, its windows long gone, the roof caved in.

There was no sign of anyone, nor of a vehicle.

It had to be behind the building.

He had to be behind the building.

She realised she wasn't breathing, her heart in her mouth.

What would she find?

A burned-out wreck, all hope lost?

She rounded the corner, and there it was.

A silver van, side on and, to her relief, not showing any sign of fire damage.

She stopped the car, climbed out and walked to the back of the other vehicle.

Both doors were closed.

She grabbed the handle, pushed it down and tugged.

As she pulled it open, her life with Luke flashed before

her eyes. The time he'd collided with her on his first day at Filchers, the tingle she'd felt when their eyes met, his resistance to asking her out, their weekend in Paris.

Was this how it was all going to end?

She pulled the door wide, saw him, and the bottom dropped out of her world.

He was on the floor, facing away from her, held upright by chains through his elbows. His wrists were cuffed together, and there was blood on the back of his head, on his shirt, a pool of it on the floor.

She put her hand to her mouth.

"Luke!" she gasped.

"Hi, Sam. You took your time."

Chapter 79

Fred stood up and clapped his hands when Luke entered the meeting room on the 3rd floor at 25, Gay Street.

James and Glen did the same and, after a few harrumphs, Filcher joined in. Unlike the others, however, he remained seated.

Luke held his hands up to stop them.

"Thanks, guys, but there's no need."

"You deserve it," Fred said, and gestured to the bandage wrapped tightly around Luke's head. "How many stitches?"

"Twenty-two."

"Twenty-two!" Glen said. "Very imperative."

"Impressive," Luke said. "The word is impressive."

"It was a woman, though," Filcher said. "A woman saved you!" He shook his head in disbelief. "What is the world coming to? Ah… Sam, wasn't it?"

"Yes," Luke said, surprised that, for once, Filcher had got her name right. "If it hadn't been for her, I don't think I'd be here. Not just her, though, the entire team."

Filcher stuck his chest out.

"I do what I can."

"I was thinking of the Ethics team, Mr Filcher. Maj, Helen and Josh all played their part. There were others, too. Many others."

"Yes, but I enabled you. I am your manager. Your overseer. You acted under my supervision. And she… Ah…"

"Sam."

"Yes. Sam. She works for you. You work for me. All working at my behest. Within my purview. I am responsible for your actions. For your achievements."

"Do you want us to applaud you too, Mr Filcher?" Fred asked.

"Well, I…"

The door opened, and Ambrose stepped into the room. Filcher closed his mouth, then opened it again.

"Ah… Come in. Please. Come in."

He jerked to his feet, stood ramrod upright, then turned to the others and waved his hands towards the door as if cajoling unruly pigs into leaving their pen.

"Out! Out! Our Chief Executive wants a word with me."

"I want to speak to all of you," Ambrose said.

"Yes. Ah… Of course you do."

He turned back to Luke, Fred, James and Glen.

"Return to your seats."

No one moved, since none of them had stood up.

Filcher looked back at his uncle, stepped to one side and indicated his chair.

"Please, Uncle. Be seated."

"I'm okay standing, thank you, Edward."

"Yes. Hah! Stay standing. Yes."

"I wanted to pop my head in to thank you, Luke."

"There's no need, Ambrose."

"Nonsense. And please pass my thanks on to Sam, Helen, Maj and Josh. It was a splendid job all round."

"Thank you," Filcher said.

Ambrose ignored him.

"Are you sure you're ready to return to work, Luke?"

"Yes. A week off is plenty. I had concussion, but fortunately he didn't fracture my skull."

"Two days would have been sufficient," Filcher said.

"Two weeks would have been more sensible," Ambrose said.

"Or three weeks," Filcher added hastily. "Or four."

"Stop creeping, Edward."

"Ah…"

"As I was saying, Luke, it was a wonderful team effort. Have you heard what the latest on Miles Barrington is?"

"Yes. I spoke to the assistant chief constable this morning."

Filcher nodded his head.

"ACC Scarrott," he said knowingly.

Ambrose glared at him.

"If you don't have anything valuable to add, Edward, keep your mouth closed."

"Ah…"

Ambrose turned back to Luke.

"Please continue."

"Barrington's told them everything. As well as Zara Opray, he had two other accomplices, code-named Draco and Gilderoy. Draco turned out to be an accountant living in Birmingham, real name Michael Adams, and Gilderoy was a senior software engineer employed by IBM. He was from London and his name is Raj Patel. They've both been arrested and are in custody."

"Excellent. I assume Barrington will be charged with murder?"

"Yes, among other things."

"What about Zara and the other two men?"

"They'll all be charged with various offences under the Online Safety Act, and they're probably looking at custodial sentences. However, the police don't believe any of them were accessories to the murder of Dominic Watts."

"And the sexual extortionists? The ones who caused Jack Pickford to try to take his life."

"Also arrested. A sextortionist in Nigeria has also been linked to Mr Killjoy's SexIt service."

Ambrose turned to the Head of Human Resources.

"James, have you heard how Jack is?"

"He's doing well, Ambrose. They're hoping to discharge him from hospital in the next few days. He'll need some time at home to fully recuperate, but I've arranged for him to join a different account when he does return. I think it will make things a lot easier."

"And his mother?"

"Also doing well, I believe."

"That's good news."

He turned back to Luke.

"Did Jean mention what's happening with Arwyn?"

"The police are still debating whether to press charges."

"Evil man," Filcher said, shaking his head disapprovingly.

"I feel sorry for him," Ambrose said.

Filcher didn't even blink as he reversed his previous statement.

"Indeed. Poor man."

"The company is funding the rehab clinic for him as you requested, Ambrose," James said.

"I only hope it's effective." He smiled. "Thanks for your time, everyone. And don't forget to thank your team, Luke. Now, I have to get back. Sorry to interrupt."

"Not a problem," Filcher said as he rushed to the door before Ambrose could get to it. "Any time. Any time at all."

He was practically bowing as he opened the door and watched his uncle leave the room.

Once he'd closed the door, he marched back to his seat and picked up his printout of the meeting agenda.

"Where were we?"

Luke stood up.

"You'll have to excuse me, Mr Filcher. I need to pass on Ambrose's thanks to my team."

"Of course. Yes."

James stood up.

"I need to leave as well. I need to ensure everything's in place for Jack Pickford's return."

"Ah…"

"Do you need help, James?" Fred asked, as he too stood up.

"Yes, please."

James bent forward and nudged the Head of Security.

"Glen?"

Glen looked up.

"Yes?"

"Could you help me? We need to sort access out for the new Head of IT."

"We do?"

"Yes." James nodded his head subtly towards their boss. "Now."

"It's impressive that we do it now?"

"Imperative," Luke said, and glared at him. "It's imperative we do it now."

The penny dropped, and Glen nodded.

"I see. Of course."

He also stood up.

"Before you go…" Filcher began.

The door closed before he could finish, and he looked around at the four empty chairs, then at his printed agenda.

After a few seconds thought, he buzzed through to Gloria.

"Yes, Mr Filcher."

"Tee time, Gloria."

"With biscuits?"

"No. Not teatime. Tee time! I don't want that ruddy brown stuff. Call my golf club. Book me a tee time."

"Very well, Mr Filcher." She paused. "Oh, I nearly forgot. As he was leaving, Ambrose said he might be in to see you later this morning."

"He did?"

He thought he heard a snigger from her end, but decided he must be imagining it.

"Ah…" He swallowed. "On second thoughts…"

"You don't want to play golf?"

"No. Changed my mind. Too much work."

"I understand. Would you like me to bring you some

tea?"

"Weak?"

"Most definitely, Mr Filcher. Very weak."

Chapter 80

Josh was seated at one of the hot desks when Luke walked into the room the Ethics Team were sharing on the second floor. He looked up and smiled.

"Good to see you, guv."

"It's great to be back, Josh."

Helen walked over, gave Luke a hug, then gestured up at his bandage.

"Ach, I'm not so sure the wee wrap-around is a good look."

"I'm sorry to say it'll be there for a few days. Still, it could have been a lot worse."

"Aye, it could indeed."

"Where's Sam? Maj too, for that matter?"

"Isn't it obvious with the laddie sitting there salivating like a St Bernard?"

"They're fetching cream cakes," Josh said, and grinned. "Doughnuts too, with any luck."

Luke heard the door, and turned around to see Sam and Maj.

Sure enough, each of them was carrying a white cake box.

"We bought an assortment of six different ones," Maj said.

It didn't take long for Josh to do the sums.

"Two for me?"

"One for Leanne," Sam said.

"Ah… Right. Gotcha."

"Give her a ring then."

"I could take it home. She can have it there."

"Josh!"

He sighed, his hopes of two sweet delicacies torn

asunder, then rang down to the ground floor and asked his fiancée to join them.

Sam looked at her watch, and then up at Luke.

"You did well. You were only in Filcher's meeting for twenty minutes."

"I've got Ambrose to thank for that. He popped in, and it gave Fred, James, Glen and me an excuse to leave. Ambrose asked me to pass on his thanks to all of you, by the way."

"All in a day's work," Helen said, "although I cannae say disarming an armed man was front and centre of my paralegal training."

"You were fantastic, Helen. If you and Sam hadn't stopped him, Barrington would have thrown Zara into the van with me and set fire to it." He shuddered as he remembered being shackled to the floor of the vehicle. "Mind you, I thought my days were over when that timer counted down to zero. He set it up purely to scare me and hadn't connected it to the road flares."

"Everything was about power," Sam said. "More than the money. Barrington liked to be in control."

They heard a noise and turned to greet Leanne.

"Can we have the cakes now?" Josh asked, a pleading note in his voice.

Leanne walked over to him, smiled, and grabbed his hand.

"Not for me, Joshy. I need to be careful."

His grin returned at the thought that he could have hers after all, then he hesitated and turned to her, one eyebrow raised.

"Why, Leanne? Why have you got to be careful?"

"I don't want to put weight on, that's all."

"Oh."

He sounded disappointed.

"You don't want me to put weight on, do you? Or do you want me to have a curvaceous arse like Mandy?"

"Ah…"

"You do?"

"No… Well, yes…"

"You want me to be fat?"

He swallowed.

"Not fat, no… Ah…"

Luke decided to change the subject before Josh's blatant broodiness got him into even more trouble.

"I spoke to Mark this morning, and he gave me an update on my father."

"How's he doing?" Maj asked.

"So far, it's not impacting him too much, and he's been prescribed some drugs to manage the symptoms. With any luck, they may even slow down the disease's progression."

"That's good news."

"Right, let's make a start on these cakes, shall we. I think I'll have two."

"Two?" Josh squeaked.

Luke smiled.

"Only kidding, son. Only kidding."

Afterword

As with all my books, this is a work of fiction. However, some of the scenarios and crimes are based on real life, and I thought it worth explaining where I drew inspiration from.

The idea for **ByteIT** came primarily from two tools providing services to criminals: FraudGPT and iSpoof.

FraudGPT, available on the dark web, is advertised as an all-in-one solution for cyber-criminals. Its features include writing malicious code, producing phishing pages and fraudulent messages, and creating undetectable malware. Subscription fees start at $200 per month, and there have been more than 3000 confirmed sales. The person behind FraudGPT goes by the name CanadianKingpin.

iSpoof was a complex banking spam created by Tejay Fletcher, a Londoner who was sentenced to 13 years in jail in 2023. Over £100m was conned from victims using his website, which enabled criminals to appear as if they were calling from banks and tax offices. At its peak, iSpoof had 59,000 criminal users, and up to 20 people per minute were being targeted by callers using technology bought from the site.

Sextortion is a type of online blackmail, often targeting people through dating apps, social media, webcams, or pornography sites, using a fake identity to befriend the victim.

Samuel Ogoshi, 22, Samson Ogoshi, 20, and Ezekiel Ejehem Robert, 19, from Lagos, Nigeria, targeted hundreds of teenagers and adults in the United States. They posed as young women whose accounts had been hacked on Instagram. One victim, Jordan DeMay, 17, committed suicide after they threatened to release a nude photo of him if he failed to pay them $1,000 US. The Ogoshi brothers were extradited to the United States and were sentenced to 17.5 years in prison in September 2024.

In 2024, **Deepfake Technology** was used to trick an employee in a multinational firm in Hong Kong into paying out over £18m to fraudsters. The elaborate scam saw the member of the finance team duped into attending a video call with what he thought were several other members of staff, but all of whom were in fact deepfake recreations. Believing everyone else on the call was real, the worker agreed to remit a total of $200 million Hong Kong dollars, equivalent to £18.6m.

The **National Crime Agency** (NCA) is the UK's lead agency against organised crime, trafficking, cybercrime and economic crime that goes across regional and international borders. The National Cyber Crime Unit (NCCU) is a unit within the NCA. The Interpol National Crime Bureau (NCB) for the UK, based in Manchester, is also part of the National Crime Agency.

Mr Killjoy

Thanks for reading 'Mr Killjoy'. It would help no end if you could leave a review on Amazon.

This is book 9 in my Luke Sackville Crime Series. If you read it as a standalone, please take a look at the first eight books: Taken to the Hills, Black Money, Fog of Silence, The Corruption Code, Lethal Odds, Sow the Wind, Beacon of Blight and Tiger Bait.

Want to read more about Luke Sackville and what shaped his career choices? 'Change of Direction', the prequel to the series, can be downloaded as an ebook free of charge by subscribing to my newsletter at:
sjrichardsauthor.com

Acknowledgements

I want to start by thanking Penny, my wife. Without her help and support, not to mention her amazing cooking, I wouldn't have finished book one, let alone got as far as this, book nine. She's also given me critical, but constructive, comments on all my first drafts which have been invaluable.

My beta readers have again provided fantastic feedback. Thanks to Chris Bayne, Deb Day, Denise Goodhand, Jackie Harrison, Sarah Mackenzie, Allison Valentine and Marcie Whitecotton-Carroll.

Thanks also to my advance copy readers, who put faith in the book being worth reading.

Yet again, Samuel James has done a terrific job narrating the audiobook, while Olly Bennett designed yet another 'brillianto' cover. His interpretation of Mr Killjoy's nerve-centre is perfect.

A shout-out to Bruno and Ruby, our two lovable cocker spaniels. They're not a lot of help with my writing, and on occasions a hindrance, but without them Luke wouldn't have Wilkins as a pet and I, for one, would miss him no end.

Last but not least, thanks to you, the reader. I love your feedback and reading your reviews, and I'm always delighted to hear from you, so please feel free to get in touch.

Printed in Dunstable, United Kingdom